The Platinum Chain

D. X. Logan

Published by D. X. Logan, 2026.

This is a work of fiction. Similarities to real people, places, or events are entirely coincidental.

THE PLATINUM CHAIN

First edition. June 1, 2026.

ISBN: 978-1967423019

Written by D. X. Logan.

To my wife, Luna. Never once did you doubt my success as you stood by my side through it all. I owe much to your support.

To Val, though we've lost touch you helped me overcome the uncertainty about if this book would have an audience. You showed me that though the book didn't fall into the worn tracks, it still had a place on the journey.

Chapter One
The Appetite of a Griffon

It felt stellar to deck the smug noble, no matter how stupid doing so was. Erica stared up at Llwanna in furious disbelief through her functional eye. The other had already swollen enough from Llwanna's punch it couldn't open. Other students stared from where they stood on the university grounds.

"You dirty commoner!" Laethem raged from beyond his fallen friend, but he didn't move into striking range. "You'll see the lash for this."

"I don't care." Llwanna struggled to keep her voice level. "I'm tired of yer constant harassment. I tested into Magus training the same as both of ya."

"The peasant assumes she's our equal." Erica scowled with her working eye, holding the blackened one as she rose. She dusted the yellowed earth from her clothes as best she was able with her free hand.

"What's this all about?" The crisp tones behind Llwanna belonged to the Groundsman, Marv. He was a stout man with a mane of coarse gray hair, known for never smiling. He was also the only faculty who wasn't a Magus.

"She attacked me!" The slimy bully had the nerve to wear an astonished expression now. She'd made Llwanna's first month here hellish and thought she could play innocent?

Llwanna opened her mouth to protest, but was cut off.

"It's true," Laethem interrupted to back up his friend, of course. "We asked her how she was and she lashed out at Erica."

It was such a blatant lie, Llwanna fumbled her retort. Marv must have taken her failure to reply with rapid clarity as an expression of guilt.

"Llwanna, this behavior is unacceptable. Civility is vital to train here and to apprentice under a Magus. We don't allow trainees known for violent behavior to apprentice."

"If so, those two won't remain here for long." Yet another voice joined in. This time it belonged to a thin, but confident young man. He spoke in a manner that seemed above everything. Not better than others, just too focused on some ephemeral thought to bother with petty things like the real world.

"Cellis?" This time it was Marv caught unaware. Anger seethed in the eyes of her tormentors. The two bullies focused their anger at this new arrival with more intensity than they'd ever directed at her. Marv recovered from his surprise. "This is a private matter between faculty and the students involved."

"Do as you wish, but they started it. I was watching from there when it happened." He gestured behind him to the only tree in the campus green. Was that a tiny smirk in the otherwise disinterested expression? "Would you like to have one of the Magi question me for verification?"

"No," Marv seemed grudging, "As the student with the highest rated potential, I can't imagine you'd risk disciplinary action over this." Despite Marv's own heritage, his tone seemed to add the word 'serf' at the end of his sentence. She'd heard the word far too often since her arrival here. With a huff, Marv concluded. "At least not for someone you don't spend time with."

Cellis extended a hand of invitation to Llwanna. "Shall I see you to your class?"

"Alright." She wasn't sure how to feel about this shift in her situation. Taking his hand, they strode away. Behind them, the sound of Marv lecturing her tormentors on honesty began. She studied Cellis out of the corner of her eye, uncertain of what to expect. Until now, every other student had either harassed her or ignored her. It was hard not to believe he had some ulterior motive.

DROM STRUGGLED TO RETAIN his composure as his breath caught in shock at the offer from the stout man who'd been inspecting items in his shop.

"Sir, thirteen oscrape isn't enough to buy a vase from an apprentice potter." He used the formal name for copper beads, mirroring the term the customer had used. "I only deal in rare antiquities here. This item's Fresnian craftsmanship. It's a near-perfect example of Houryun era work."

"I understand what it is. What would you ask for it then?"

"For a vase of this quality, I ask for four gold crowns, though I imagine I could go as low as three since you're pressing." Drom could haggle down to a luminous scepter if it meant a sale. Always best to start at the high end of value though.

"Ridiculous!" The man's face distorted. "If I'd realized you priced things so high, I'd not have bothered. At most I'd offer a fifth and four oscrape." Six beads more value than his first offer. Just shy of 40 times less than a luminous scepter.

Drom struggled to remain composed. He disliked haggling with people who tried to low ball. Such direct conflict made him uncomfortable. Any other time he might have told the man to move on.

This was his first customer in over a month however. At least the first who'd shown more than passing interest. This month should have been his busiest time of year.

"I see. Why so low? If you want papers to authenticate the vase, I have them. They even bear the seal of the historian Graecus. I don't deal in anything but authentic goods."

"Neither does the guy across the street. He offered the same sort of papers. This vase has a pattern I like more, but not enough to pay so much more than he asked for his."

Drom's eyes bulged at the thought. "Sir. No one who sells authentic Fresnian craftsmanship will ask such a low price. It's an obvious fake. Trust me, if you want the real thing, this is it."

"You want the truth of it?" The man tugged at the embroidered sleeve of his shirt. "I couldn't care less how authentic it is. I need something attractive to impress my guests, not something I expect to sell again down the road. Thanks anyway."

He wanted to shake the man. Instead he watched as the customer moved to the door, his shoulders feeling weighed down. The hollow *tink* of bones came from the door chime as the man left. Only the faint hint of pipe smoke lingering about him remained behind. At first it had reminded Drom of his grandfather's smithy. Now it was the smell of failure in his nostrils.

He walked to the bubbled glass windows. Though low quality, few stores on this end of the market square had glass windows at all. It marked his shop as a point of interest. Through the rippled surface, the distorted forms of citizens walked by at intervals.

He moved to the door and pulled it open to stare out across the street. Few people gave his shop more than a glance. At the same time, the shop across the street was active. Shutting the door, he inspected the meager front room. Dust had built up on the shelves. He'd neglected them in the absence of active customers.

"A thread and four beads." He marveled out loud at the audacity. Walking to the vase, he ran a finger over the lip and hesitated. "Maybe I should have taken it. There's only have a few weeks left."

The month of Varr had seen a sudden drop in sales and this first week of Jasentt was already shaping up to be the same. The two busiest months of years past were instead desolate this year. He'd been counting on them to recover from the expenses of the previous year. Tax collection would start at the end of the month. At best, he might have a few extra weeks before they made it to his shop to collect on his barter license and other taxes. His shop would be forfeit. Worse, he and Arasha might end up on the block if their stock didn't cover the debt.

Drom walked to the back room where the stairs led up to their apartment. Arasha wasn't home from the market yet, but she stood in his mind as clear as if she were there in the flesh. The most amazing woman he'd ever met. Why she'd fallen for him was a mystery, but he thanked every one of the gods she had.

Arasha was born to house Griffin. Hers was the second house in the line of succession to the throne. Not just any Griffin either, she was the firstborn to the Earl of her house. Despite having the choice of almost anyone to marry, she'd picked the houseless son of a merchant.

It hadn't been his confidence as he'd never been what anyone would call bold. It hadn't been his money since his own shop made less in a year than her father paid his carriage man. Even meeting her had been a fluke. Still, here they were and he couldn't be happier for it. He wanted to make sure she never regretted choosing him.

There was the sting of his situation. He'd spent money they really couldn't afford to make sure she had exquisite things. She always protested, saying he was all she needed. Drom never doubted her. What he doubted was himself. His guilt tormented him for reducing a woman who might have one day been the Princess to a freeman's wife.

He'd reassured himself he could always make back what was spent when the busy season came. Now the busy season was proving to be a loss. He slumped against the wall, fighting back the urge to cry. Men don't cry. It was a viewpoint his father had pressed on him for years. Drom cried anyway.

He chastised himself for not checking with his preferred merchant guild to make sure they knew about the other shop. They couldn't have helped him undersell of course. Still, at least they might have warned him about a criminal business and maybe notified the authorities. Even if they could do something, it was too late now to recover the lost sales and make up the difference. Not with those prices next door. There was no way. The authorities could close the other shop tonight and it wouldn't save him. The stout customer had driven icy dread strait into his heart.

The door opened again. He pulled himself together and wiped his arm across his eyes to dry them. Plastering a smile on, he stepped out of the back to face the new arrival.. He was met with his beloved wife gliding towards him with a warm expression. Despite the cheap trade cloth dress, she had all the grace of the royalty she might have become. Everything about her spoke of her noble blood. Long blonde tresses hung in bouncing coils cascading down her shoulders and shone like liquid gold. Her violet eyes flashed with a bright glint despite the dim lighting of the store. She was as a vision no mere mortal such as he was ever meant to have.

Chasing the dour thoughts aside, he met her halfway. They embraced, kissing one another. Drom forced himself to relax. He didn't want her to worry and ask questions. The last thing he wanted was to distress her. It was still the second week of Jasentt after all.

"Hello my dove. What brings you to the store today?" He tried to sound playful, pretending he had never seen her come back home in the middle of the day.

"I couldn't stay away from you, love." She returned, playing the game. When the words slipped from her lips, he couldn't help but believe she was sincere. Her angelic voice made him want to melt.

"Excellent, because I can't stand when you're away too long." Drom kissed her again. Arasha giggled before murmuring something about having to put things away. Drom hadn't paid attention to the basket hanging at the crook of her arm until now. He'd have failed to notice the building was on fire if she was in eyesight.

He followed her to the back and watched as she climbed the stairs. She paused, looking back.

"Oh, do you need me to bring down some Sassweed tea? You're a little pale today."

"No, it's alright. Thank you." To which she responded with a smile before she walked out of sight.

Two weeks to earn what took two months to accumulate under normal circumstances. How would he make an honest living so long as he was being undersold for beads on the scepter? If only the merchant guilds had unified as the Magi had, it would be different.

Drom paused as the implication of those thoughts sank in. No chance of making an honest living. That only left a dishonest one. As soon as the thought came, he was pushing it aside.

The more he dwelt on it, the more he fretted. For any hope of keeping his business, his wares, and their freedom, he'd have to do something desperate. There was no other way. He spent over two hours waiting in a vain hope for a sale. While he did, his mind searched for something that might help. Inspiration, however, wasn't favoring him.

AT NOON, HE GAVE UP. Locking the shop, he climbed the stairs. His intention was to tell Arasha he'd need to pick something up. The evasion was unnecessary as he found her asleep on the straw-packed mattress they shared. Sprawled there, it was how he imagined a dryad would rest on a bed of pine boughs. The bland and dimly lit room seemed brighter for her presence.

"I love you, my sweet. I won't let anything happen to you. I promise." Drom kissed her forehead.

He pulled out a thin bit of parchment and cheap gall ink from the drawer of the end table. It took him a bit to locate a quill.

The note took only a moment. He wrote he'd shut down the shop early to take a walk and would return soon. As he waited for the ink to dry, he frowned at the cheap writing supplies.

"How does a Griffin write a simple letter?" The words spilled from him in rueful tones. Every local child grew up with these joke-riddles. They'd tell them to one another and laugh when they heard the answer. Few youngsters understood the significance until they were adults. They represented expressions of the typical nature for each noble House.

"A Griffin sends a hundred men in every direction to seek the finest paper, richest inks, and a quill from only the rarest of exotic feathers. Once gathered, only then can he write a 'simple' letter." Why he bothered answering to himself out loud, he couldn't say.

It felt clunky. Without grace. The answer was longer than the question with many of those joke riddles.

Each laid bare a facet of society. This one, in particular, gave an apt description of the nature of Arasha's family. Everything was decadent. They never settled for anything but the best. None of them but Arasha.

He'd let those stupid stereotypes convince him Arasha needed fancy things. Never once had she requested more for herself than the simple trappings that are typical of her new-chosen station. He'd let unspoken fears of not measuring up drive him. In hindsight, his dealings with other Griffins had nothing to do with the reality of who she was.

With the ink dry, he set the note down. The table wobbled as he did so. He slipped downstairs quietly. Experience told him he'd have an hour before she woke. It would be another two hours before she would make dinner from the items she'd brought home.

He'd written he was out for a walk. It was the truth, just not the whole truth. It nagged at him to be even that false with her. He just didn't wish to burden her. He could only hope inspiration would strike like a bolt of lightning. If he found a way to navigate through the tax season they could recover everything over the next year.

The shop downstairs remained as he'd left it. He knew the bone chimes wouldn't be loud enough to wake her, but logic didn't outweigh caution, so he disabled them. Even the faint whine of the hinges bothered him. A wave of sound hit him as he opened the door, loud enough to undo any attempt at quiet he might have thought he'd managed. He turned to secure the door behind him.

Scents from strong perfumes, unwashed bodies, and night soil washed over everything here. Such smells existed to varying degrees in all parts of the city, but the high traffic here concentrated them. A solid rain would wash away the scent of human waste for a time, but it hadn't rained since the start of the month. He'd grown used to the pungency of it all, though it always hit him when he first stepped out. He'd heard stories that centuries ago, Magi used spells to improve the situation.

His shop sat nestled into a transitional place between the main market district and where the cheap shops trickled deeper into the city along the fringe. Being along one of the primary lanes led to a strange mix of individuals passing through. People from all walks of life wandered by. He'd made sure his shop offered something for each. Having a store one street over might have cut down his visitors enough he'd never have stayed afloat even in a good year.

That dark introspection drew his attention to the shop across the street. He watched several people stop there while his shop drew scarcely a glance. He studied his rival with greater scrutiny. The sign above the shop bore the proud proclamation 'Bezzal's Artifacts and

Oddities' with a picture of a crumbling stone tower painted in the center. He frowned up at his own worn sign. He'd need to have it repainted soon. The lettering read 'Rare and Precious' in flaking gold and pale red so worn it was hard to make out. The painted jewels that had once been vibrant had now worn to the point they weren't visible at all.

When all the buildings bore similar light brown sandstone in near-identical constructions, you need to stand out. Signs aside, everything else about this location should have made it perfect. No expensive apothecaries or Magus shops to draw away the eyes of the well-off, but nothing so cheap as a chain brothel within a block or two. Even better, the taxes were lower because it was so far from the prime areas of the market district.

"Boil them!" He moved, working into the crowd. "I have to manage a short while longer, then I can turn them in."

This drew a glance from a heavy-set fellow in a fancy silk doublet. Drom returned the glance, taking him in. Embroidered onto the chest of the doublet was the blue and purple badge of his station as an Advocate. Even without the badge, the man exuded authority as so many of his kind did. Drom wanted to explain himself, but let it go. There was no chance of affording the legal fees of an Advocate if he couldn't afford the taxes outright.

Drom shrugged at the man who returned to studying the modest baubles being sold by a blanket trader. Blanket traders were more common the farther from the center of the market you were. Here, they lined every spare patch of ground to the sides of the street where a door didn't open into a shop or a crude wooden structure wasn't erected to serve as a storefront. The glass of Drom's store meant it had no wooden structures built there. Instead loud hawkers often set up their blankets there. Thankfully today the blanket trader was just a quiet older man.

He started walking. Without a set goal, he moved a bit slower than the rest of the crowd. It afforded him a glance from the lone Guardsman standing at the nearest intersection. The man leaned on a tall halberd marked with a blue tassel. With a forced smile, Drom nodded at the man. Picking up the pace, he followed the flow of the crowd out of sight. No sense risking that sort of attention.

This led him out of the market rather than deeper in. The crowd didn't vary much. Here a woman in a muslin dress with a hand-woven basket walked a pace away from a man in satin bearing heavy embroidery. The ratio of blanket traders to wooden structures shifted and the total number of beggars asking for copper beads increased by a measure. The salesmen you could find in a location informed more about where you were than the shoppers.

Despite the diversity of the crowd, his attention drew to one particular individual. He focused closer on the one who'd caught his eye.

The man was thin to the point of frail with ill kempt mouse-brown hair. The man's clothing were a dingy canvas pallium and billowing canvas braies in even greater need of cleaning. This was most true of the knees, which were stained a dingy brown and frayed. For shoes, he had little more than patches of leather tied into place with hemp rope. Everything about him was out of place in the city. Even beggars didn't dress in that manner.

His clothing screamed 'serf'. A farmer from outside the city. Even among the houseless, there were degrees of social standing and serfs were only a step above slave. For most citizens, this put them beneath notice. Even the lowborn of the city were stepping around him rather than allowing themselves to brush past. An unconscious gesture of distaste.

He might have done the same in the past, but Arasha'd altered his outlook. Someone beneath his station wasn't beneath his notice.

He tried to decipher why the man was standing still in the middle of the churning crowd.

Like a rock in a river, others flowed around him. He didn't seem to notice. The man lacked even enough caution to keep a hand on the money pouch tied at his waist. Drom approached to get a better angle for determining what had the man's focus.

Once he figured it out Drom couldn't help but laugh, which drew the attention of the other fellow. Only now did the man show caution, eying Drom as if expecting trouble.

"Can I offer you some advice?" Drom lifted both palms to show he wasn't up to anything.

"I cain't stop ya from talkin'."

"Fair. Don't let your hand leave your funds there unless you believe a cut-purse deserves the money more than you and you wish to donate to their cause."

"Aight." The man's hand shifted down to rest against the strings of the pouch where they were tied to his belt.

"New to town or been this way before?"

"I live outside the walls. Pa's the one who brings in the harvest, but needed a hand t'day. Figgered I'd look around while he's sellin' things."

"I see." Drom took it to mean the man had come to be standing here by pure chance. He indicated the sign the man had been studying. "Safe to say you've never been into a place like the Rainbow Dove?"

"Naw." The man turned his eyes back to the vibrant sign bearing a naked woman dancing with two multi-colored feather fans. "T'ain't nothin' like this back in Druhr Creek."

Drom never paid attention to the chain brothels of the town. Beyond the inherent dangers they posed, they struck him as terrible places. Not everyone agreed with him, but he'd never the stomach for them.

"I wouldn't go in there if I were I you. I realize it's tempting, but if all you can afford is this, head somewhere else. Maybe find an agreeable girl back home."

"I can handle myself." The man scowled and puffed up. It was like watching an underfed puppy try to appear fierce.

"I'm sure you can, but this place isn't like a regular brothel. Have you heard of a chain brothel kid?"

"I ain't no kid. I'm a full seventeen years." When the young man attempted to swell his chest, Drom decided not to comment. After a hesitant moment, the man added, "What's a chain brothel?"

"A normal brothel, they're full of women who make a choice to ply the trade. They want to supply you with attention in return for your money and their attention doesn't come cheap. This isn't that. This is where the women don't have a choice in the matter. The prices aren't much lower unless you're willing to take the least healthy option possible."

"Slaves?" The man seemed surprised, as though they didn't have them outside the city walls. Perhaps Druhr Creek didn't.

"Yes. Humans who've lost their rights as a matter of justice or Elves."

"Elves? They got them short wood folk in there?"

"Not real elves." Drom tried to find a way to explain this. It was apparent whatever limited place this man was from was far removed from the city. "Were you taught what a Hormunculus is?"

"Hormies? Yeah. Old man Tucker has a Troll."

"Okay, well, you know how a lot of them are given nicknames like 'Troll' instead of their actual names?"

"Wait, it ain't a real troll?

"Does it look like a bloated humanoid and turn to stone in the sun?"

"Naw. It's all thick and four-legged creature with floppy ears and a long nose with ten fingers on the end."

"Then it isn't a true troll. It's a Tj'vhot."

"Tudj vot?" The young man interrupted. He wore deep confusion as he tested the pronunciation.

"It's Magi speak. If you'd been educated in the city, you'd be aware of it. The fact it's so hard to say is why so many have nicknames. Since the Tj'vhot name starts with a T and they have similar skin, people took to calling them Trolls."

"And so Elf is short for Hormie?"

"No, it's one of two names used for Ill'ln. Elves are the ones who are dangerous."

"Why'd anyone wanna bed with somethin' like a Troll?"

"Ill'ln aren't like Troll's." Why was he wasting time with this? He had his own problems. "They're similar to humans besides their strength and the long, pointed deer-like ears. Made to be intelligent servants and always attractive."

"Oh I seen some of them. Sounds great. They made a Hormie for people to have at! I love the city."

"Aren't you listening?" Drom had the urge to correct the man's assumption Ill'ln were created for sex, but focused on the more important aspect instead. "They have no control. Listen, if you can afford one with a piercer chain, do what you decide is best, but if you can't, don't risk it. These brothels don't bother with piercer chains. They pin an Ill'ln down with real chains and let you at them. If it can hurt you, it will. I'd not blame them if they did either."

"Well I'll pick the other kind then."

"The other kind are Nymphs. Those take a powerful spell by a Magus to make docile. There's no way you'd be able to afford one even if you found a brothel using them. Lords, Ladies, and Magi are the ones who keep those. Few chain brothels even have Elves in piercers, let alone a Nymph. You'll certainly find none of them in this part of town." The process to make one would require only an hour as he understood it, but Drom had never heard of any in a brothel.

The cost of doing so was beyond the gains for anyone not looking to keep one as a status symbol. Something to do with the casting quota system used by Magi.

"I see." The man frowned, studying the Rainbow Dove. "So they need one a them piercer chains. How'll I know if they have um?"

"Count her not being chained to a wall or floor and trying to kill you as a favorable sign." How little were the children of serfs taught? Didn't they want their children to accomplish more in life? He dropped the idea. Did it matter? No doubt they were taught other things. Things important to life as a farmer.

"Okay, officially piercers are called homunculus control bindings, but I've never met anyone who called them that. I heard someone say the term piercer came from the pain they cause, but others claim it was due to the piercing screams of the Ill'ln." Both explanations weighed heavy on Drom. Either version of the story was uncomfortable at best. He continued.

"A piercer chain limits their actions, so long as you're careful. Since Nymphs were cost prohibitive and bound slaves are worthless outside of chain brothels, piercer chains are the standard in the kingdom. They are thin silver, gold, or platinum chains around their necks." As an afterthought, he added, "Don't ever take those chains off either. If an Elf managed to break its bindings or piercer chain, they would lash out. Violence seems to be bred into them."

"Alright." The man swung his attention between the chain brothel and Drom. There was an awkward silence, so Drom took the hint.

"Best of luck to you and your father."

"Thanks. I appreciate you takin' the time to chat."

"Don't mention it." Drom left the man to his choices. Part of him regretted the lost time, but it always felt good when he helped someone else. He neared the next intersection, this time heading deeper into the market district.

Over his shoulder the crowd had grown thick between him and the young man. Only the top of the man's head was visible, moving towards the Rainbow Dove. Foolish. He'd done what he could to help the man. It was up to the young serf to keep himself safe now.

Drom tried not to dwell on it, but couldn't help envisioning it. The dirt farmer would enter and ask what his coins would afford him. They'd either laugh, or take them all and send him in with an Ill'ln chained to the floor. No matter what happened, the Elf would have to suffer. As for the man, he'd would be enjoying himself and get careless. He'd forget the warnings about the danger such a creature posed, even in its restrained state. He would put a hand too near to her mouth, or let his hand touch hers or, worse yet, some more intimate portion of his body. She would bite, break, claw or whatever else she was able to manage. He'd live, but he would wear the scar of his exploits for the rest of his life. The line of consideration brought up frustrating memories for Drom.

Arasha'd told him a story of her youth. She'd been an adolescent when a servant Ill'ln in her home escaped from its piercer chain. It ripped the arms off of a manservant in front of her. To this day she was terrified of them.

He empathized with the pitiable creatures. To be treated as lower than an animal was not a fate he would care to wish upon a sentient being. Slavery was appalling enough, but even slaves were treated with more respect than Ill'ln. Still, who was he to alter society? Maybe one day they'd stop breeding them and create some homunculus less aware of its situation. How much intelligence was necessary to fill minor servile roles?

Shaking his head Drom walked on. The brothel sign passed from sight soon after. He remained no closer to resolving his problems.

"Where to go?" He mumbled as he followed the flow of the crowd. Like a river of human and animal flesh, the people all milled towards the market square along Market Street or outward across

Hawker Lane. A horse here, several cattle being led there. It wasn't so crowded etiquette could be ignored, so each person was careful to avoid more than brushing contact with the next. For a moment, visiting his parent's supply shop near the South gate came to mind but it would've taken too long to reach. Instead, Drom let himself be drawn along by the movement of the crowd.

DROM EXAMINED HIS OPTIONS. Even if the town Guardsmen were not watching for cut-purses and muggers, he would have been unable to manage either task. He wasn't so deft he thought it possible for him to lighten someone's purse without being horribly obvious about it. Mugging was out of the question. He couldn't physically harm another person. It just wasn't in him to do so. What options were left?

There was the possibility of buying and selling stolen goods, but it was risky. Maybe not so risky as he might have thought, given his rival. Even if the risk was low, it took time. Time was something he didn't have. Perhaps he'd try his hand at gambling, but his luck wasn't the best, as recent events made abundantly clear. Losing would put him in even worse straits. He might find a way to serve as a middleman on a smuggling run, but it suffered from the same problem as selling stolen goods. It took too much time. There were the special tobaccos meant only for nobles. The black market for those was strong among lower classes. Drom wasn't sure he felt any more comfortable being involved a deed than he was with mugging. Especially when a noble would have the right to cut his head off if he was caught.

Before he could run through more options, something roused him from his speculations. All around him others bore signs of discomfort. A piercing scream cut through the awkward quiet that had washed over the crowd. It was a scream of unbearable pain and raised the hair on the back of his neck. The source had to be an Ill'ln. He'd heard similar in the past. Gray eyes scanning the area, Drom found her through a break in the crowd. The Elf girl wore a silver chain around her throat.

One of the least powerful piercer chains. Silver chains only caused pain in four situations. Attempting to remove it, attempting to flee, attempting to harm a human, or with a command word known only to the owner.

She was curled in the street clutching at herself. Her pale skin, smoother than was natural, was stained with splattered mud. Shimmering blonde hair was now matted in brown patches to her skull, making the sharp angle of her ears stand out. Those pointed, doe-like ears quivered as a peel of screeched agony ripped from her throat and past her strained lips again. In truth, all of her trembled, but the ears stood out. She was beautiful as all of her kind were, even through her horrified pain.

A third ear-splitting scream echoed between the buildings and the crowd increased the wide berth of avoidance to what was going on. The unfolding events became clear the instant there was an opening in the crowd. He'd missed how it started, but it wasn't a stretch to guess at what had happened. Three boys stood laughing over the pained woman. One who stood a foot or so taller than the other two sneered down. The pale scar along his left cheek formed a deep crease. He appeared to be taking great joy in seeing the Ill'ln's suffering. Drom had no way to be sure what the boy said, but since the Ill'ln cried out once more, it seemed likely he was using the command word for her piercer chain.

The sheer cruelty in ones so young unsettled Drom. Everyone had their own opinions about Ill'ln, but taking such clear pleasure at the suffering of such an undefended being shook him. The youths weren't hesitating. Sympathy for Ill'ln was seen as uncouth at best, but this sort of cruelty was barbaric. Before Drom decided how to act, a door slammed open hard against the silence of the crowd. A counterpoint to the agonized cries.

A tremendously muscular man tore out from a doorway. He first eyed the crumpled Elf, then the boys. Righteous anger flared in the massive man's eyes and their laughter stopped cold. All three turned as one and ran into the crowd. The last piece fell into place, allowing Drom to fathom what had occurred. Those boys must have learned the command word for this Elf and decided to have a little fun. From the sadistic glee the leader had taken, the boy may have previously suffered at the hands of Ill'ln. It was possible the scar he wore was a constant reminder of such an encounter. Her owner failed to show a proper level of disconnect in his initial reaction, clearly concerned. By the time he reached her, he'd regained a bit of composure. Whatever he felt, he didn't go so far as to comfort her, hold her or do more than offer a hand.

Show done, the crowd dispersed. Her master wouldn't be able to show her proper compassion even if he wanted to. To show excessive kindness to Ill'ln was a tremendous sign of weakness on the part of any person in the city of Fairmar. The man's anger could be passed off as a matter of anger over his property being tampered with. No one would call him out on it. Too much more and people would talk. When people talk too much, things begin to tumble downhill for the target of the rumors.

Life was not smooth for anyone seen as weak. Even as people avoided involvement in such scenes, some gave inward cheers for those who caused pain in an Ill'ln. There were people who held a deep hatred for Ill'ln despite how much a part of life they were in the city. Drom wasn't thrilled with the sadistic streak in some of his neighbors. He'd never understood it. Ill'ln were dangerous, but it was their nature. You don't hate a dog for chasing chickens even if you had to put it down to protect your flock. It existed as an animal following its nature. Hatred didn't change anything.

Still, no one could alter what was. Nobles and Mystics might have their hands on the wheel of fate, but simple men such as himself didn't shift the balance of the world. He might pity the Ill'ln, but only in private. He didn't need rumors on top of his other problems.

Absently Drom considered that this was the second situation of the day to involve Ill'ln. Two thirds of an omen. The thought passed just as quickly as it had come. The discomfort of that last situation continued to linger in him though.

MEMORY OF THE SUFFERING Ill'ln wasn't the most pleasant thought to have while puzzling through his issue. He no longer tracked where he walked as his mind wandered. What was he going to have to do? Time passed in a haze, each new idea was as lousy those before it. The flow of the crowd deposited him near an alley. He looked up to recover his bearings.

To his shock, he was on Brant's Road only a short way from where he'd started. Market Street was even visible from here. Glancing skyward, the sun had moved down by an hour and a half. He'd ended up circling back by following the stream of human bodies. Drom shook his head at the improbability.

His frustration peaked for a moment and he muttered to himself, "Maybe I need to pay more attention to where I go. Wasting time going in circles isn't doing me any favors." Thus resolved, he trudged toward his shop, defeated.

He drew short as he passed close to Bezzal's Artifacts and Oddities. A tall male Ill'ln was standing beside the building of the rival store. The creature stood watching the crowd pass by. His expression was passive and bored behind a few shocks of black hair hanging over his eyes. By himself he was nothing of note, but he wore no restraint of any sort. No piercer, no heavy chains, nothing. His dark skin wore no tan lines to imply there had been any such restraint on him for a long time. Drom might have missed him, dressed as he was, if not for the obvious ears. He wore quality silks, much in the way a noble servant might dress. A loose cap covered much of his head though it hadn't retained all the dark locks. Whenever someone looked his way or passed close, the Ill'ln would lower his tan eyes as a show of respect. There were no signs of struggling to restrain himself as he stood docile by the door. Almost human if not for the ears and unearthly flawless features of his kind.

He was a Nymph! A 'Nymph' being present meant that someone powerful indeed must be inside the shop. The wealth required to afford such a creature boggled Drom's mind. You never ran into them through this section of town. Anyone rich enough to own them would have come from the other end of the market and wouldn't have passed the center. To realize its master was in the shop of his rival was too much to be believed. Even on Drom's best day, no one came in his store who had enough to afford their own Nymph.

Drom cursed. Loud enough several nearby people were compelled to shoot dark glances in his direction. He stepped back against the nearest wall and watched. It wasn't long before the owner returned from within and Drom's eyes bulged at the sight. It wasn't just a person of wealth, it was a Master Magus Aeromancer! No way of determining his specialty, if any, but he wore his white robes in the cut of his rank. The pure white of the cloth served to testify he was Master of the Airy Element.

If it hadn't been enough to prove him powerful, his familiar verified it beyond all doubt. It was what looked like some sort of pygmy wyvern perched on his shoulder. It might once have been a lizard or serpent, but now bore a dragon-like head, complete with horns. That head swiveled in constant observation of its surroundings. It shifted on the Magus's shoulder, tiny clawed feet clutching the cloth. Leathery wings were folded against its narrow body, but they would have spread three feet to either side when unfurled. It rested there like a twisted parody of a falcon, fierce and observant. For a familiar to have evolved so far the original species was uncertain indicated powerful Magus indeed.

The white clad man tugged his neat black beard, scanning the street before snapping his fingers and moving off. The docile Nymph followed meekly. Drom's mind raced. Why was a Master Magus at his rival's shop? Did he buy anything? If so, what and why? A Magus should be able to recognize a forgery right? What other reason would there have been?

Drom pressed hard into the crowd, cutting across the street and rushing towards his door. He fumbled with cheap brass key twice before managing to unlock it. In a daze, he latched it back, adding the wooden crossbeam after.

He stumbled into the back and pulled himself up the stairs with all the grace of a blind man in unfamiliar territory.

It wasn't until he reached the top of the groaning staircase that the real significance of the days events struck him. Forget his rival's possible sales. He'd been granted a sign things weren't as dreadful as they seemed. Three times he'd had his attention drawn to something unusual. Every time the point of focus had been identical. In each instance, it had been about an Ill'ln of progressively greater value. First the chain brothel, then the Elf girl in the piercer chain, last was the Nymph he had seen only moments ago. It was an omen! Drom was so lost in the implications, he failed to notice when Arasha came over. He startled when she kissed his cheek and asked if he'd found what he was seeking.

He burst out in a laugh before he could contain it and offered a broad grin, "Yes love, I did. Everything's about to start improving for us. The gods have blessed me with an omen of wealth and prosperity. Soon our lives will transform for the better. I'm sure of it! Perhaps I'll finally be able to offer you all the things you deserve."

"Drom." Arasha studied him. Her brow knit with concern, either at his reaction to her kiss moments before or his words now. He couldn't be sure. She gazed deep into his eyes, her voice strong and sincere, "I don't need anything but you. As long as I have you, nothing else matters. If I'd cared about material things, we'd never have even spoken to one another."

"I understand beloved. It's why you deserve the world." He gave her a tight embrace. She returned it and motioned to their undersized table.

"Come. Tell me about your eventful walk."

He sat down and spoke without reflecting on how it might come across to her, "I saw an omen. Three Ill'ln of greater fortunes." He stopped there. Not because it was all he had to say, but because her expression had soured the instant he used the word Ill'ln. He'd kept her from worrying about their financial woes, but with the mention of Ill'ln, he'd undone it all. 'Greater fortunes' mattered little to her in the light of 'Ill'ln'.

Chapter Two
The Knowledge of a Shingu

"Each of you have been chosen because you displayed an aptitude for magic. This is the final set of courses before full apprenticeship. Those who do not pass will proceed no further along the path of the Magi."

Llwanna's mind refused to focus on Magus Sylvador's lecture. Instead, the presence of Cellis' eyes on her consumed the whole of her attention. Moments like this made her want to believe he felt something for her. Something besides friendship. Alas, he'd never once tried to be more than that. Even when she'd bucked convention and hinted at her openness to it. She remained indecisive if it was fear or a sincere lack of interest in a relationship.

"... Will be a review. Let's start with the nature of portents and omens." The teacher droned in a monotone. Llwanna had to say something to Cellis. If for no other reason than to stop the disconcerting sidelong study of her face at least.

"What?" She whispered in exasperation. The boyish smirk he gave made her face flush. What was he contemplating?

"I'm glad you made the cut."

"Idda been more impressed if scum like Erica and Laethem hadn't made it too." Was that all? He had to stare at her for this?

"They've grown skilled at hiding their bullying."

"Way to make me feel better 'bout it."

He shrugged, "There's still one hurdle before apprenticeship. Perhaps they'll slip up and not make it past wizard status. Either way, they don't matter to me. You do."

"Oh?" More of his infuriating near-flirting. If he was interested, she wished he'd be out with it already so she knew how to take things.

"You're my best friend."

"I'm yer only friend."

"No one else has proven worth my attention."

Her face was growing warm again. She stumbled for a response. "I... ya realize nothing says either of us is gonna make it either. I doubt I'm wise enough to call myself a wizard though. If I don't make apprentice where does that leave me?"

"I'm certain you'll make it. Try not to forget about me when you become a member of the Circle."

"How could I ever forget the noble hero who rescued me the first day we met?"

"Perhaps. All I did was point out facts. If I need to do something impressive to be remembered, one day I'll make sure you have an epic adventure. The sort you're always claiming you want. Right out of those bardic tales you love so much." He chuckled.

"Cellis." The Magus' voice remained monotone despite an increase in volume. "Is something humorous about the laws of magic and the rules guiding our Order? Perhaps you can repeat to the class what I was saying?"

Llwanna's hair stood on end at the interruption. Magus Sylvador was infamous for harsh punishments when students failed to pay attention. She whipped her attention forward. Hazarding a glance at Cellis who wore an unfazed expression. How could he be so calm?

Cellis looked forward, acting as though he'd been paying attention the whole time. As it turned out, it wasn't an act. "Thorin quantified his second law of fortune as 'The Rule of Three'. Magical energies tied to the flow of fate manifest in sets of three. Thereby allowing the observant hints about what the future might hold."

"Superb. Please refrain from further interruptions." Their instructor's attention returned to her review lecture. Llwanna'd not heard a word of the review, but didn't doubt Cellis had spoken verbatim. He was already skilled to the point of being intimidating. What was he capable of if he bothered to work hard?

"Yes Ma'am." Cellis managed to remain expressionless, though Llwanna let a tiny smirk escape despite herself. Arrogant and respectful didn't play well in the same tone. She had no idea how Cells managed it.

"I'll hold ya to that promise one day." Llwanna let it drop. Still, she couldn't help noticing Cellis continued to watch her from the corner of his eye. If only she could read his mind.

"OH MERCY NO." ARASHA gripped the chair she'd pulled out as though she might fall if she let go.

"I'm aware you don't like them. I understand. It isn't about them though, it's just how the omen manifested."

"It's an ill omen. You need to be careful." There was visible strain in her eyes.

"Please dove, sit." Drom did so as well. "Take a minute to breathe."

"What?" She remained standing at first. Trembling legs won out, and she lowered herself into the chair.

"It's not an ill omen. How could it be with such symbolism of increasing wealth?" He shouldn't have mentioned the Ill'ln. It had spilled out in his excitement though.

"There're magical laws to omens. Neither of us was trained in magic, so how can you be sure?"

"The gods send us omens to interpret or to guide us. If they are guiding me, it can't be bad. If they were warning me they'd make certain I knew how to interpret those warnings. Right?"

She didn't reply at first. Instead her hand slid towards his own. Her grip was firm though her hand trembled.

"Drom, promise me you'll be careful."

"There's nothing to worry about." He didn't mention why the increased wealth was needed. That would have just been further cause to worry her.

"I don't care. Promise me. Wealth doesn't matter to me, you do."

"Okay. I will be careful." Drom wished he were better with words to reassure her.

"I," She started, but stopped and reconsidered how she'd say it. "Is this omen going to help you find yourself?"

"What?" Drom didn't understand where the question had come from.

"I'm not oblivious." It wasn't spoken as an accusation. Even so it stung to have it pointed out. "I see it when you smile, or when you talk about anything downstairs. I recognize something's been bothering you for a while now. You don't have to hide things. It breaks my heart to see how hard you work to hide your fears and worries from me. You can be yourself with me. Never forget that."

"I know." Drom hesitated. Part of him wanted to confess everything. He should. Fear gripped him though. More than anything, he wanted to do what was right for her, not lay troubles on her. Troubles that only existed because she'd chosen to be with him. As if she were reading his mind, she spoke again.

"Drom. I love you. I love you for who you are. You never have to feel like I need you to be anything more than exactly what you are. Okay?" Her grip had become more solid, the trembling gone. "I'd give up everything for you."

"You already did." His words fell bitter on his tongue.

"Why can't you see yourself as I see you, love? Objects mean nothing. Expectations can burn away for all I care. You're kind and honest. You put me ahead of everything else. You're amazing. If you can't see it, trust me when I say you're perfect as you are. I want to be certain you're safe far more than I ever cared about material things."

Gazing into her eyes, he'd never question the sincerity there. She was laying everything out, and he knew it.

"Alright Arasha. I'll be careful. Let me do this for us. I made some mistakes, but I am going to fix them. I realize I've been caught up in giving you things and I understand those aren't why you're here with me. I know I've been an idiot. Grant me a little time to compose myself and to deal with this omen. Tomorrow I expect to have everything I need to say worked out."

"Of course." She didn't even hesitate.

"Thank you. I'm sorry."

"There's nothing to forgive, love. I'm glad you're willing to open up again."

The rest of the night was uneventful and Arasha didn't try to pry anything out of him. Her trust he would speak of it when he was ready was absolute. Drom marveled at how blessed he'd already been by the gods in meeting her.

DROM HADN'T SLEPT WELL. His mind ran an endless circuit around what the omen meant. He would need to pay attention to everything today. It felt certain that he'd run across the source of the omen. He'd need to be ready.

When the first rays of dawn broke, he rose and moved to the table, cutting a piece of yesterday's bread. Glancing to his wife laying in her undertunic like a sleeping dryad, he clasped his hands together in excitement. He was going to be able to fix things. It would be a new beginning for them both. Overnight, he'd decided he knew what the omen meant. There was no doubt in his mind the omen meant he would find progressive improvement of fortune. His life would improve from here forward due to some event in the coming days.

Arasha made a soft sound, reaching for the empty spot where he'd been laying. Gentle eyes opened and a soft smile crossing her lips, she whispered. "Good morning, love. You're up early."

"Yes, dove. I thought I would start right away since today's going to be so important."

"You shouldn't let yourself become so excited. Omen or not, it isn't wise to let yourself act without understanding." She rose and stretched. "Remember, you promised to be careful."

"I did promise, and I will."

Her beaming expression could have melted a stone heart. "I wish I'd been able to apprentice in the Order's school." She laughed. "If so, maybe I could have offered something more helpful than to worry. I guess I wasn't paying close enough attention to their lessons." There was a hint of regret in her voice. He'd noticed it before when she talked about her failure to apprentice as a Magi.

"I paid attention," Drom offered, "So what's my excuse? I'm not sure I would have liked being a Magus anyway. They never seem to be cheerful people, no matter how powerful they might be."

"As long as I still had you, I can assure you I'd be a joyful Magus."

Chuckling, he cut a second slice of bread. She let the sheets fall away as she sat up to take it. "I've decided today I'm going to travel around the town for a bit and see if I have a premonition. I don't expect there is going to be a lot of business today. Still, would you want to run the shop for me?"

She made a surprised sound, brushing her hair back quickly pulling the bread from her lips. After swallowing the petite bite, she made a small sound somewhere between a chirp and squeal, "I don't believe you've ever asked me to help with the shop before."

"I'm sorry. I thought you might want something to do, I didn't mean to imply you weren't doing enough..."

He'd only thought her smile had been powerful before. The expression that blossomed on her face put the previous to shame. She cut him off with, "No, no, no. It isn't a negative thing. I'm glad you believe I can handle it. I understand you want me to remain comfortable, but it's satisfying to see you haven't concluded I'm helpless either." Batting her eyes sidelong at him, she added, "Just because I grew up pampered doesn't mean I didn't learn how to do my fair share of the work."

Drom felt his cheeks flush and inspected his feet as if they were interesting. "I didn't mean for it to feel like I thought you couldn't. I apologize."

With a musical titter, she set down the bread and drew him in for a kiss. "Stop apologizing. You worry too much. I love you, nothing else matters." Again she kissed him, soft and slow this time. "You go ahead and take your walk, I'll take care of the shop. Who can say? Maybe I'll even manage to haggle a better price on something down there than you could."

They settled in at the table to enjoy a light breakfast of bread and strawberries. Arasha lamented the lack of fresh cream to enjoy them with, but she'd not liked what was at the market when she'd bought groceries the day prior. They talked about the upcoming day. There was no further talk about the omen or his plans though. Instead, the conversation focused on what running the shop would require. She already knew most of it from watching him work, but it might help to refresh her. It made sense if for no better reason than to take his mind off of the future for the moment.

When they finished, they exchanged sweet nothings. She kissed him goodbye and saw him to the door. Glancing back to wave as he walked into the street, he noted she remained in the doorway to watch until he passed from view. Everything she did reminded him of how lucky he was to have her in his life. It also drew his mind into sharp focus. Today would solve all of their problems.

HIS EYES SHIFTED FROM person to person and place to place. Drom never imagined himself as a hunter, but today he was. He didn't even perceive his prey yet, but was sure he'd recognize it when he found it. If he recalled the Order education right, the key elements of fate would all be linked to the omen. The signposts would relate to the Ill'ln in some way. Something about them was at the center of the omen itself.

He was so intent on hunting for some visual sign he nearly missed the conversation between two women in front of a large stand as he passed through the market square. The stand bore bolts of fine cloth laid out in neat piles, but not so valuable the owner could afford to buy an actual storefront instead of the cheaper wooden stand.

The two women were dressed in a style that spoke of fair wealth. They wore well-tailored garments with a great deal of cloth involved in the designs, but at the same time, the cloth was not of the highest quality.

Also, while the embroidery of both was fancy, it was sparingly used. Drom determined them to be Baronesses at most. Such appraisals were a natural skill that came with his business. They were on the upper end of well-off. The upper tier of what he could have expected to enter his shop.

That was not to say the women wouldn't be due proper respect by a freeman such as himself. They simply weren't of high enough station to take great notice of unless they spoke to you. The city was full of various members of lesser Houses. In general, anyone of lesser rank than a Duke or Duchess was unnoteworthy outside of the moment. Noble without a doubt, but too low to hold real power.

It was a stray word that caught his ear and made him take pause. The word 'Ill'ln'. Drom tried not to be too obvious as he walked to the stand beside them. He made a show of studying the pottery before him, but his real attention was on the conversation to his right.

"So what did he say?" the golden-haired of the two in the high collared tan houppelande inquired, the gown-like garment swaying as the motion of the passing crowd stirred the air.

Her companion glanced around, fingers fidgeting with the folds of her dark blue cotehardie where it flared from its snug place at her hips. Her long sleeved dress didn't sway at all, speaking to the heavy material it must have been made from. "He told me I could find what I sought if I went to a Magus' shop."

Drom knit his brow, trying to determine what they had been talking about before this point. Magi ran all sorts of shops, but they always focused in some way either on components used in castings or items of a magical nature.

"Do you suspect we could afford that though?" The first woman almost spit the words, bearing open disgust at the idea of being unable to pay for anything she wanted.

"I don't know. Maybe if we head to one of the lesser shops, they don't always have as powerful wares, but it might be sufficient for our needs. Certainly the price is going to be a bit more reasonable." The second woman seemed equally offended.

"So okay, assuming we can afford it, which of the shops do we pick?"

Glancing around yet again as though part of a conspiracy, the woman in blue spoke so low Drom almost couldn't make it out. "There's a shop tucked into the southeast corner of the square. Farthest out from the other shops run by Magi. I bet they would be able to help us. Come let's see, shall we?" and she gripped her companions arm, drawing her away from the stand.

Drom frowned, letting himself be distracted by the nature of their discussion. He failed to follow them right away. He wasn't going to let them out of sight though and waded into the crowd after them. Thankfully the woman in blue had vibrant red hair held high by pins and combs. Otherwise he might have lost them in the initial lapse of attention.

Their destination was now his own. It seemed clear the fates wanted him to visit this shop to complete his destiny. Perhaps his fortune would come from meeting someone there, or perhaps some great inspiration would hit him from seeing the way the shop was arranged. He was not a Magus, so he wouldn't be able to sell magical artifacts legally any more than a Magus could sell mundane artifacts in their shops. There must be some other aspect of importance in this place.

The women traveled in a straight line. As straight as the market allowed anyone to travel at least. Drom however was forced to weave a bit more through the crowd to make his way after them. He doubted they would notice him following, but his status was visibly lower so fewer people stepped aside for him. He almost lost them at one point, but fate intervened.

A strong wind came up from behind them, tugging the lirapipe attached to the woman in tan's headdress into her face. As she paused to pull the long tail of cloth back into its proper place, he was able to recover some distance between them. Drom thought silent thanks the gods for their aid in guiding him and once more pressed onward after the women. Now he was sure this had to do with the omens.

It wasn't long until Drom stood before a shop with no picture painted on the sign. Instead it had brilliant golden lettering painted onto the stonework. Drom was unfamiliar with the language. That wasn't unusual for shops run by Magi. They seemed to believe anyone who would be able to afford their services would also be able to read ancient tongues, or at least realize the archaic languages were indicative of mystical workings. On reflection, that might just be a correct assumption.

Taking a few deep breaths, Drom pushed the heavy door ahead of him and stepped through. There was no chime or bell to announce his entrance, but there was a slight creak from the hinges of the door itself. The room was square, but the shelves were arranged in a circular fashion. An opening strait to the back of the shop parted the shelves in the middle, with a stonework circle decorating the center-most floor of the room. While the outside of the building had been the same sandstone as the rest of the market buildings, the interior floor was polished marble. The opening through the center of the shelves led strait to another heavy wooden door at the back wall. The pungent scent of clubleaf tobacco filled the room and there was a faint tapping sound sensed more than heard.

His eyes immediately went to the back of the shop where the two women whom he'd been shadowing were talking in hushed tones with an elderly man. All Drom was able to pick out around the other two was the man's brow, graying hair and a few hints of his robes. Those robes were a dark purple, so while they were respectable, they gave no indication of his abilities. No attention was directed his way, allowing Drom to sidestep and let the door close after him.

A convenient shelf stood near the door, creating an aisle with items on either side. Here Drom tucked himself out of sight to collect his thoughts. Before he could gather any however, a soft squeak brought his attention to an aged metal cage on a pedestal near the door. Its contents were out of place with what one would expect of such a store as this. Rather than some fancy bird, a sickly rat was sitting on a mat of straw and staring right at him.

There was something disturbing about the creature, perhaps it's apparent poor health, or maybe the way its eyes seemed to focus on Drom as if it held dark intelligence. 'The Magus' familiar?' Drom wondered to himself. It didn't seem likely considering the condition of the animal and the fact it was being caged. Maybe something special about the rodent made it important to Magus. A component to some specialized casting, perhaps?

Rather than dwell on this, Drom instead focused on the surrounding shelves. Fate had guided him here, but why? He browsed several of the items to his left. Some bore cramped writing in Laehnish on little cards to explain what they were. Not a common language, but one he knew. Most however bore cards in the same archaic writing as the sign outside. Most even had numbers accompanied by the symbols. Drom guessed these were the asking price of the items they accompanied.

Drom didn't frequent the shops of Magi. He'd never been able to afford their wares, but he knew they didn't haggle. It was a strange practice he'd never fathomed regardless of his own dislike for haggling. The only possibility he could imagine was whatever they happened to be selling might be unique to them.

Drom couldn't guess at this Magus' business practices. It was clear he didn't stock components by the contents of the shelves. Instead it seemed this shop focused on items crafted by Magi in the past, along with a few specialty items. Not unlike a magical version of Drom's own shop.

He peered through the thin opening between two of the curving shelves. The women and Magus were still talking though now they were moving towards a shelf near the front of the store. It was likely the Magus was guiding them to whatever it was they sought. Drom made a mental note of where they went. It might be important if he didn't find something meaningful on the nearby shelves. He also made a closer assessment of the owner. The Magus' face bore the marks of great age, but was somehow unweathered. It was abnormal for a Magus. Most of them maintained a young appearance while extending their lives.

It was clear this man had extended his own years. Few made it more than several dozen years without growing worn down. It was rare for someone to extend their life without including youthful appearances to be a part of the casting though. It made him appear elderly only at a passing observation. His fluid movements spoke of a spry fellow. It was as if he were still a young man cloaked in a perfect costume of an aged one. Contemplation on the subject was interrupted by noticing the man had fixed a stern gaze in his direction. Offering what he hoped was a reassuring gesture, Drom moved to the next shelf, putting it between the Magus and himself.

"It's alright, you aren't doing anything wrong." Drom assured himself in a whisper. "He must assume I'm browsing without intent to buy because of my clothing." Drom inspected the simple clothing he wore and muttered, "He's not wrong."

Drom wiped a trickle of sweat from his brow with a quick motion. He braced himself against the nearest shelf where it touched against a wall. Several drawn out breaths brought his frayed nerves back into check. Glancing between the shelves again, the Magus' attention was on the two women once more.

"Why did I react like that? He's still only a person, Magus or not." Drom chastised himself in a harsh whisper. His upbringing had enhanced a sense of deference to authority figures. Even without such upbringing, it was in his nature anyway. The idea this Magus might think ill of him bothered him more than he liked admitting.

As Drom lowered his eyes, he noticed there was a reflective glint. There on one of the shelves, where a corner conjoining walls should have been, was a platinum piercer chain! Platinum chains were an exceptional rarity, hard to create and expensive beyond belief. Silver chains were common, gold a bit less so, but a platinum piercer chain was capable of something the other two weren't.

If worn long enough and in the hands of a skillful trainer, they could make an Elf into a Nymph without the typical spells. It was an expensive tool, but could be used over and over. To find one on the shelves of a low end Magus' shop like this seemed improbable at best. How on earth did the old man come by this?

The significance of the discovery was almost lost in his mind against the surprise of finding it here at all. In the back corner of this ancient shop was another sign of his destiny, but what did it mean? His mind struggled to comprehend until his eyes fell on a card resting on the shelf above it. In Laehnish letters were the words 'Idol of the Golden Nymph', without any indication of what it did or what its price might be.

He reached for the six inch tall statue without consciously deciding to. It was crafted from gold-striped marble, carved and polished into the form of a woman. Whatever hand had carved it was skillful. The figure would convince him it was a real woman in miniature, if not for the cold, textured surface and color of the stone. She was poised in a shy, yet evocative pose. She wore nothing though her long hair flowed over her form in all the right places to uphold a hint of modesty.

"May I help you?" A harsh voice came from over his left shoulder. Drom was so startled he almost dropped the statue.

"I..." he stuttered, hunting for words as he recovered from the sudden appearance of the senior Magus. Whatever transaction the two women had required must have concluded. "... I was browsing. You have a substantial selection of items."

"It would be more impressive if I had fewer random gawkers and more customers." The aged fellow grumbled. Drom could empathize with him. Doubtless, it was irritation at what appeared to be a loiterer in his shop. Even when there wasn't another customer, it was frustrating to deal with. "Are you interested in buying anything or would you prefer to wander around touching everything?"

"I'm debating a purchase for my wife. I have saved up a reasonable bit of money to surprise her with after the taxes are dealt with." It was as acceptable a lie as any though he felt sure he'd be called on it.

The man's demeanor shifted in such a slight way it might have been Drom's imagination. "Alright. I apologize." he didn't seem convinced. "Ah. I doubt you'd want to gift her with the idol. According to legend when properly used the possessor becomes irresistible to the opposite sex. If legends are to be believed, it isn't discriminating, however. You might find she draws in someone she likes more than yourself." It struck an uncomfortable part of Drom's self-doubt, stabbing at a buried fear.

"Yes, well..." Drom tried not to let the sting of those comments show. Arasha'd been open about her emotions as long as he'd known her. She might find other men who she saw as more attractive in the physical sense, but she loved him. She wouldn't discard him for someone else. Fears aren't rational things however, which kept him dwelling on the Magus' words far longer than he wished to admit.

Once he'd suppressed the nagging doubts, his mind returned to the statue. Perhaps he was meant to sell it, or at least possess it. Was a woman assigned as the Prince's Sheriff to their portion of the city this year? He didn't comprehend why he needed it. He only knew fate had led him to it.

"How much are you asking?" He asked, ignoring the cutting nature of the Magus' comment.

"The set price is 700 Royal Notes." There was no way for him to afford it as things stood. There was no way he could pay for it even if he saved up for a few years. He wasn't going to be able to buy it, but could he back away now? Especially being aware it might decide the difference between ruin and fortune for his wife and himself. "I believe you're correct about it being a poor gift choice. I guess I should keep looking. If I have any questions about anything drawing my eye, I'll seek you out."

"I see." The venerable man reviewed Drom in a manner that made the hair on the back of his neck stand on end. Aged or not, this man was not to be trifled with. The lone glance spoke volumes. "If and when you find anything you can afford and seems to fit your criteria, please do inform me." He departed down the row, seeking out a chair near a door on the back wall.

Drom stepped out of sight as the man walked away, in case he looked back. The Magus didn't bother to track him, so Drom tucked the statue into the pouch on his belt instead of putting it back. He made a point now of wandering and inspected various items on the shelves. Sure to stay in sight of the man from there forward, Drom made a show of browsing the names and prices listed. At least the ones listed in Laehnish. He made a show of the fact he had no chance to take anything, using the time to reflect.

His conscience nagged at him as did the warnings of caution from Arasha. He needed this statue. Fate itself demanded he have it. He wasn't a thief. Could he bring himself to steal something? Which god was it who'd sent the omens? Not every god was a benevolent one. If he knew more about magic, he might be better able to gauge the situation. For that matter, didn't everyone say 'gods' regarding matters of omen and fate? That implied it wasn't any individual god.

He put a hand on the pouch, fingers tracing the bulge where the statue rested. Drom could swear it was radiating slight warmth. He'd already committed to the course of action. Why was he hesitating now? Putting it back while the man was watching would net him in trouble as surely as stealing it would.

Over and over, his mind tumbled through fears, hopes, and the words of his wife. Still, if gods were on his side, there was no way for his fate to be turned aside. He was destined and so he set himself to follow-through with what he'd started. Resolved to action or not, those worries refused to release their hold on him.

"I'll have to give it some thought." Drom tried to sound disinterested as he strode toward the exit. "Thank you for your time."

"That's what I figured." The man grumped, not even bothering to rise and see Drom out. It seemed the Magus hadn't questioned the sincerity of Drom's performance.

Drom bit back a snide reply. Was it reasonable for him to be cross? The fact was the man was right about his unwillingness to buy something. It would be especially foolish to antagonize the man in light of the fact he was about to steal from the poor fellow.

Again Drom mentally thanked the gods for their help. They'd led him to an abnormal Magus' shop, a vulnerable one. As far from the center of town as this shop was, the Magus couldn't afford any assistants and there was no visible warding against theft. He'd never have found it if not led here. This wasn't even something he'd have considered trying.

As he opened the door and stepped through, the thanks was cut short. There wasn't enough time to register more than recognition of a shrill whistle. Before he could run, his entire nervous system burst into flames of pain. In the same moment, a force knocked his breath out, hurling him backwards. He landed in the center of the room on the circular pattern of tile he'd noted when he arrived, though his recognition of the situation was limited in light of the forceful relocation.

Gasping for air at the residual pain and unable to move, Drom's awareness turned inward. The pattern at the center of the room, which he had originally taken for decoration of stonework, turned out to be the focus of a ward spell. A spell now pinning him cemented to the ground.

His vision blurred, but Drom was sure the form that now loomed was of the aged man. Something was being said, but he couldn't make out what. His ears were filled with a strong ringing. His jumbled mind managed to focus only long enough to question how the omens could have been wrong. Numbness replaced the pain as darkness overtook him.

DARKNESS SHIFTED INTO a red hot pain. It was as though he was waking into a nightmare. His entire body ached and burned as if it had been bathed in a fire until it charred even his bones. His insides were curled up and twisted into frayed knots. The surface of his skin felt as if it was being stripped away by thousands of razor-sharp blades.

Time didn't exist. He knew nothing of how long the eternity of suffering dragged on, but at some point it finally dulled. When it withdrew enough for his mind to return from the brink of insanity, his perception of his surroundings returned once more. Albeit in a slow ebb. The first thing to catch his attention was something unpleasant caked on his skin. This was followed close behind with the overwhelming odor of human excrement and the knowledge he'd been rolling in his own filth for however long he had been here.

He gagged, though nothing but a thin string of bile was brought up. He'd spent the rest of his stomach contents during his torture. There was a vague sound. A voice. As his senses returned to him it resolved, clarity slow in coming. His eyes opened to blurry shapes and vague forms. Fighting to focus allowed the voice to clarify some. It was the Magus from the store and the clear source of his current state. Drom was still too sick and in pain to do more than strain at listening. He did so only as an escape from the lingering suffering.

"... never understand it. All of you seem to have this idea you can get away with whatever you want." The wizened voice was in the process of ranting. "Damn the laws of the Order and the separation of the world of mundane and magic. You couldn't have grabbed something mundane like coins so I could put you through the courts? No, your kind always goes for real valuables. Do you have any idea how much quota I had to expend to enact a 'fitting punishment' in accordance with Circle law? Fitting punishment means it has to match up. Sympathetic magic. Damned rules. You could have at least had the decency to steal the Flailing Stone. I could have beaten you with a cheap flogging spell and been done. If I hadn't learned this spell..." It trailed off into grumbling.

There was a sound of something being moved, a chair maybe. Drom tried to speak, but no sound came out from his raw throat.

"Ah... regaining control it would seem. Marvelous, that means you can understand what I'm saying." The man let out an irritated sigh. "The previous thief caused just as much frustration. Changing someone's form isn't as simple a task as people envision. A few more thieves like the two of you and I'll be out of quota for the rest of the year! I even have to use my own quota for it in case the Circle asks questions. Such a waste."

The blurry shapes were resolving. Drom could make out enough to realize the room he was in wasn't the storefront. Instead, the majority of the room this room was an empty space. The walls were close enough that the heat of his own body reflected back at him, faint but there. A person seemed to be sitting in front of him, between Drom and a door. Given the voice, it had to be the old man unless there was some assistant Drom hadn't seen before. Again he tried to speak, but only a faint squeak emitted from his throat. Progress at least. Anger welled up to fill the void where the pain had been a moment before, fighting with the remaining pain for his attention.

"Regardless, it's done now. It is now for me to find a way to turn some profit from it. At least your transgression allows for future gains. I don't have the quota needed to do it all with magic, but I can do the rest through simpler means. What's a decade or two after all?"

Whatever the man was talking about, it didn't matter. Drom was going to resolve this situation as soon as he could regain his full faculties. A strange sort of other-ness welled up inside of Drom, different from mundane anger. It was as if there was a spirit of overpowering hatred whispering in his ear. It drove at him, demanding he break the man's neck or tear out his throat.

The instant he decided to listen to the suggestion however, a pain every bit as atrocious as the one he'd suffered only a short time ago lanced through his body. A ragged scream tore from his own throat, which sounded inhuman and nothing like his own voice. Now twitching and gasping for breath on the ground, Drom could only stare with bulging eyes.

"I can only assume you were fool enough to direct aggressive thoughts toward me. Your platinum piercer chain won't allow those. You should already be aware of such. Mind and body are bound by anything I designate, and I made sure to set a few orders in place the moment your transformation was complete enough for it to work. You can't even imagine harming me without suffering excruciating pain. Any direct thoughts or actions of escape are off limits and of course you must do whatever I tell you unless you want to deal with pain beyond human understanding." The man's voice, though hard, was tinged with a momentary blend of disgust and sympathy. "I don't envy you your new life, but you brought it on yourself thief."

Drom grew sick again, reaching up to his neck to touch the chain there. How? Piercer chains didn't work on humans, only on homunculi. Drom realized his shirt was gone. He hadn't brushed his shirt collar when he'd touched his neck, and it occurred to him his fingers hadn't touched any clothing at all. In fact, there wasn't the sense of it against his skin either. His vision was still too blurred to recognize more than the color of his flesh as he looked down, but it seemed wrong. He wasn't able to identify how. The shape was distorted in ways he couldn't fathom.

Before he could ponder further, the Magus spoke again, "That's right, you aren't human any more." He followed the statement by answering the obvious question. "I've transformed you using spells which haven't been cast on anyone for over a hundred years. It's not common knowledge Ill'ln are born of human stock, but now you comprehend it through firsthand experience." The old man gave a startled sound and add, "Lest I forget, I order you never to tell anyone else about who and what you were before this day."

Drom managed in a rasp entirely unlike his own voice to say, "I'm not a thief."

The man scowled. "You tried to steal from me. That makes you a thief. As per the Order's code of laws, I am doling out a punishment befitting the crime you committed. You attempted to steal the Idol of the Golden Nymph, so a Nymph you will be. Your body is now Ill'ln and in a decade or so the chain will have broken your will. I'm unwilling to waste the quota on further spells. Making the physical transfiguration cost enough as it is. Since platinum piercer chains are the only other way to manage such a mental reform, I'm lucky I had one in stock. It's slower, but just as effective in the end. Also, since that was an idol representing a true nymph and the quota cost was the same regardless, I decided it's only fitting your form match a true nymph."

Anger welled in Drom again as it all came together in his mind. That was why the chain worked. That was why he appeared odd in his blurry vision. "Bastard!" he screeched, unable to even consider doing more without a tingle of pain. It hit him why his voice sounded odd. It was a higher pitched.

"Now now, that's no way to talk to your new owner." the aged man grumbled, not seeming to enjoy this as many others might. "This can be an uncomplicated situation, or a difficult one. Accept it and you'll have a fairly mild life without struggles, but don't imagine I'll go gentle on you if you fight. This is nothing personal and I take no pleasure in it. It is simple justice. Now, what was your name?"

"Drom." he responded after a short pause. The whole situation weighed on him and he wept in frustration. The strange voice of hatred remained, oddly untouched by the chain regardless of what it whispered, as though it were separate from himself. It seemed it was only when Drom listened there was any pain. Right now however, all he felt was hopelessness.

"Drom... I see. It derived from the language of Rewessin, meaning 'Warrior of Pride.'" The man mulled it over. "I doubt you ever knew, I've never heard of a well educated thief."

In fact, Drom had known thanks to the study of history he'd done as part of his work, but was too overwhelmed to bother explaining. Instead, he continued crying to himself in a filthy heap.

"Not a fitting name for an Ill'ln woman such as you are to become." The overt statement of his reassigned species and gender only made it worse for Drom. "I believe I will take another word from the same dead language. One similar in sound, but far different in meaning. From here forward, you are Droya. It means 'She who Serves.'" The man's tone might be dour, though Drom was too focused on his situation to muck out the subtleties. "Now, let us clean you up. You're coated in Aporrhoea. A week such as you've had needn't be made worse by ending in such a dispirited state."

Realizing how much time had passed only made it worse. Drom laid limply, his vision might have cleared by now if not for the tears. He closed his eyes and dejectedly waited. The old man stood and with surprising ease, lifted Drom's limp body. He took Drom over to a medium sized basin, already filled with water. Drom could do nothing but whimper to himself as the filth and grime was removed from his skin and hair. The weight of this situation threatened to consume him. More so than the previous pain had.

What hurt wasn't that life as he'd known it had ended. It was the intense realization his precious wife was going to suffer for his stupidity. He'd been so horribly wrong about the omens. He'd been delivered warning signs and mistaken them for guideposts.

Chapter Three
The Thorns of a Bristletree

"Laethem and Cellis, you'll both be working on a report on the Law of Finite Matter." The words of Instructor Dorn hung like a lead weight on Laethem's chest. Of course he'd be paired with the one person in class he couldn't stand more than any other.

Cellis sat down beside him. Neither acknowledged the other. Both remained silent as the rest of the class were assigned into pairs. As the last of shifting desks and shuffling chairs faded, Cellis broke their silence.

"Finite matter shouldn't be too difficult." Cellis spoke without tone. "Matter isn't made or destroyed. It's reformed based on the casting. Done."

"I would say it is more nuanced than that."

"Of course you would." What an arrogant troll turd. "Gods above help us if you ever missed a chance to prove yourself better than the rest of us."

"I don't need to lord over others. It's just important to have a complete grasp of the fundamentals if we're to master them."

"Obscure nuances are never going to matter. In a practical sense they are worthless. Men like you and I have the potential for great power. You waste your potential on trivialities and houseless scum." Laethem wasn't sure which aspect annoyed him more.

"Llwanna has as much potential as you or I."

"Lowborn trash will never be my equal." The false-calm expression Cellis wore made Laethem's blood burn. "You're equal only because you debase yourself."

"Your prejudice is antiquated and foundless."

"Rabble like her aren't..." The slam of the teacher's hand on the desk, along with some choice words, cut Laethem's comment short. Boil him if he would lower himself below his station. What did he care how Cellis felt about the matter?

DROM WATCHED CELLIS with a customer. Two weeks spent in a form not his own, two weeks here being forced to accept a subhuman role. He refused to envision himself as an Ill'ln, a female, or a slave, regardless of what form this Magus had reshaped him into. Drom knew he would find a way to become himself again. It was the belief that had sustained him through this situation. Those first few days had been tearful and devoid of hope. Even now it threatened to drag him into despair if he didn't keep himself focused.

Thoughts of running away or of assaulting the man always brought pain, but thoughts of someone else harming the man were fair game. He had spent his time here trying to figure out the limits to the piercer chain's hold on him, with only minor success.

For as strong as a platinum piercer chain was, he'd found clear limits. The chain reacted to thought. By focusing on his individual options, he'd been able to find out which did and didn't bring pain. The orders Cellis must have enacted while Drom was unconscious were fairly basic. Don't contemplate harming the designated owner of the chain. Don't do direct harm to a human without just cause. Don't intentionally damage property of value without just cause. Lastly, don't run away from your 'owner'. The first two might have some leeway he hadn't yet found, but he was certain the last did not. As to the third, 'just cause' seemed to be anything which was intended as an aid to Cellis or ordered by Cellis.

Beyond these, the aged Magus had only set the limit Drom could never in any way indicate who or what he had been. It meant he had to respond to the new name he'd been given. He couldn't indicate his past in any way, so was limited in finding a way to escape. No chance of sending a message to his wife without violating the rule. At least, not that he'd worked out yet.

In the absence of anything else to distract him from the problem, he inspected his ill-fitting apron-dress. It was cheap, poorly-made and held together at the sides by only a few stitches. The fibers were a rough home-spun linen. Cellis had tossed it at him the first day, grumping he didn't need excuses for more gawking customers. Drom hadn't asked, but assumed he must have gone out to purchase it in the period of transformation. Either the spell didn't control proportions or Cellis hadn't been willing to wait for something specific to be tailored. Money didn't seem to be an issue for the Magus, only quota, so wasn't the likely cause for the ill fit.

Despite the shoddy clothing, his new form was one of unsurpassed beauty as all Ill'ln were and it showed in spite of what he wore. Making servants attractive seemed a needless waste. Drom hadn't put much thought into it before. That Ill'ln were designed to serve nobles must have been the cause. The unquenchable desire to have every bit of their property take forms pleasing to the eye. Land, objects, or the living alike. His stomach twisted and bile threatened to rise every time he considered exploring the implications. Insult had been added to injury through being made into this feminine form. He'd not been particularly macho in life. Arguably he'd made a poor showing of traditional masculine traits. Still, much of his identity was tied up in his male form.

Drom returned his attention to Cellis. Within his time here, the Magus had avoided eye contact with almost religious fervor. If he'd made Drom this way out of some personal desires, he wasn't taking advantage of the view, let alone the control. What few times he did glance at Drom, Drom sensed a pain in his expression. After the conversation post-transformation, he'd never spoke to Drom outside of ordering something done. Those rare moments of direct speech were never lengthy. Gather an item from the back. Step aside as he was seeking something. Where other men might have gloated or savored Drom's situation, this man seemed put off by it. Though Drom wasn't inclined to be understanding, there might even be regret in those moments of direct interaction. Maybe. He wasn't going to forgive the man, no matter what might slip in those brief expressions.

For Drom's part, he felt similarly disinclined to talk to his captor. In the past two weeks he'd studied the situation with quiet focus. He'd decided the man might let him go, but only if he could present his case well. Those moments of avoidance and possible regret could be useful tools. Drom knew there was no pain when he thought about asking for his freedom, so it might offer a way around the no escape rule of the piercer chain.

As the current customer moved towards the exit, Drom moved from his standard spot along the wall near the front door. It was the spot he'd been ordered to stand when not needed, so close to freedom he could never reach for. The tiny voice, which had become a constant companion, was whispering in Drom's mind. It seemed bent on escape and violence. No wonder Ill'ln were such violent creatures if this was something all of them suffered through. It was strange since it wasn't his own anger, but something other. As far as he knew, Ill'ln hearing voices wasn't something anyone had ever told him about. Was it himself alone or did they all suffer from strange voices in their heads?

"Cellis?" Drom kept his voice soft, only speaking at all after making certain the customer was gone from the store.

The Magus blinked in surprise. Apparently he'd not expected Drom's previous silence to be broken. Drom had hoped for this. It would increase weight of his words. "Yes Droya?" In an afterthought, he added, "It occurs that if you will be speaking with me in public, you should refer to me as Master or Sir, as would be the case with other Ill'ln. We should cultivate the habit now. Consider it an order."

Drom grated at the use of the new name. He glared as he was told to use 'Sir' or 'Master' when talking to the Magus. Two weeks ago, he'd have defaulted to 'Sir' without a second thought if he'd been talking with a Magus. It would have been a show of social respect. As a subhuman and a slave, it was one more sharp reminder of his current reality. "We're not in public." Drom hissed. With an effort, he forced the welling anger down before it could interfere. It wouldn't help him succeed in convincing the old Magus to free him. "I told you before, I'm no thief. I wanted to explain to you why I was stealing from your store."

Cellis said nothing. There was a cautious glint in his eyes as though expecting a deception.

"I am... was... a merchant. I made a few crummy choices because I thought I could make up for it during the busy months. You see, my wife was highborn, and I wanted to supply her everything she'd given up by marrying me." He paused to allow it to sink in.

Cellis frowned, but otherwise gave no signs of his thoughts beyond perhaps a tightening around and narrowing of his eyes. "Proceed."

"Another store opened across from my own and was selling items cheaper than possible for a legal business. You, being a business owner, realize the Sheriff will be collecting taxes soon. I didn't have enough to pay them. There wasn't time to make up the difference even if I did bring the other shop to the attention of the authorities. I had to find a way to cover the taxes you see." He let out a breath, the tightness in his chest released as he confessed. "I believed I had a favorable omen about Ill'ln, one of impending fortune... but I was wrong. Fate pointed me here, and that's how we came to this point."

There was only silence from the Magus so Drom continued. "It isn't for myself I'm worried. It's for my wife. Without me there the best she can hope for is being homeless, but given the way things were going she's going to end up on the auction block along with our wares. She deserves better."

Drom stopped and waited. Silence filled the room for a long time. After a pause, Cellis shook his head. "I pay my taxes to the Order for the record, but why should I trust the word of a thief? Even if I did, it doesn't matter. There is nothing I can do for your supposed wife. As you can tell from your time here, I don't make much myself." It was true. Drom had seen many people enter the store, but only two bought anything. Of those, only one bought an item Cellis seemed pleased to be counting the coins for.

Not wanting to press his luck yet, Drom offered, "I felt you should be aware." and took a step backwards, lowering his eyes respectfully. Drom hoped the old man would consider the situation and it would play on his sympathies enough he might do something for Arasha before it was too late. With a little luck, he might even restore Drom's life.

Drom cast a furtive glance to the entrance as the aged Magus moved towards it. It was almost half an hour early for him to be shutting down. Maybe he always did so on this day of the month? Cellis latched the door into place without putting any form of a sign into the window. Drom had never paid much attention to the shops of Magi, but through the last week he'd learned much about how they differed from a typical merchant. Most of it was little things, such as not placing signs out to show they were closed. Drom could only assume it was another aspect of their aloof nature. It was hard to be certain if it was the true cause or if he was missing something.

ONCE THE DOOR WAS SECURED Cellis moved to the back rooms and Drom followed as he'd learned to do at the end of each day. It might have been an order, but Drom never tested it. He preferred to keep close. It allowed him to watch the Magus for any hints about how to escape. The back room was composed of a primary area, used for the storage of a few eclectic items, and a series of three smaller rooms which branched off. One was where Cellis slept though it hadn't crossed Drom's mind to ponder what was there beyond that. Drom counted it as a mixed blessing not to have been taken in. There might be useful hints about the man there, but it also meant Cellis wasn't one of the sort to use an Ill'In for personal gratification.

The second was the near-empty room Drom had awoken in and which served as a sort of casting room for the Magus. The last had an ornate rune-carved door leading to a room far larger than seemed possible for the compact building. It was used to store overflow stock for the storefront. It doubled as Drom's bedroom now with a thin straw pallet in a corner near the door.

Even as Drom let the door shut behind him, Cellis was drawing a cloth from off of a smoky gray quartz sphere at the center of the primary room. This was something Drom hadn't seen Cellis do before. Lest he be sent to another room, he feigned obliviousness. He wanted to find out who the old man wished to contact. Anyone would recognize the sphere for what it was, a communication orb. Still, aside from the few public spheres, only the wealthy or Magi could afford to own one. They could be activated by anyone, but only if the internal reservoir of magical energy was sufficient. As a Magus, Cellis could use it without restriction. He could power it with a portion of his own quota.

If there was one thing Drom had learned in his time here, it was that quota was everything. At least to Cellis if not other Magi. It seemed a constant weight on the man. He would often mumble to himself in irritation about the quota required for this or that. If such a device was being employed, it must be with someone well away from the city to warrant the cost in quota to Cellis. In all other things, the Magus grumped over the least use of quota. With this, the quota must be well worth it to him. He never once complained to himself about it, but instead seemed intently focused. In different circumstances, Drom might have laughed at the absurdity of a tight fisted Magus throwing quota at something as minor as conversations.

That line of thought was broken by a string of incomprehensible syllables. Some chant to evoke the sphere's power no doubt, which only stood to further prove this particular sphere wasn't the sort used by the mundane community. Still chanting, Cellis uncovered a modest bowl filled with shaved garlic and sprinkled it around the sphere, the scent flooding the room. This continued for a full minute. Without warning, it stopped. The globe grew clear as though the smoky colors were simple mists. What filled in the sphere as the mists rolled away was the face of an attractive woman with burning red hair, save for a single platinum shock near the left temple, and fierce green eyes.

Her lips were curled into an expression like a rictus sneer as she spoke, "I was starting to suspect ya were going to be late ya ancient coot!" She was either a dear friend or someone of greater power. Who else would call a Magus anything but their proper title?

"I do wish you wouldn't call me that. You're technically older than I am Llwanna." Cellis grumbled with a scowl, eyes wavering a moment in a glance towards Drom.

"Then pony up the quota to make yerself look as marvelous as ya feel! It ain't as though it's hurting anyone to appear younger."

"And it isn't hurting anyone for me to show my age either. Are we going to retread this whole argument again or are we going to talk about something important today?"

The face in the globe gave a quick, wry expression and offered, "Alright, alright Cellis." She rolled her eyes... "I trust ya found the last shipment to yer liking?"

Cellis absently glanced at Drom before responding. "I can't say if I liked it, but I have already put at least some of it to use. Please be more careful what goods you're 'liberating' in the future. Some of those items would stand out if I put them on display right away."

Drom couldn't help but frown at the way this conversation was progressing. Was Cellis a dealer in stolen goods? Did the magical community even have something equivalent to a fence among them? If so, it meant the woman he was speaking with some sort of smuggler. It was an unusual concept Drom would need to explore further at some later point. For now he needed to listen and glean what information he could. His now-sensitive ears picked up on the muffled sound of firm knocking from the front, but the Magus either was ignoring it or couldn't hear it.

The woman giggled and disappeared from view for a moment, leaving a blue background behind. Sky, perhaps. When she returned, she wore a wide brimmed black hat that hid all but a few stray strands of coppery hair. "But if we only went for the safe cargo, I'd never have anything noteworthy to send to ya. What would be our excuse to keep in touch then?"

Before Cellis could respond, a thunderous pounding at the front entrance sounded, replacing the original knock. Cellis called out with surprising volume and clarity, "I'M CLOSED!" His sharp tone spoke volumes of agitation. There was a pause as if the culprit had left and the Magus prepared to speak with the woman in the sphere. Before he could open his mouth to do so, the pounding returned anew.

With a hiss of frustration, Cellis told her, "I will contact you later. I need to determine who's so desirous of being transformed into a toad."

Llwanna rolled her eyes yet again. "Oh lord, that old cliche? Have fun with yer guest Cellis. I look forward to talking with ya again next time."

"You as well. Stay sweet." Cellis offered in an uncharacteristically friendly manner, going find out who was pounding. He gave a hand motion for Drom to follow.

"Ya do the same..." Her voice echoed as she faded back into the smoky quartz of an inert crystal.

THE LOUD HAMMERING at the door continued and Cellis stormed to the front with a fury to match it in equal measure. Showing uncharacteristic savagery, he pulled the latch free and tore the door open. "What sort of pixie-brained pond whelp disturbs a..."

He didn't finish before a sharp "Enough." forced his rant to die off before it could build steam. The owner of the voice that had quelled the Magus' ire struck Drom as familiar. Something about the way he stood and the neat trim of his abyss-black hair and beard.

Cellis regarded his visitor for a time with a wary and guarded expression before asking, "Decide not to bring Vlax along?" Inspecting at the clean yet simple tunic the visitor wore, he added "Or is it incognito this evening?"

"Are you going to invite me in or shall we exchange pleasantries on your doorstep all evening?" It was spoken in a dry tone which bordered on bored.

It wasn't hard to recognize the disdain for one another these two held and Drom was sure a confrontation must be brewing. The nagging suspicion he should remember this visitor still picked at the back of his mind. He remained silent however and listened, contemplating where he might recognize this man from.

"Very well Count Laethem, do come in. To what do I owe the pleasure of a visit from the High Seat of Aeromancy?"

"The formality is unnecessary" Laethem stepped inside, closing the door behind him in a smooth motion. Rather than answering right away, he studied the transformed merchant as one might study some unusual bobble, causing Drom to averted his eyes. It was more out of discomfort than any show of respect. "I see you've overcome your aversion to owning servants. About time you grew up." Extending his hand, he brushed the platinum chain that encircled Drom's throat with a single finger. "And such an expensive means of control as well. Platinum piercers aren't particularly common."

Drom shot a surprised stare as the reason this man looked so familiar struck to him. He was the seat of Air Magic! This was the Master Magus he had seen at his rival's shop as part of his omen!

Laethem made no show of noticing the expression, "Rarer still of late, after the cargo of the 'Red Wind' disappeared three months ago. Quite a mystery. One would imagine piracy, but only a Magus could have taken the ship and that, of course, would have been detectable through a Magus' Identification Crystal." The official name of quota crystals. "I should hate to assume we have a Sorcerer in our midst."

Cellis regarded the other man with much the same cautious narrowing of eyes by which one wild Apsuhound watches another. He remained silent and guarded, so Laethem continued.

"Of course there are ways around those crystals, or so I'm told. Didn't you used to have a job making them for the Circle? I imagine those who've made the official crystals could counterfeit them and provide them to a pirate sorcerer. Oh on another note, how is Llwana, by the way?" It was a seamless transition with clear implications. It was Cellis who gave a startled slip of surprise this time before recovering his composure. Laethem sneered like a cat who had cornered a mouse. "Does she still hold the same grudge against me you do?"

"She's no concern of yours Laethem."

"Oh? As a member of the Circle, it is my duty to ..."

"Enough of this game of banter." Cellis cut him short, "Be out with it, what did you come here for?"

"I wronged you and Llwana both in the past more than once." His tone softened. "You most of all were the better Magus in those days and I am wise enough to admit it now. I have a great desire to make things right." Laethem offered, "To date, the best I have done to help was through turning a blind eye on the two of you and your 'activities.'"

"Still," Laethem made an absent gesture, "That was more out of pity than regret. To see such talent squandered as the two of you have done is heartbreaking. She might have managed to attain an advisory position to the Prince and you could have been sitting among the Circle!"

Drom struggled with his emotions regarding Laethem. The man had been part of the omen and now he was here. What did it mean? Was it a coincidence?

"Power and politics never interested me Laethem. I can't speak for her motives beyond simple wanderlust." Cellis countered, "Not that we can take political positions in mundane society, but even the title of Prince itself wouldn't interest me."

"No? And what if I told you society was about to undergo a dramatic upheaval? That you could be helping to improve the world and you could have a meaningful place in the new order of things? Your displeasure with Order law isn't a secret. If the separation of mundane and magical power bases were to be removed, Order laws would need adapted for certain. You could have a direct hand in reshaping our society."

All of this sounded to Drom like a rebellion or uprising. He recalled the history lessons growing up well enough. There were many rebellions after the world's magic went away. The ancient societies fell to ruin. It had been generations before order returned along with magic itself. He couldn't recall many peaceful rebellions.

Those few peaceful ones still meant a great deal of unpleasantness for the kingdom involved. If he didn't already mistrust this man who'd in-part led Drom to this demeaning fate, talk of rebellion would have closed the deal.

Cellis made a silent study of Laethem for a few heartbeats before shaking his head. "I would say the Circle should attend to its own affairs before meddling in those of society as a whole." The corners of his lips twitched downward, causing a significant portion of his beard to shift with them. "Or I might say you're still a bully. You just happen to use more subtle means these days."

"You ungrateful son of a troll!" Laethem bellowed in sudden rage. "If not for my intervention, the two of you would have found your way onto the end of a Red Machtha's blade by now with the Order's blessings!"

Cellis gave a polite, if smug smile, as though he'd won a game of stacks between the two of them, while Laethem visibly worked to reign in his temper.

"So be it Cellis," Laethem's words were slow after regaining composure, "You have time to reconsider. Don't dwell on it too long though. One of the keys is nearly in order. Once I have," He stopped himself. "Once the last bit falls into place, things will rush forward. If you decide to be reasonable, contact me. I will send someone to convey you so we may discuss the details as civil equals."

Drom suspected between the difference in the ranks of these two and the clear animosity being shown by Cellis, calling them equals was a ploy on the part of Laethem to gain agreement. Arguing Magi were a fearful sight and Drom was having a hard time keeping his wits strait enough to unravel the situation. Did all Magi allow slaves and Ill'ln to observe conversations no freeman would ever have access to? The answer was likely yes, since slaves weren't people in the minds of the powerful, they were property.

Cellis made a noncommittal gesture. "I am more than reasonable, though I doubt I will be taking your offer."

"That is your choice Cellis, but you won't interfere either. If you do, I won't keep protecting you from Order justice."

"I'm far too intelligent to be interested in entangling myself in your, or anyone else's, politics. Initiating or interfering alike. What reason would I have to play such games as you do?" Cellis huffed, "Go do whatever plotting or coup you wish and understand I have no desire to have any part in it. Unless it is restructuring the order law to end foolish practices like the handling of 'justice', I don't care."

Laethem opened his mouth to respond, but instead shook his head. In the place of whatever he had been about to say, he offered, "Perhaps I will return in a few days time. Your stance may yet evolve."

"Unlikely." Cellis held open the door.

Without a word, Laethem bowed and stepped into the evening chill. When the door was again secure, Cellis let out a deep breath and rushed to the back of the store, ignoring Drom. Unsure of how to take all of this, Drom followed.

He considered saying something about recognizing Laethem as the Magus he'd spoken of seeing at the rival shop. Cellis' expression was sour however and Drom couldn't imagine how speaking of it could hold value to the irritable Magus. He let it go and focused on watching Cellis work his spell.

A haphazard casting later, the surprised face of Llwana was showing in the center of the crystal sphere. "Cellis?" She studied the agitated Magus, "Since when do you call twice in one day? Or week for that matter?"

"Since today. Llwana, we have a serious problem."

Chapter Four
The Honor of an Apsuru

Maria brushed a strand of hair from her eyes and turned the page. Though Laethem was with her in the library, he wasn't studying.

"I'm telling you, it will happen."

"Mm Hmm." Her attention remained focused on her studies.

"Why do you do that?" His voice dripped frustration.

"Do what?" She lifted her attention from the book. The neat trim of his black hair and goatee spoke of a recent visit to the barber. Two weeks earlier than usual. He must be trying to impress someone.

"Mumble meaningless phrases. I've been trying to have a conversation."

"We aren't all prodigies. Some of us have to study."

"I've seen your scores, you never miscast. You don't need to study."

"I never miscast because I study." She emphasized 'because'.

"Bah." He was going to sulk, meaning she'd never manage to focus on her studies unless he spoke his peace.

"What were you saying?"

"Oh? Now you care?" But he was placated enough to relax. "I'm going to be on the Circle one day."

"The Circle?" It wouldn't help to mention directly he was a slacker, so she offered, "You'll need to become an elementalist first. You'd have to become a Master Magus. I never figured you to want more than

Enlightened Magus status. That is, if you'd choose to go beyond just Magus at all."

"Have I ever been content with the common? I'll find the right element for me and master it. I'll become one of the best."

"Alright. Can we study now?" Maria couldn't resist imagining what element might suit her. It wasn't something she'd put thought into. No time now though. She forced the thought down and returned to reading. Focus on attaining her apprenticeship first. The remaining rungs of the ladder could be reached for as they came up.

"COME, WE ARE GOING to the market." Grumped Cellis. Unlike most people in the city, he only went to market once a week and had last went two days before Laethem's visit. Drom was at a loss to explain how the old man kept the things he bought fresh outside of magic. As tight as he was with his magical quota, it seemed doubtful.

Such minor curiosities were all Drom had to distract himself from his plight. Attempting to adjust the apron-dress for greater modesty without success, he wished Cellis would buy something with a better fit. He moved to follow, wondering if he should ask for a replacement dress.

"And don't forget the basket." the aged Magus added.

Drom complied, staying silent as he'd learned would keep him from drawing the man's attention. They left without a further word and the crowd parted around them without seeming to notice. Even so, Drom would have sworn every eye was trained on him. It was the first time he'd been taken out of the store and it made him feel a horrible sense of exposure and awkwardness.

The powerful whisper inside of his mind had become a constant companion urged him to flee, heedless of the disabling pain that would result if he complied. So much as even allowing himself to listen brought the first tingling burn under his skin, so he pushed it down with an effort as was now second nature.

"Gather enough vegetables to last the week Droya. I have to attend to something." Cellis avoided eye contact. "And when you've done so, meet me by the auction stand. Don't dawdle, I expect you to be there no later than an hour from now."

"Yes," Drom grated in a tone barely civil. "Sir." Irritation at both being ordered, and the required use of 'sir' causing a hesitation. If not for the piercer chain, he would have spit at Cellis, Magus or not.

The old man walked off, leaving Drom alone at the Northern edge of the market square. The gap between himself and the sea of people shrank in as the Magus departed. This left only just enough room to move, so it felt claustrophobic despite no one touching him. Imaginary glances became a reality, making him wish the aged man hadn't left. Contempt, curiosity, fear and even lust rode in the sidelong glances and lingering stares by those in the crowd. Each was sickening to him for reasons all of their own.

"Make way Elf." The booming voice of a man sounded behind Drom. He had just enough time to jump aside as a man riding a massive chocolate stallion rode over the exact spot he'd been standing.

"Dung scraper!" Drom cursed at the rider out of reflex. It wasn't until the horseman pivoted his steed around that it occurred to Drom where he sat on the social ladder. To anyone seeing him, he was a mere Ill'ln. It also became clear the man he'd insulted, however mild the wordings, was a noble. At least judging by his attire and attitude. Drom might have noticed sooner had his mind not been occupied with the near trampling he'd avoided.

Drom had only a moment to contemplate at how the insult hadn't caused pain. It would seem there was no 'harm' in such a social disgraces. That, or perhaps it was the intent had been more of an exclamation than an insult, regardless of its end result. Even so, the words couldn't be taken back and now Drom would have to deal with them.

"Your name and owner Elf!" Not so much a question as a demand from the irritated horseman. He tugged at his gipon's lower hem as he stared down his nose at Drom. From the rich purple color of the quality cloth and the heavy blue embroidery worked into it, he was certainly a member of the House Apsuru.

"Droya," Drom stated, unable to relay his real name thanks to the chain. His mind raced for something to help keep this from growing worse. House Apsuru was legendary for their ferocious response to any perceived insult to their honor. Perhaps realizing the owner was a Magus would do the trick. "And Cellis of the Order."

"Cellis?" The horseman's brows rose and his tone shifting to one of surprise.

"Yes Sir." Drom offered. Short and to the point should help avoid making further mistakes in judgment.

"And since when does he keep servants?"

"It is a recent decision to do so, as I understand." Drom's curiosity gained the better of him and he couldn't resist adding an inquiry. "You two are acquainted?"

The horseman frowned down at Drom. He shifted to scan the crowd. "Only in so much as a favor once granted me." His voice growing less harsh. "I should cut you down where you stand. Be thankful for your master Elf. Were you anyone else's property, I would have made an example of you and reimbursed the owner minus the cost of the sleight." He glanced in the direction he'd been going. "I do not have the time to relay a message to him myself. You will carry a message to him for me instead." Again, it was not a question, but a demand.

Drom only nodded. As much as he wanted to lob a series of harsh words on this man, his threat wasn't a hollow one. Several members of House Apsuru had been known to execute slaves over minor offenses. Not just their own slaves, but anyone's. Owner complaints were rare as they were almost always granted a more-than-fair compensation, but he had no wish to be the loss in question. He was lucky the horseman seemed rushed or he might have suffered a public whipping for good measure.

"You will tell him Kirk, Earl of House Apsuru sends his regards." The horseman knit his brow again and added, "And his chosen pet is ill mannered. See he learns of your insulting behavior and is made aware I expect you to be punished."

The Earl of House Apsuru! Drom would never have imagined grumpy and hermit-like Cellis knew the leader of the House second only to the ruling House Sphinx. Much less on favorable enough terms the man would allow himself to be insulted by a slave and take no direct action because of it. What sort of favor could have elicited such an allowance?

Kirk reigned his horse back in the original direction, but twisted his torso and head, speaking to Drom one last time. "And should I find you didn't carry my message, I'll reconsider your assault on my honor." Not waiting for affirmation, the man set off at a steady pace. The crowd parted as if an invisible wedge pressed ahead of him.

DROM WATCHED THE DEPARTING horseman. He tried to imagine how the insignificant Magus could be on such intimate, if sometimes unpleasant, terms with such powerful people. First with a member of the Circle and now with the leader of such a powerful House. Circler Laethem had spoken of wasted potential and offers of rank. Earl Kirk had more or less admitted being indebted to him. What else about this enigmatic Magus was hiding behind the image of a withered and underachieving Elder? He was at least an Enlightened Magus in rank, but what about Grand Magus or Master Magus?

Not comfortable lingering there further, he set off on his task. The incident with the horseman put him behind and he had no desire to find out how the chain around his neck would react if the task took longer than the hour limit he'd been given. Thankfully, vegetables were plentiful still at this point in the year. The last of seasonal harvesting would be ongoing for a few more weeks. It meant starting prices were fair, the crops were in prime condition and it was easier to haggle a favorable price.

While purchasing goods with promissory notes from a pouch sewn into the lining of the basket, Drom returned his mind to his situation. There had to be a solution. Unlike the iron smith puzzles he'd always enjoyed however, this puzzle refused to unbind. Aside from his original idea of asking for freedom, every other idea which might have a chance at success brought pain the moment he focused on it. Each time it did, he would let the idea drop before the sensation could intensify.

Tiring of the jolts of discomfort and pain, he focused on a different train of thought. What was the best hope to save his beloved Arasha? It couldn't be more than a week before the tax collectors began making rounds and the collecting of the debts from the previous year's use of a barter license. At least on this end of town. Was there some way to obtain enough money to placate them? It only needed to be enough so her freedom wasn't added to the debt. If so though, how could he get it to her in his present condition.

These thoughts were still circling in his mind by the time the purchases were finished. He went to the middle of the square where the auction stand was, and found a growing crowd milling there. He waited on the outskirts of this group for Cellis and examined the promissory notes remaining in the basket. Outright theft brought pain. Theft was a form of harm he deduced, but what about if he borrowed them with every intention of seeing they were returned? No pain. Drom had found a loophole, albeit a tiny one.

A flash of pain hit as Drom thought for a moment about not returning it. The moment he was certain about seeing it returned, the pain was gone again. The old Magus hadn't made any orders about borrowing from him. Indeed, why would one realize the need to do so, considering Drom's new form and station? Cellis also believed he was a thief and what thieves ever took something with the intentions to return them? Would any of them have even had the idea of borrowing anything in Drom's situation? There was also the fact he couldn't have done anything with whatever he would have borrowed anyway. It meant there was no visible motive. Without a motive why would the aged man have placed a rule against it?

Still, it felt like theft even if the loophole would allow it. Theft had put him into this position, was he willing to risk making it worse by doing so again? His morality argued no. His common sense and his sense of self-preservation agreed to the same. Love of his wife however, disagreed vehemently and refused to listen to the other three. As for the strange voice at the back of his mind, it was ignoring the whole line of thought in favor of whispering to run away for the forest.

"DROYA." THE MAGUS' voice caught him by surprise and nearly caused him to drop the basket. Cellis wore a distracted frown. In his hands was a joint of cured meat, but there was no way a single joint of meat was what occupied the man's time while the two were separated. It wouldn't have accounted for the time.

"Yes... Sir?"

"Don't stare at people, it makes them uncomfortable."

Drom hadn't noticed he'd been staring at anyone while lost in his thoughts. Thankfully Cellis hadn't taken a tone of order, but instead one of statement. For a reply, he gave a simple nod, giving a quick glance to try to determine who he could have been staring at.

"Time to be home." Cellis didn't say so, but Drom knew he would be calling Llwanna when they returned. He had done so every night since Laethem's visit. Drom wished he knew what it was they spoke of, but had been sent off after the contact was made on the first night and hadn't been allowed to listen in since.

Following the aged Magus, Drom caught a momentary glimpse of golden curls like Arasha's through the crowd. He couldn't imagine her being in a crowd of people waiting for an auction to begin. Still, he couldn't help himself. He'd seen the glimpse near the stage where a man was now standing and speaking. He stopped for a closer scan in that direction.

"By the law," the man was saying, "Debts must be paid either by the value of one's estate or by the value of one's freedom."

This must be one of the first rounds of tax auction for the year. From the area of the Port District where the tax collectors would already have started he was guessing. One week for each of the five districts starting there and ending in the Crown district. If not there, one of the outlying sections beyond Fairmar where the more rural areas of the kingdom lay. Arasha might indeed be present if that was the case. She knew Drom's habit of attending these sorts of auctions to help stock a few items on the shelf for the coming year. Maybe she didn't believe he'd abandoned her. She must be hoping Drom was still planning to return!

In the corner of his eye, Drom saw Cellis come to a stop. He scanned the direction he'd come from, but Drom remained fixed. The majority of his attention was fixed on hunting for any sign of his precious wife in the lake of human forms.

"Yesterday's estate auctions failed to alleviate the debt of only two such businesses from the first of this year's tax evaders." the auctioneer was continuing. "The first is estate number thirty seven."

Cellis seemed to have spotted Drom, a sharp scowl forming as he backtracked through the crowd. Drom was aware of it in a vague sense, but nothing else mattered. The old man's lips moved as he spoke, but the words no longer registered to Drom. The entire world washed from his senses, leaving only one vision behind. His breath caught in his chest and his heart pounded like thunder in his ears. There was Arasha, clothed in a simple cream chemise and tan supertunic, yet as radiant as the sun at midday. It wasn't her beauty holding his attention fixated, but instead it was the manacles which enclosed her delicate wrists and the fact she was being drawn up to the stage by a chain attached to them.

"We will start at seven Silver Scepters." The words rang out like a whip cracking as it lashed his soul. Drom stepped forward and was met by a fiery pain that drew him up short.

"I said, follow me. Now!" Cellis put heated emphasis on the final word. Momentarily stunned, Drom followed on reflex. It only took two steps before he regained his wits.

"Cell..." Pain forced him to restart the sentence. "Sir, we must stop! It's urgent. Please, I must speak with you. It can't wait!"

It was the first time Drom had insisted on anything and he was glad he hadn't tried until now because it had an immediate effect on the Magus. Cellis stopped, his bushy white eyebrows lifting at the near demand of the tone. "Must we? Must I?"

"Yes." Making sure he was close enough to speak freely with the Magus and not risk being overheard, Drom pleaded, "My wife, Arasha, it's her on the auction block! They must have levied taxes earlier than usual in this area of town this year." It had to be the case though Drom hadn't seen a collector anywhere near this end of town once yet. Then again, Magi shops might be exempt from the normal yearly taxation and licensing, which would explain it. Cellis had no windows and Drom hadn't been allowed outside until today.

"That nonsense again? Persistent in your tales aren't you thief!" The aged man shook his head. "True or false, she isn't your concern any more. Come Droya, we are going home." He once more walked away.

"No." Drom's harsh whisper sounded more like the feral voice inside his head than his own, but it was his own feelings spoken before they were even thought. His skin grew alive with pain. It increased with each passing moment. Still, he set his feet to remain. The sensation had him certain his flesh was being peeled away by white-hot blades, yet the reality of Arasha being sold into slavery gave him a strength he could never have mustered in his own defense. "We have to save her." he wheezed.

Shock flashed in the expression of Cellis' withered features at Drom's resistance. How visible was it Drom was keeping from curling into a screaming ball of pain by a thin thread of willpower? Either out of curiosity or concern about making a scene, Cellis' gaze flickered to the ongoing bidding, and he spoke. "Order retracted."

Relief from the torture was immediate, as though being doused in an icy river after being in a burning building. Drom gasped for breath, eyes turning to the auction stand. The coppery scent of blood told him the warm moisture in his hands wasn't sweat. It was the aftermath of his own nails digging in. In the background, the auction was continuing. Drom wasn't recovering swiftly enough to speak, so Cellis did instead.

"Why do I have to do anything? Especially for you who would have robbed me of my valuables, has robbed me of quota and continues to rob me of precious time?"

"I love her. None of this is her fault, it's mine. She shouldn't suffer for my mistakes."

The old Magus's face softened, showing honest sympathy in something more than a sidelong glance for once. Sighing, he shook his head and offered, "I'm sorry she is suffering for your actions, in truth I am, but what is done is done. Perhaps she will be bought by someone kind."

Drom's eyes bulged. Desperation filled him and in a rush of words he offered the only semblance of bargaining power he had. "Save her and I stop resisting. I will be a Nymph as you intend, but without having to wait years for a return on the value of the quota you used on me."

"Oh?" was all Cellis responded with.

"Going once..." the auctioneer drew out the words baiting for someone to making one last bid.

"Wouldn't you offer the same in my place if it were Llwanna up there?" Drom pled.

"Going twice..."

"You have my oath, Master." Drom bowed low and lowered his eyes. The title grated even worse than 'sir' did, but he kept his voice even.

"Fifty Royal Notes." Cellis' voice lit over the crowd and brought a sharp silence and turned a fair number of stunned faces his direction. Even the auctioneer was left in a stunned silence as the bid was four times higher than anyone would have paid for a tax debt slave under normal circumstances. They were too prevalent at this time of the year to warrant a high price, pretty or not.

Drom had to struggle to keep his head bowed, only managing it for fear of ruining everything. His wife's only hope was for him to uphold the oath he'd sworn. Out of the corner of his eye, he noticed Arasha staring in their direction as well.

"Fifty Royal Notes from the man in the rear. Do I hear more?" the auctioneer called as he regained his own wits. After a suitable pause, "Going once..."

"I'll hold you to your oath Droya." Cellis mumbled, low enough for only Drom's sensitive Ill'ln ears to catch. "This bargain may end up costing me more than I am gaining. It's Laethem's man I just outbid, and he doesn't appear as though he's pleased about the matter."

Drom lifted his head, abstaining from eye contact with the Magus. "She's worth it many times over Master."

"Going twice..." was called without anyone answering a new bid. One man among the crowd scowled and stormed away at a brisk pace. Probably the man Cellis had mentioned outbidding. "Sold." Arasha was led off of the stand and the next debt slave was brought up for the next round of bidding.

Cellis motioned for Drom to follow and they both circled the crowd to settle the account. Drom's stomach churned and his muscles tried to falter. His wife was safe, at least from the risk of becoming a chain brothel whore. It was a common fate for tax slaves as attractive as his wife. The pressing issues now were his inability to tell her who he was and the fact they were both slaves.

It wasn't until they were in her presence an even greater problem presented itself. The raw terror in her eyes as they approached drove into him like a lance. He bore the form of her worst nightmare. Drom was Ill'ln now and the oath he'd sworn ensured nothing he could do would convince her otherwise. Even without the oath, the order to hide his ever having been human was still being enforced by the piercer chain.

While Cellis was paying his bid, Arasha strained against her bindings to stay as far from 'the Ill'ln' as possible. Drom kept his eyes down-turned and his cheeks grew damp with tears, hidden only by the veil of hair over his face from bowing his head.

Chapter Five
The Value of a Slave

"I'll be your master for the duration of the apprenticeship period. Whatever your peers may be doing is irrelevant. You must accept I will be starting you on weak spells. All magic ripples through the fabric of reality. Even the weakest spell may refashion the course of events in countless ways. As such, I expect the utmost respect be shown for magic at all times." The words of the senior man, Master Ulrin, struck Erica as fascinating.

"Really? Has it ever happened?"

"Indeed. The catalyst for the war between the Dolani and Mins-Kovan Kingdoms was a perceived insult from a rain aversion spell. The caster only offered it to the primary dignitary. She took insult her entire entourage wasn't offered the same treatment."

"Wait," Erica's mind spun with the implications. "Doesn't that imply the ripples in reality can also come from mundane circumstances also?"

"Very perceptive young apprentice. Magic has stronger ripples, but every action ripples at least some. All things are connected."

"Can the ripples be anticipated?"

"Divining spells are rooted in the anticipation of how ripples will flow."

"Is it possible to guess how it will ripple without casting a spell?"

"I've not thought on it." Master Ulrin seemed startled at the question. After some time, he spoke again. "I suppose one could do so.

With enough information, it might be possible to perceive the flow of events. Why bother though? Divining uses almost no quota for short-term events and long term ripples are too complicated to accurately predict for certain. Even with magic, long-term events often fail to match with predictions."

Rapid thoughts washed over Erica in a torrent. She'd have to gather data on how ripples flowed. It meant creating events whose effects she could make direct observations of. Dozens of possibilities came to her.

Ulrin returned to laying out rules and expectations. Erica made sure to commit them to memory. Even as she did, she worked out a plan. She'd set a fire. With a few well-placed words to Laethem and Cellis, she should be able to twist them from rivals into enemies. Watching the flow of events between them would be educational.

She would learn to recognize the path of events which rippled from the actions. With enough information, she might be able to ensure all of her spells created the greatest shifts. She hoped without expending quota on trivial things like predictions. Laethem was proving to be a useful tool yet again.

"BRING HER TO THE ARKHEK Arcanum when the auctions have concluded." With a furrowed brow and down-turned mouth, Cellis studied Drom's struggling wife. "I have one last task I must attend to and a squirming slave would be burdensome. There will be a bit extra in it for you."

Drom followed in silence as Cellis strode off towards the shop. One last glance back before the auction square was out of view showed Arasha calming down. She was staring after the two of them with reddened eyes. This was going to be torture for them both, each for a different reason.

"I am surprised at you Droya. You haven't thanked me yet." Cellis glanced back at Drom without a visible expression. "Regardless however, you are indeed welcome."

"Thank you Master." Drom couldn't bring himself to muster a proper tone in light of the terrible situation he'd led Arasha into.

"Tell me again," Cellis glanced back to the auction now a little way behind them. "What was it you claim caused you to steal from me?"

Drom spoke without putting thought into it, repeating the abbreviated details of how he had used up his savings on Arasha and how the rival shop had undersold him by an exceptional margin. His regrets had made constant circles of it, so the words came without effort. He didn't have to think to relay it, instead remaining focused on Arasha. Unpleasant thoughts finally sidetracked as Cellis spoke at the end of the woeful tale.

"Bezzal's Artifacts and Oddities, you say they were underselling by a great margin? Odd they evaded the notice of the Guardsmen this time of year. Are you certain in your belief they were selling counterfeit goods?"

"What else could it have been? There wouldn't be a profit there otherwise."

"What else indeed?" Cellis stroked his beard, eyes distant. "What else are you aware of regarding the owner and store?"

"Nothing else. I've never been inside." Drom wrenched his mind away from Arasha. "Si... Master, why is it you're so interested now? I didn't think you believed me." Despite how poor his wife's situation now was, he managed a respectful tone. Regardless of his fate, Drom was grateful the man had been the one to purchase Arasha instead of someone else.

"Because I'm wondering what is Laethem's stake in all of this. The man we bid against was his if you recall."

"Laethem?" Drom was startled by the connection. "You suspect he..." Trailing off without finishing the sentence, he blurted out the next. "He was there! He was part of the omen! The Magus I saw at the other shop was Laethem! I recognized him when he came to talk to you."

"Why didn't you say so previously?" Cellis whirled on him, his face marked by agitation. "It would have saved us half of this conversation."

"I didn't expect there was any connection. It seemed like an odd coincidence."

"You couldn't possibly be a thief by trade. You don't consider implications beyond people's surface actions." Spoken in a manner free of tone, so Drom couldn't be certain if it was a statement, a compliment, or an insult. "I need to contemplate this matter."

They traveled the rest of the way to the shop in silence, Drom focused on this new take on recent events and how the pieces fit together. When they were safe inside the shop, Cellis took a moment to make sure the rat's water remained full before he spoke.

"Lathem doesn't realize I transformed you, I am sure of it. That much of what has occurred wasn't any part of his plotting. He would have been more pleased with himself when he came calling. I also suspect this rival store of yours wasn't selling forgeries. It seems probable they were selling real antiquities with Lathem subsidizing the value for some reason." They moved to the back room. "He is skirting dangerously close to breaking Order laws with his actions. By some interpretations, he's already broken those laws. The overwhelming question is why?"

Drom listened to all of this, deciding it was best not to point out Cellis was becoming caught up in the politics he claimed to abhor with such venom. Instead he asked, "Master, you believe me? About everything that's happened."

"Yes." Cellis busied himself moving containers from the central back room to the room beyond the rune-covered doorway. He motioned Drom to do the same. This flurry of item relocation was something new, and he wasn't sure what the purpose could be, but he complied all the same.

"So," Drom ventured the words with caution, "Why not undo all of this? I can do something to repay the debt I owe you both for the quota you have had to use up and for your bid on Arasha." He held his breath, still moving items as he had been ordered to.

"Your reason for stealing doesn't alter the fact you stole. I am still bound by Order law to uphold your punishment." Cellis didn't even pause in his work. The response was upsetting. Even more so considering how it was obvious Cellis didn't mind sidestepping Order laws when it suited his own interests. With a faint shift in tone Drom couldn't interpret, Cellis continued speaking. "Besides, counter spells for creating homunculi don't exist. They would be a wasteful use of quota without any substantial gains, so no one ever bothered to craft them. Regardless of how you, I or anyone else may feel about the fact, you are an Ill'ln for the rest of your life."

In those few short sentences, Drom's world collapsed. He had held out hope of convincing Cellis to restore him, but the hope died in the span of a heartbeat. Faltering, Drom kept himself doing the ordered task only with difficulty.

"What about just Arasha?" He persisted. If he couldn't save himself, perhaps he could save her, "The price of a Nymph will be more than enough to cover the additional cost of the auction."

"It will, but if she's free, what assurances do I have besides your word you'd continue to display the docile behaviors?"

Drom wanted to protest, but Cellis was correct. There was nothing he could say or do to prove he would keep his word outside of his love for Arasha. Cellis nodded into the silence.

"Disbelieve it if you will, but I regret what I've done to you. I have since the moment your transformation. It was an action taken in anger and far too extreme for the crime regardless of Order law. Those words mean nothing in the end, since it's in the past and can't be undone, but try not to assume my present actions are out of cruelty. I won't deny I'm protecting my own interests, but where I can, I'm doing what I can for you and your wife as well. Take some solace in that if you can."

Abstractly, Drom had suspected the man wasn't pleased with the situation on a personal level. This was the first time Celis had admitted as much openly though. He'd thought knowing for sure would help his resolve. Instead it only showed the Magus wouldn't act on those feelings any more than he already had.

"She'll not be mistreated." Cellis paused in his work to study Drom.

"I understand Master." Indeed, he wouldn't have oathed away everything if he didn't believe Cellis would show a greater degree of compassion and kindness than the average owner. No, he would have since she could have ended up in a brothel. He still didn't believe Cellis would mistreat her though.

"You don't need to call me that anymore." Cellis seemed a bit uncomfortable as he once more set to moving items. "Only whoever buys you."

"I gave my word to act as a Nymph. I intend to do so perfectly for Arasha's sake. Will you be making it an order however Master, or a preference?"

"Preference." Cellis sighed. Drom had been hoping it would be otherwise, but didn't wish to say as much. "I can't imagine the self-control it takes to overcome your Ill'ln nature without the piercer chain being the cause. It is out of character for you from what I have observed since we first met."

"Master?" Drom left the rest of the question unspoken. His confused expression must have filled in the rest of the question for him.

"Historically, Ill'ln have been unable to control their actions without the aid of a piercer. The original Ill'ln were crafted from criminals. It wasn't understood until too late that unlike most homunculi, Ill'ln retained knowledge of who and what they were before the transformation. Most wrought havoc before they could be killed or restrained.

"As a stop-gap measure, piercer chains were developed, but every new Ill'ln suffered the same violent streak regardless of how their creators attempted to refine the process. One such variation was to alter the gender of the Ill'ln from their human self as all the initial variations were crafted from males. After all, the majority of death-sentenced criminals were and still are male. It didn't work, but did create an additional manner of punishment for those criminals being used, as you are intimately familiar with. Years later it was discovered Ill'ln were unlike most homunculi in yet another manner as they were able to breed true.

"Regardless, they never found any way to erase the memories or remove the violent nature from any new Ill'ln they crafted. Even the most docile and compliant slave turned semi-feral after the transformation and required a piercer chain or a strong spell to be kept under control."

Surprised to learn so much about the history of Ill'ln, Drom listened. With the whisper in the back of his mind it was a little wonder they were all violent. At least if the voice was typical of the side-effects that came with the transformation.

Cellis stopped to study the room's contents before moving a few more things to make better use of the space and allow for more to be fit in.

"I have not created any orders regarding your new oath, yet you remain firm in it. I can't imagine the spell worked for you as it had never worked for any previously created Ill'ln. To the best of my knowledge, there is not one account of such a case in all the history of your breed of homunculus."

"You've never struck me as strong-willed. I should say for certain you've not shown such strength of will before now to overcome the base nature of an Ill'ln. It tells me you love her more than most people are capable of. How else could you defy the most basic nature of the Ill'ln?"

Drom opened his mouth to respond, but a firm knock on the front door interrupted. Cellis pivoted toward the front with a soft curse.

"Boil it all." The Magus set his box of trinkets down and picked up a twisted bit of wood on his way to the front. "I would have hoped for more time. Perhaps it's only your wife being delivered, but it seems too soon."

HE WAS HOLDING THE wand of wood in much the way a dagger-man handles a blade and gave Drom the impression it was far more dangerous. Staying a step behind, Drom followed Cellis into the store proper and watched as the door was unlatched and opened. It took a moment for Drom to recognize the clean cut man in the vibrant green and gold of House Griffin who towered in the doorway scowling. It was Arasha's father! They'd only met twice before in the flesh, neither occasion being pleasant for Drom.

"I have come to negotiate the return of my daughter as your man indicated. What is your price?" A voice laced with anger bellowed from the Earl of Griffin.

For a moment, Cellis lapsed into an expression of confusion before setting the wand aside on the same table as the rat cage by the door. "You seem to have the wrong location Sir. I have no man-servants or apprentices and you can be certain I'm no kidnapper."

The Earl scowled. His eyes flickered to the chain around Drom's throat, appraising the value no doubt, then the rest of the shop beyond the two of them. "Don't play games wizard. Your man sent me to seek your place of delivery from the auctioneer. I am here, so speak your price and return Arasha to me."

"Wizard indeed!" Cellis wore an expression like he had bitten into dung. "Wise I may be, but you are addressing a Magus, not a mere scholar."

Drom's brow climbed in surprise. It appeared that indicating Cellis was anything less than his proper station would elicit so harsh a reaction. From what he knew of these two men, this could be quick to turn ugly. Arasha's father was vicious and cutting towards those he disliked. Drom had experienced it firsthand on both prior meetings. Cellis for his own part, had a stubborn streak that grew more obvious when faced with an unpleasant guest. The interactions with Lathem had illustrated the fact as clear as day.

"Your station means nothing to me. The only thing of import is my daughter's freedom. Now discontinue your foolish denial and name your price!"

"So now I am a fool? Look around you Sir, the only servant here is Droya."

"Master," Drom ventured in as humble a tone as he could manage. "A word privately?"

Both of the others stared at him as though he had turned bright purple and sprouted antlers, but Cellis gave a curt gesture of compliance. Nymphs were rare to interrupt unless it was something the owner needed to be made aware of. "One moment." He offered to his guest and moved to the far end of the room out of hearing range at a brisk stride. "The answer is no." Cellis looked like he might spit.

"But," Had his thoughts had been so obvious? "He will pay enough to cover every bit of my debts twofold and you would still have myself for sale." He was resigned to his fate at this stage.

"This isn't about the coin or the quota."

Drom stared uncomprehending. "What other..."

"Laethem. Until I comprehend what he's plotting, I can't comply with her father's desire to have her returned. It might be playing into some greater scheme. Consider this an act of compassion."

Drom couldn't find the words, so gestured he understood even if he didn't agree. They returned to the door where the Earl glowered with ever-greater impatience.

"I assure you I have no knowledge of the man who contacted you, or of the message you received, but return home and after I have come to the bottom of this situation, I will contact you." Cellis let out a slow breath.

Arasha's father on the other hand, if anything, grew less calm and collected than was already the case. No small feat. "You're turning me away after all but kidnapping my daughter and sending the barest hint to have me hunting through half of the city to find you?!"

"I sent you nowhere and I've kidnapped no one. Now, leave my premises unless you wish for me to enact proper legal recourse." The Magus' hand edged as though to regain its grip on the wand.

"So be it." The Earl didn't fail to notice the motion of Cellis' hand. With a snarl, he continued, "Whatever else may come, you will bear the full of my ire." It was no minor threat, considering the powerful position the man held. The door slammed shut behind Arasha's father before Cellis could reply.

CELLIS SHOOK HIS HEAD. "I'd almost forgotten how melodramatic Griffins can be. Thank all that's divine they rarely frequent my shop." Not moving from where he stood by the door, the old Magus stared at its wooden surface for a time. After a long pause, he relatched the bar and began in the direction of the back rooms. "Keep moving items as before, I must make contact."

Drom nodded, returning to his task, forced for a time to dwell in silence with his own emotions. Arasha was safer, but unable to be freed or return to her family. Drom himself was no help for her situation either. He'd never felt so helpless in his life. Any distraction would have been welcome.

One came a short time and pungent spell later, Cellis spoke with Llwana in the orb, so Drom listened in when he could.

"I'm beginning to feel like you're making excuses to talk to me Cellis, what is the latest?"

"Where are you docked?"

"We aren't. We're at sea, why?" She frowned. "Speak plainly."

"I can say with fair certainty Laethem is going to try to eliminate me. Probably you too. If I don't contact you at any point soon, head south."

Drom lost whatever was said next as he was in the other room. Something about the room seemed to muffle outside sound more than the other rooms did. Even his enhanced hearing wasn't helpful. He returned to discover Llwana wearing a confused expression.

"Supplies for six months! That would take up the full measure of our hold, most of the crew quarters and half the top deck. What sort of ship do you imagine we're sailing?"

"Fine, as much as you can afford the space for." Cellis didn't seem pleased. "We're going to need it if the situation becomes dire enough to require heading east."

"Are you expecting to circle the continent?"

"Not quite." Cellis smirked. It reminded Drom of a young boy. "I owe you an adventure. I might fulfill my oath yet."

Again the conversation was lost as Drom hauled a large unlabeled box he was sure should have been heavy despite the fact his frail-seeming body had no trouble with it in the least. The conversation was drawing to a close by the time he was out again.

"I'll try Cellis. Michael isn't going to like it and the crew isn't so loyal I'd trust them not to mutiny by the second month."

"I trust your powers of persuasion Llwana."

"That makes one of us." She rolled her eyes as the globe clouded over and her face faded from it.

Cellis sighed. "Let's hope I'm being over-cautions." Drom remained quiet, continuing to relocate boxes. Cellis resumed as well, letting the silence linger between them.

Halfway through packing the room with all sorts of chests, crates, and loose items, another knock sounded from the front of the building. This one was firm, but not insistent.

They exchanged glances and Cellis nodded. Both moved towards the front. Hand hovering near where he had left the wand, Cellis motioned for Drom to lift the bar of the door. When he had done so, the Magus inched the door open.

Cellis let out the breath he'd been holding and withdrew his hand from the wand. Drom's heart skipped a beat at the sight of Arasha beyond the opening. Even bedraggled as she was, she looked like the Princess herself to him.

The moment was ruined as she realized how close Drom stood and let out a heart shattering scream.

Chapter Six
The Justice of the Circle

Cellis studied the toad-like creature as it folded its wings upon landing. They'd taught the basics of homunculi in the classes. Ill'ln and Trolls aside, this was the first he'd seen up close.

"What is he?"

"Hmm?" His master, Gosen, glanced up from the tome. "Oh, Ren? He's an Imp."

"Isn't that someone who puts feathers on falcons?"

"Yes, but this is a different sort of imp. Called Imps because of their usefulness in minor tasks. The official name is Khal'van."

"I've never encountered one."

"They've fallen out of fashion. Few are crafted these days. Quota-heavy to convert and most Magi prefer to cross a room when they need something minor."

The Imp's little frame seem frail, despite having seen it cross the room with the heavy tome. Cellis was torn between revulsion and fascination. It bore warty gray skin, leathery wings, and solid black eyes. The being gave the impression of a miniature demon. Gosen's words sank in only after he'd stopped staring at it.

"How can Ill'ln be so common? Wouldn't they use more quota than this diminutive Imp did?"

"Ill'ln breed true."

"Oh. I'd read some homunculi do so, but the texts didn't specify which ones. I wish I'd had you there when Laethem argued with me

about that point. I assumed he was trying to sound smart since I've never seen a pregnant Ill'ln."

"The Circle insists on all births happening in a controlled environment. Young Ill'ln are raised the same way." Gosen peered up from the tome he'd been reading as he spoke and frowned. "Laethem? That's the bed-wetter apprentice?"

"No. That's Erica. They tend to hang around one another. You were aware of that?"

"I researched each apprentice before choosing."

"Laethem is the one who tried to blame me when his trunk caught on fire." Cellis' pride swelled at the idea of being chosen rather than assigned.

"Ah yes." The corner of Gosen's lips quirked upwards. "If Ill'ln surprise you, you may not have learned about hippogriffs yet."

"They were homunculi created as battle steeds, similar to wild griffins but more controllable." He liked being able to answer something obscure.

"Absolutely correct. Griffins, however, are homunculi as well." When Cellis stared, the Master clarified. "They were crafted before the sixty year war, but bred true and naturalized after escaping. Hippogriffs were an attempt to recreate them. Documents were lost and the proper base creature was never rediscovered. It worked out better anyway. While less fierce, they are much better steeds. They're also sterile, which helps keep enemy kingdoms from creating their own without the quota costs."

Cellis stood in awe. There was so much his new Master knew. He couldn't wait to learn it all. No doubt he'd been chosen for their shared love of rare knowledge and magic.

DESPITE EVERYTHING, Drom had almost forgotten his new appearance. Without making a conscious decision to do so, he took a step towards her. The way she recoiled kept him from taking any farther. His form and situation had grown too familiar, allowing him to ignore the shape and sensitivity of this new body until now.

Arasha's fear when she looked at him brought it all back in full force. He couldn't comfort her, couldn't tell her he loved her. He couldn't even act as anything but the Elf woman he now was, thanks to the chain and his oath. All he could do was stand there with his eyes passive and downcast in the hope she would feel less threatened.

Cellis studied Arasha, then the two guards from the auction who were now tensed to prevent her from struggling free. He produced a two bronze buckles, coins each worth about two copper buttons, from his coin-purse to tip the men for bringing her. With a motion for Drom to move farther inside, the Magus took Arasha's chain and drew her in with an effort.

"Enough of this." Cellis shut the door behind the departing guards. "You were a Lady of House Griffin. Convey yourself with more dignity than some fresh-bought brothel girl."

Arasha's eyes blazed with fury as she rounded on Cellis, "You never," but she trailed off. Her eyes softened back into resignation and fear. She stopped struggling to evade Drom though.

"Better. Now, I don't comprehend why you have such an aversion to Droya, but she is of no harm to you."

"Ill'ln have been known to escape the piercers. She is anything but harmless." There was a hesitation, followed by a detached "Sir."

Drom couldn't help but look up. He was taken aback at his wife's willingness to fall into speaking as an inferior to anyone. How many times had she ranted to him about the wrongs of intelligent homunculi, slavery, and the arrogance of the Magi? Yet, here she was showing no passion against slavery being imposed on her. Only her fear of Ill'ln seemed to retain any strength at all.

How could she be willing to bow her head and call anyone short of an Earl 'Sir'? Had he been wrong all this time about her strength of conviction? Then again, a month ago, he would have asked the same question regarding himself.

"Droya is a Nymph. She is nothing to be feared."

"Nymphs wear no piercer chains." Arasha managed a sideways glance towards Drom.

"That is a slight misnomer. Magic-broken Nymphs wear no chains. Those broken through a platinum piercer often retain the piercer chains."

Arasha didn't respond.

"You will recognize the truth of this in due time. Chain-broken Nymphs are almost never seen in the current era, but there was a time when they were the only sort of Nymph to exist."

Drom struggled for some way to affirm this. Nothing came to mind that couldn't be attributed to the chain itself. Arasha was looking away now anyway.

Another knock sounded yet again. This time a single light rap on the door. Any further discussion was halted as Cellis cursed "Erosana's Tit!" and snatched up the wand again. After tossing up the crossbar, he pulled the heavy door open.

"How many times..." As the door swung open Cellis froze, his sentence unfinished. It was not a pause or double take. He just stopped all motion of any sort. It was as if he'd become a statue.

Three men in red and black leather rushed through the door. They rounded their weapons on Drom, but he was too puzzled to react. Arasha screamed at the sudden appearance of armed men rushing them. She fainted, landing hard on the stones of the floor. Drom could only imagine how harsh this day had been on her mind. Had the armed men not been between them, he'd have rushed to catch her.

A fourth fellow slipped in. Tall and thin, he dressed in the same colors as the others, but with an insignia Drom didn't recognize. The way he carried himself removed any doubt he was the group's leader.

He was followed by a stout man in robes of the group's colors. This last fellow had eyes only for Cellis, deep concentration marking his face as he focused on the Magus.

"Fool." the commander sneered at Cellis as he shut the door behind them. "The idiot never gave the Ill'ln an order of defense. He didn't even have his wand up." The commander cleared his throat, causing the armed men to relax their weapons.

"At the command of the Order, you are now in the custody of the Red Machtha. You will remain in custody until you can face trial on the charge of high crimes against both the Order and the kingdom." The commander paused as if Cellis would respond. He couldn't of course.

He turned his attention on Drom and the unconscious Arasha. He brushed a strand of black hair behind his ear. "All of your property and assets are now forfeit." The formal tone dropped as he glanced back at the robed man. "So that went well. The Circle will be pleased."

"Sir," It was one of the armed men, "What of these two?"

"It appears the Ill'ln is under no order to defend her master, so you can lower your weapons now. Laethem needs the woman, but as long as she's uninjured, anything else is of little consequence." The commander seemed disinterested. His eyes fell on the door to the back room and he gestured. "We aren't expected back for a short while. You men deserve a reward for a job well done."

The guards sheathed their blades. One bent to lift Arasha's limp form from the ground. The other two grinned at one another and approached Drom. It took a few heartbeats to identify the glint in their eyes. Lust. Lust directed at him, or as they believed, her.

The two took a grip of his arm on either side and drew him towards the back room. The third was carrying Arasha in the same direction. Revulsion welled up in Drom at the realization of what they meant to do. It was unlike any fear he'd ever experienced. More intimate and terrifying than even the fear of death.

The leader of the men spoke in quiet tones to Cellis, who remained frozen in place. A superior expression inched across the tall man's face at whatever it was he was saying. Drom only gave it a moment of his attention, however.

What was about to happen to him? Worse, what was about to happen to his wife? The primal voice in his head, faint since the market, came back now in force. Pain blossomed for even listening to it and flared brightly as his own thoughts aligned with it. Violence was allowed to protect Cellis, but this wasn't about the Magus. It was about Arasha. A seething rage boiled up in him. It didn't drown out the pain, but he didn't care if his body burned away from it. They would not do this to Arasha!

As one of the men released Drom's arm to open the door anger spilled out into action. His mind was filled with the voice. It moved his body as though he had the reflexes of a feral animal. A beast intent only on destroying everything before it.

The man still holding him didn't finish the scream from the breaking of his arm as Drom's own arms wrapped around his head and broke his neck before he could. Shifting momentum, his hands drew away the blade from the sheath of the falling body. He spun, driving it into the second man turning to see what the sound was.

It all happened in a fuzzy state of consciousness. His mind was detached from his body, leaving him to vague curiosity. He'd never fought a day in his life. How was he taking on trained men? His body followed new reflexes, rounding on the third guard, but now the pain levels peaked. His mind scattered before the pain, all thought, and emotion dissolving away.

Deprived of anything but pain, he locked up in agony. As the haze of unconsciousness fell, he was powerless to take direct action about the third man dropping Arasha to draw his weapon. Drom's own body fell, but he managed enough effort through the pain to shift his weight so he fell below where Arasha would land. As blackness overtook his sight, a sound like muted thunder clapped. Then there was nothing.

HAZE GAVE WAY TO THROBBING awareness and the sound of Cellis' voice.

"Get up, damn you both! We don't have the time for this." The voice sounded like it came from another room.

Drom's eyes opened, and he lifted his head a bit. Making a scan of the room as his ability to focus returned, he couldn't recall the last thing that had happened. As he saw the bodies, it came back to him. The remaining men who'd been standing when he fell were now sprawled on the floor unmoving. Unlike those Drom had killed, they didn't lie in pools of blood. In fact, there was no indication of what might have dropped them. He'd have thought they were unconscious if not for the lack of breathing.

A soft moan escaped Arasha, who remained on Drom's back where she'd fallen. Cellis came from the rear room. The Magus grabbed a handful of items from shelves as he spoke.

"Excellent! You're awake. Rouse her. Be quick about it too. At best we have an hour or so before what has happened here is discovered. If we're caught again, they won't be so easily undone." Again Cellis passed through the door into the back of the store. Drom was left trying to puzzle out how they'd survived.

He was hesitant as he opened his mouth. "Arasha," He shifted to slide her from atop him and caressed her shoulder. It took more effort than expected not to add 'my sweet' or 'dove' at the end of her name. He wished to say so much more, but instead he backed away. He knelt with his hands on his knees and his eyes downcast in the classic servile pose of a passive slave. Anything if it would ease her fears. "My lady."

He had to repeat it several times before she stirred. "Cellis wishes for you to wake. I believe it's his expectation that more men will be coming." He kept his eyes downcast.

Arasha blinked in confusion, unfocused in the half-conscious state. Her eyes opened and closed several times as though she wasn't clear-eyed enough to recognize who was speaking. Those eyes settled on the bloody bodies of the two men Drom had killed, then onto the others laying lifeless.

Fear spread over her face, directed at Drom and she scuttled back on all fours, putting space between them.

"You," her voice cracked, "Killed them!" No hint of question in her tone. She spoke it with absolute certainty. Before he could reply, Cellis returned.

"No, Droya did not kill these men," Cellis didn't look their way as he continued his work. His voice remained casual. As though he'd been in the room the whole time. "I did. Droya merely distracted them."

Drom studied where Cellis was selecting items from his display shelves in a rush. Why was the aged Magus lying for him? Pity, regret? Some other reason? Arasha seemed uncertain of how much she trusted what had been said anyway.

"Be thankful she did too. They had intentions on your virtue." Cellis motioned at Drom, indicating he should rise. Drom did so, moving to where the aged man was nearing another shelf.

Arasha watched Drom like a hen watches a feral cat. Her only response was, "Oh." The tone of which sounded far from convinced.

"Both of you, gather anything from the shelves that bears this symbol on the tag." Cellis pointed to a large tag in front of the spot he'd grabbed from. The symbol on the upper right-hand corner resembled a bullseye with three lines forming a vague triangle around it.

"Yes sir." Arasha was again being uncharacteristically timid as she rose from her spot.

"Yes Master." Drom spoke in the same moment. He still had a hard time grasping his wife acting so passive. She was inconsistent with the woman he'd married. Acting passive himself was awkward, but he had no choice at all. Even without the piercer chain, it was for his wife's sake. No, he had to do it. What made her?

There weren't many items with the indicated symbol, but finding them consumed time. Arasha avoided areas where the red and black clad bodies lay as well as anywhere Drom was working. For his own part, Drom avoided looking at her directly or any other act which might cause her discomfort. When all the items were gathered, Cellis returned to the front and picked up the rat cage.

"Both of you bring these to the back stock room and meet me in the casting closet. Droya is aware of the location." The old man and the rat eyed one another through the bars as Cellis lifted the cage level with his face.

Both complied without speaking. Drom led the way, carrying the bulk of the items. He knew it had to be heavy, but the strength of his new form made the burden seem light.

When the clutter of mystical artifacts was secured in the correct room, they went to the casting closet. Arasha remained a respectable distance from Drom through the entire task. They found Cellis chanting over a large bowl. Incense smoldered on either side and stank of stagnant water. He passed his hands over the bowl several times as though stroking a nervous cat.

Arasha seemed to forget her fear of Ill'ln, moving closer for a better inspection. Faint squeaks rose from within the bowl as Cellis finished chanting. The Magus glanced at the two of them now.

"Quick. Bring the two barrels from the front near the East wall."

Drom left without a second thought to carry out the task. It wasn't until he had the first barrel lifted that Arasha's absence was noticed. He'd have to carry them alone it would seem. Judging the weight, he decided he could manage both, so gathered the second with care. Even with his new-found strength, the barrels proved awkward to carry. He had to set one barrel down long enough to open the door again.

The sound of the rodent was much louder now, and it seemed to be squealing in pain. Little sound penetrated the front shop from the back rooms. Especially the strange storage room. Until now, Drom hadn't thought about it closely. Not that there was much reason for him to worry over it.

Arasha was almost beside the bowl now, peering with apprehensive curiosity into it. Drom's arrival prompted Cellis to wave to hurry him over.

"Quick! Open the first and begin pouring it into the bowl."

Unsure why they would be torturing and drowning a rat in a bowl, Drom complied. He pulled the knobbed lid from the first barrel, releasing the scent of rotting fish. Arasha's nose wrinkled, though she didn't shy from the bowl, and Drom's own senses were overloaded for a moment by the foul stench. Recovering, he lifted the barrel and poured.

The syrupy stuff oozed out in a thin yellow stream. Glinting metallic flecks suspended in it sparkled in the light as it flowed into the bowl. Drom was careful to avoid any of it escaping the bowl as he poured. How long before the rodent drowned in the sticky fluid? It seemed cruel, but he didn't have any real choice. The rodent convulsed within the ever-deepening slime.

"What are you doing to it?" Arasha spoke Drom's own curiosity. The level of the fluid in the bowl wasn't rising with the speed it should have, though Drom was pouring at a steady pace. peeking into the bowl again, the rat seemed larger than it had been.

"Providing mass to fuel his return to a previous form. Without doing so, the transformation would consume whatever matter was at hand. Possibly yourselves included." Cellis didn't look at her though Arasha stepped back from the bowl in an instinctive gesture. Drom would have liked to step away as well.

"Transitions in form," The wizened man explained, "Mean the physical material of whatever is being altered must increase or decrease to match the matter contained in the new form. Living forms do so though digestion or excretion if it can be done within the limits of the spell's duration. If they can't do so, they absorb elements from whatever happens to be nearest to them instead."

As much as it reminded him of an Order school lecture, Drom was glad to have it spoken. The information was new to him, so must have been something taught only to students slated for an apprenticeship. It explained why Drom had woken in such a soiled state after his transformation.

"What are you making it into?" Arasha's eager curiosity was greater than Drom would have expected. She loved to learn and was fascinated with magic. Still, it was like she forgot her current circumstances. "A horse to ride on?"

"Not at all." Cellis chuckled. "He was once a human. I intend to see him return to human form and make him an offer. A deal in exchange for the return of his freedom. I suspect he'll be glad for a way to pay off his debt to me."

The contents of the first barrel had slowed to a trickle, so Drom set it down and opened the next. By now the rodent filled the bowl and was about the size of the average dog. Its body structure was shifting as well, and it now crouched upright. It dipped its head low to gulp in greedy swallows at the fluid.

When Drom tipped the next barrel up, the creature leaned forward as if compelled by unseen hands, the narrow snout driving into the sludge. He had to fight back nausea at the thought of drinking the foul fluid from these barrels. The stink alone would have been too much for Drom's senses a few weeks ago, let alone now. Blessedly he'd learned how to tune out some sensory input having grown familiar with stronger senses.

Arasha no longer asked questions, instead content to watch the slow transformation with fascination. She was transfixed and for the first time since her arrival, some spark of the passionate woman Drom knew shone through. Her eyes were alive with thought and wonder. Drom was elated, beaming despite himself before turning his attention back to the rodent.

The rat was now more man than animal. It had a grizzled countenance evoking an instinctual fear. The gleam of hate still danced in dark eyes, but now it had a form able to act on that hatred. Were the half-man creature not gulping down the repugnant fluid, would it instead be attacking Cellis. Was there wisdom in returning this beast from its low station into a state where it might take revenge?

"Amazing!" Arasha broke the silence in an excited whisper.

"Transformations oft are." Cellis frowned, studying to the woman. "Arasha, behind you there is a weathered cloak. Gather it up and bring it to me." He spoke her name as though trying to decide if he wished to continue using it in the future. At least that's how it sounded to Drom. It could have been his imagination. Some people renamed slaves, but Cellis had only done so to Drom due to gender and linguistic issues. Hadn't he?

Arasha was hesitant as she complied, making an effort not to miss a moment of the transformation. The rat's tail was now gone, and the face was reshaping. Most of the hair was thinning away, leaving it more human by the moment. Drom's wife stepped wide around him and handed Cellis the cloak as she returned.

The old Magus walked behind the transforming man and waited for him to stop gulping. Only a quarter of the second barrel remained as Drom lowered it. He had pictured the human-turned-rat as a crouching sort of man who must have resembled a rat even before his transformation. Instead the man was tall and almost regal despite the weary stance and the mess of fluid that had missed his mouth. He was well-muscled, though not so much so it would impede limber movement.

He was gasping for air after wiping some mess from his face and chestnut brown hair. Black eyes were now a pale shade of green staring out past a noble nose. Dark olive skin marked him as foreign, Lithkanian perhaps. Drom knew his look if not personally. Enough to grasp this was the sort of man who had played on the hearts of many a doting woman.

A pang of jealousy hit Drom as Arasha was studying the man. Cellis dropped the cloak over his shoulders, hiding some of his indecency at least. Drom knew from her sidelong glance, Arasha found this man attractive. Always before, if she'd glanced the view of another man, he brushed it aside with ease. After all, she'd chosen Drom, and he never doubted her loyalty for a moment. She'd sacrificed everything to be with him. How could he not trust her?

Things were different now. Arasha must believe Drom had abandoned her. He himself could never tell her the truth thanks to the geas set on him. How long would it be before she gave up hope of his return forever and become receptive to the advances of another? Assuming Cellis allowed his slaves such diversions anyway. At what point would the expression in her eyes become a meaningful thing?

"You have a choice." Cellis was scowling at the now-cloaked man with sparkling syrup coating his features. He was met with a venomous expression in return. "You may either agree to aid us as payment for the remainder of your criminal debt to me, or you can return to your rodent state forever."

"Some choice." The man grumbled before spitting out some slimy residue from his mouth. "As though I have any real options."

"There is always a choice." Cellis' expression was impassive. "Even if the choices aren't what we would like."

"So be it. I'll do what I can to help you." The man's eyes were now staring at Drom rather than Cellis. There was something in his expression which unsettled him. Tearing his eyes away, Drom watched Arasha. She was smiling! Part of him was joyful for having her smile return, but contemplating why it was there unnerved him. Made a slave, sold to a man who owned her worst fear and preparing to run after being attacked. There was nothing to smile about today of all days. Was it the chance to observe magic directly, or was it the result? Drom's eyes returned to the man she was focusing her smile on and frowned.

Chapter Seven
The Skills of a Thief

"I was under the impression Cellis liked you." This conversation was veering onto an uncomfortable and personal vein.

"I don't know. We're close friends." Warmth filled Llwanna's cheeks as she answered her mentor. "Why ruin it by chasing maybes?"

"Perhaps." Master Magus Roseline appeared amused as she replied. "He is thinking like a fairy no doubt."

"What?" Llwanna was bewildered by the unfamiliar expression.

Her mentor didn't speak right away. Instead she stared out the window, watching as a sparrow took flight. She remained silent this way until Llwanna joined her.

"Years ago there was a song popular in the taverns, 'The Magus' Frog.'" Roseline didn't look to Llwanna, remaining focused on the bird as it flitted away. "The song told the story of a fairy who came upon a Magus. He'd frozen a frog mid-leap to study it. Afraid the frog would be captured and harmed, she attacked the Magus. His concentration faltered. The frog, now free, was unaware anything had happened. All it knew was it was hungry and something was buzzing nearby. With a quick lash of its tongue, the fairy was eaten, and the frog hopped into the water."

"How does this relate at all?"

"Like most men, Cellis has trouble understanding what women want. Like the fairy, he doesn't see the truth of the situation. He's oblivious to what matters." The elder Magus' smile grew, turning her

attention to Llwanna. "Men try to do what they conclude is best. It makes things worse just as often as not."

They both laughed at the assessment and returned to training. Llwanna was relieved to be off of the topic.

WHY WAS THERE A REVERSAL to the rat transformation, but not one for his own? It was frustrating, but he let it go, albeit with reluctance. There were more vital matters at present and he couldn't ask Cellis right now anyway. Arasha continued to grin at the former rat as Cellis spoke. It did nothing for Drom's state of mind.

"Exceptional. I have limited the spell so if you do not return and have a boost from me every eight hours, your form will revert to a rat." He pointed aged finger and added, "And don't assume some other Magus will be able to substitute. Anyone but myself tampering will cause several organs to burst."

"Understood." the man grumbled, shooting a smirk towards Arasha and Drom before returning his attention to Cellis. "What would you have me do, 'Oh mighty Magus'?"

"I don't need your respect, just your cooperation." Cellis wasn't oblivious to the tone at least. "Find us somewhere to stay for a week or so until plans can be clarified. Somewhere safe."

"Sure." The former rat studied Drom. "Poor Droya, you have my pity." How was he aware of names? Was he aware of everything from his time as a rat? To Arasha he offered, "Sweet Arasha, I'm sorry for your loss. Perhaps when this messy business is over, Cellis will set you free to be with a man who doesn't turn tail and leave you to rot." A flicker of his eyes to Drom was met with invisible daggers. "My name fair lady is Ries, should you need a shoulder to cry on."

"Get to your task thief" Cellis scowled.

"Of course. I assume the wash basin and clothing chest are still located in the same place?"

"No, but there is a bowl of water, a tunic, and a pair of pantaloons in the central rear room waiting for you."

With a bow, Ries exited. Arasha's expression was one of musing while Cellis and Drom both frowned after the man.

"No time to waste. Droya, pull the storage door from the wall and we will depart shortly."

Drom shot an uncertain glance at Cellis. The tingling precursor to pain surfaced at not following the order right away. It spread through his skin and prompted a quick inquiry. "Pull the door Master?"

"Yes, as in grab it on either side and draw it away from the wall."

Arasha had regained enough of her fear to be standing well away from Drom again, but her curious expression mirrored Drom's own. Drom didn't want to break his oath, let alone deal with the pain of the piercer, so he left the casting room and walked to the storage door. The other two followed though only Arasha was paying close attention to what he did. To the side, the bowl of water and a cloth sat soiled by the viscous fluids and filth. There was no sign of Ries.

There was an audible pop as Drom pulled, but the door came free in his slender hands. The wall where it had been was smooth, as if nothing had ever been present.

Cellis grabbed a large sheet of cloth and some rope they hadn't packed away, moving near. "Now to wrap it up and we can be on our way. Droya, set it down please."

Drom did as requested, stepping back. He watched as Cellis prepared to wrap the door as if it were some odd bit of furniture. Cellis acted as though it were normal. Arasha had once again forgotten her fear of Drom. She wore open curiosity as she studied. Her attention didn't waver until the door disappeared under cloth and rope. Drom knew she found magic fascinating, but hadn't understood how much she was drawn to it. It bothered him to realize there were things about her he hadn't understood.

"Gather it up and both of you follow close."

Stepping into the front of the store, it turned out Ries waited there. How had he cleaned up and dressed so quickly?

"Where am I to find you once I complete my task?"

"Granary road alley." Cellis opened the door, allowing the others to exit ahead of him. The wrapped door Drom carried caught brief attention from those on the street, but didn't hold anyone's interest long. The sight of an Elf performing heavy labor wasn't a reason for anyone to raise an eyebrow.

Ries slipped out and was lost in the crowd even before Cellis could close the door behind them.

"How did he learn my name and situation?" Arasha voiced Drom's earlier thoughts. Her eyes were lingering on the spot where Ries had last been visible with a puzzled expression. She only turned away once Cellis replied.

"His mind remained human despite his form. There is much he has overheard since I altered him. Your name is the least of it. Were he not under the geas, he would be dangerous."

They moved down the street, keeping to the side as they did. This turned out to be a mixed blessing as the door Drom carried obscured Cellis and Arasha as a party of men in the colors of House Griffin passed. Neither Arasha nor the group caught sight of one another or it might have led to a large public situation. The group was led by Arasha's own father and he had the House Magus with him!

There could be little doubt what they intended to do and part of Drom wished it had taken a little longer for them to leave. Fifteen minutes more and Arasha might have been freed to rejoin her family. Cellis was right however. As much as Drom hated to admit it, even to himself. Until Lathem's plot was clear, she was probably safer with them. What did Lathem believe ransoming her back to her father would accomplish anyway?

It was only a short trip before they arrived at the alley in question. They paused to wait for fewer eyes on them, then slipped down the narrow space between buildings. Drom was forced to maneuver around trash while balancing the awkward shape of the door. Given the scent in the air wafting down the alley and the buzz of flies everywhere, he was careful where he stepped. As was the case with many Ill'ln, he was barefoot after all.

"There is a point in this alley where it widens enough for my needs. By now, there may be at least a few men out hunting us. Masking my castings with counterfeit crystals won't do anything useful if someone recognizes one of us." Cellis had counterfeit crystals?

The alley indeed opened into a wide area as Cellis had told them it would. It was here they stopped. Drom put the door down, leaning it against an unobstructed area of wall. Arasha found a semi-clean spot to sit and clutched her knees to her chest. Drom wanted to comfort her, but knew better. Instead he stood until Cellis ordered him otherwise.

"Set up the door. Quickly!"

"Yes Master." Drom unwrapped it.

"When it's open, I will need assistance from both of you. Droya, you're going to act as a channel, since I have no familiar. Arasha, you're going to act as an assistant."

A light flickered in Arasha's eyes and the tears threatening to fall were banished in an instant. She rose with all the smooth grace Drom remembered and moved as close as her fear of him would allow.

Once the door was in place, Cellis entered and returned with a few oddities. It was various crystals, a bit of clay, and two wooden dolls. Arasha was instructed to place the crystals in a circle while Cellis sculpted some basic traits with the clay onto the wooden dolls.

One became the crude likeness of a woman, the other a man. These he handed to Drom.

"Arasha, we are going to have to both place a hand on Droya. It is the only way to make this illusion strong enough to pass scrutiny. You have my word Droya won't harm you in any way."

The visible desire to participate warred on her face with the stark terror at the idea of touching an Ill'ln. She placed the last crystal and rose with a slight tremble. By her edging towards Drom, compliance was winning out over her fear by a narrow margin. It was heartbreaking.

Cellis ignored it, feigning not to notice and Drom did nothing to draw attention to it either. The smooth touch of Arasha's hand made his skin prickle. This form's enhanced senses meant Drom could recognize the soft ridges of her fingerprints. The urge to take her hand in his own was cutting, but he pushed it down in his mind. He contented himself with her light touch on his wrist. To take any action would only frighten her and be out of keeping with the Nymph nature he had given his word to follow.

The Magus took his other wrist after retrieving the dolls, chanting with his eyes closed. Drom watched as the dolls were waved in geometric patterns before being pressed to the cleft of Drom's chest, slid down to rest between his bosom and held against his heart. The press of flesh and the apron-dress were enough to hold them in place as Cellis removed his hand. It was an uncomfortable reminder of Drom's situation.

Hand now free, Cellis continued his patterns and chanting with two fingers extended and the others curled. Drom's arms tingled where each of them held his wrist. The tingle in his limber limbs became a numbing throb seeping up. Was this supposed to happen? The grip of both tightened as there was a surge of something through him. Drom became light-headed and woozy, his heart racing and chest burning.

Three lengthy syllables in some strange language brought it all to a sudden halt. The uncomfortable feeling faded away and Drom's wrists were released. Cellis and Arasha were gone, replaced by an average looking young woman in slave clothing and a middle-aged man in a noble robe. It was cut in the manner of a Magus fresh out of apprenticeship.

"I trust you are both still well?" Cellis' new voice was deeper than the original.

"Yes Master. That was peculiar." Drom's attention was on Arasha, making a covert study of the now-brunette woman from the corner of his eyes. Freckles? Of all the adjustments, the addition of those was the oddest to Drom.

"Yes Sir. Well enough." Arasha studied the minute differences in her hands. Drom noted the illusion didn't hide the soft 'h' sound she added at the end of words with 'l' at the end. Her eyes went to Cellis, taking in all the minute adjustments that added up to a complete modification in the man's appearance. "How long does it last?"

"Until the poppets are destroyed." Cellis plucked the two dolls from Drom's chest. Both now resembled the new forms worn by Arasha and Cellis.

"What about myself Master?" Drom was curious if an illusion of his former self could serve as a makeshift solution to his inability to return to his real form. Something to consider.

"I altered the appearance of your piercer to appear gold. It should be more than enough and doesn't require any extra power to be channeled." Cellis took the dolls through the doorway placing them on a shelf just inside the room. "As it stands, I will have to switch crystals again to avoid notice. Droya, gather up the focus circle and pack up the door once you've put them away."

"Yes Master." He gathered up crystals.

"So now what?" Arasha was again studying herself as well as she could without a reflective surface.

"Now, we wait."

THREE SILENT HOURS passed, leaving Drom to dwell on many things about his situation. Few of them were pleasant. Cellis kept pacing and moving his lips as though he were talking. Arasha had long since stopped studying herself and had resumed her fetal sitting position. From time to time she would peek her head up from where her arms crossed over her knees.

It was Drom's sensitive new eyes and ears that first revealed Ries was near. Before Drom could say something to the others, the thief spoke.

"I have a location. Not suitable by far for the sweet lady slave, but just right for yourself Cellis." Drom frowned at being left out and even more at the clear attempt to flirt with Arasha. At least she didn't acknowledge the statement.

"Took you long enough." Cellis grumped, ignoring the man's jab.

"Safe houses aren't as common as you seem to believe. You're lucky the Nymph and the door clued me in to who you were. Oh, and you can thank me later about sowing some rumors."

"What sort of rumors?" The old man's new face was scowling with such sharp angles it felt like it wore his true age for all the lines it held.

"Oh, rumors the Order was trying to destroy the merchant guilds and how they are moving against the ones who tried to expose them. I figure with the rumors of the Prince and ruling Houses all being involved in similar schemes, it should throw a bit of sand in their gears."

"The Prince?" Cellis kicked a bit of trash and wrung his hands. He seemed to be talking to himself rather than Ries. "How? What does that have to do with Lathem? It must since it involves the merchants."

"Word has it a number of lesser Houses led a coup today after it was discovered the ruling Houses had all been plotting to frame the Order of scheming. I figured since we both already realize the Order was behind it, this should put them off balance."

"You fool! The rumor you started won't hold up regardless of truth. It's going to make them hunt us even harder now. The Earl of Griffin went to the store after we left. People will assume your rumor was off and it was the High Houses who were trying to silence someone."

"How was I supposed to realize that?"

"Father!" Arasha snapped out of her silence.

"He is alive, pending a trial. As are most of the House leaders." Ries assured, "You need not worry just yet."

"Most? Wait, trial?" Drom interrupted.

"She speaks! Yes most. House Shingu and House Apsuru's leaders where not present when the others were set upon. It seems neither was where they were expected to be."

"We forced Laethem's hand when he assumed I was getting involved. He wasn't ready to move or he would have netted them all." Cellis' eyes were distant as he tried to piece it all together.

"Earl of Apsuru!" The sharp squeal from Drom wasn't meant to be so piercing. It caused the others to stare at him. Even Arasha managed to pause her fretting over her father long enough to eye him in puzzlement.

"Droya?" Cellis was the first to react.

"I met him in the market. He wanted me to tell you Lord Kirk of House Apsuru sends his regards and your pet is ill tempered." It should have bothered Drom more than it did to call himself a pet, but right now it didn't seem important.

"So noted. That isn't helpful or relevant right now. It's no reason to be drawing attention down the alley either."

"But it is helpful. He said you did him a favor in the past. If he is still free, he might be able to help us." Drom was unaware of Cellis' plans, but from everything he'd observed in the time with him, it seemed clear enough the Magus intended to leave town unnoticed and meet up with Llwanna. Cellis mused this information, tapping his chin, but it wasn't he who spoke next.

"Kirk will help us! He is certain to be preparing a rescue of your father and the Prince already." Arasha's failure to say his title spoke volumes of her former station, as well as her former familiarity with the Earl of Apsuru. "He would be more than willing to help me!"

"You, yes. The man who purchased you, however?" Ries smirked. "That seems a tad less likely my lady slave."

"Contrary to your assertion, the Earl of Apsuru has never been one to ignore a clear legal claim. He will rage against the false accusations leveled on him and the other Houses, but wouldn't dream of challenging a lawfully purchased slave." The Magus' thoughtful expression broke into a one of resolution.

Arasha's eyes tightened at the reminders of her new station, but she nodded in agreement with Cellis.

"And he always repays a debt. This might be an actual blessing." Cellis beamed, no doubt putting a new plan together. "Good girl Droya!"

Drom was surprised to find himself bushing. Cellis never praised anything he'd done. Nor did the man freely extend compliments. The use of 'good girl' was degrading, but obviously heartfelt. Despite himself, it felt wonderful. After so much time feeling worthless, the sense of being valued was almost euphoric.

"Thank you Master."

"So we're going to see Kirk?" Arasha still wore a weary expression, but had a hopeful tone.

"No, at least not yet. If he's smart, he won't be easy to find until he can rally support." Cellis motioned Drom toward the door. "Ries, take us to the safe house. I will provide you with the funds to bribe whatever information broker might be able to put us into contact with the Earl. You will make it happen."

"Yes oh mighty Magus." The sarcasm was thick. "Shall I wrap him up in a bow too?"

"Please?" Arasha spoke before Cellis could react.

"For you my lady slave, of course." Ries took her hand, kissing it. Arasha blushed and Drom winced at the sudden pain earned for the thoughts that came to his mind. He'd almost followed the urging of the faint voice to snap the man's neck. That he himself had blushed only moments before despite himself didn't factor into his thoughts.

"I would be careful were I you Ries." Cellis warned, glancing from Drom to Arasha. "There are those who are worth a world of suffering and of whom your assessments are imprecise. By law, she is mine and all other bonds are nullified. It doesn't mean she is for you to toy with. Do the task I set before you and when all is finished, part company. Don't complicate this."

"Master should have left him a rat." Drom's lip curled and his eyes burned with enough intensity it caused Arasha to recoil. He was forced to soften his voice. "I could have done the work you require."

"I'm afraid not." Cellis offered an expression with mild hints of being apologetic. "You wouldn't have the contacts needed. After all, of the four of us, only Ries is a thief."

Drom was about to contest the idea he couldn't help when the words struck him. Again Drom couldn't help but blush though this time he responded only with "Yes. Master is correct." It was a minor gesture, but an important one. "He should still at least learn his place."

"Yes, I should. Such a well-behaved Nymph such as yourself would make a perfect example for me. Perhaps if I left the lady slave alone. Would you wish me to stop treating her with kindness and respect?" Ries' eyes gleamed. "Droya, being a Nymph of such beauty, you'd allow me to avail myself of your smooth and supple body as an outlet for my more carnal urges. Clearly they are why I have the audacity to treat Arasha with the kindness due from one human to another."

That stung on many levels. Even worse was if he was to live up to his oath, Drom would have to be agreeable and compliant to the suggestion.

Cellis saved him by bellowing. "Enough! We are wasting time. Everyone move and keep quiet. I've listened to enough for one day." Drom lifted the door, and they departed the alley in silence thereafter.

Chapter Eight
The Limits of the Law

Maria held the wisp of a flame in her hand. She fueled it with a minuscule stream of magic. To her it was a symbol of magic itself. Used with skill, a boon. Uncontrolled, destructive. Fire had always fascinated her and terrified her alike. Having her mentor ask if she'd make it her specialty was natural. She hesitated though.

"Well?" Mordin One-Eye pressed.

"I don't know." She knew better than to keep her temperamental teacher waiting. "If overspecialization in an element has such risks to the mind and body of a Magus, why specialize? Why require it of anyone before they can join the Circle for that matter?"

"Lack of focus is more dangerous." His lone eye was fixed in a scowl.

"How?" She was pressing her luck questioning him twice in such a short span.

"Chaos," Absently, his hand came up to touch the smooth socket on his left side. "The non-element. If it takes hold, it will spread. It will consume not only the caster, but everyone around them. Magical chaos is simpler to root out than mundane chaos, but it doesn't make it strait forward. There's always someone who suffers."

Mordin fell silent, watching the flame. Distant. When his attention returned to the present he shook off a dour expression, though only with an effort. "Chaos spells are some of the most versatile varieties known. We use them regularly. Their overuse can be lethal, however. Focusing on one of the four elements ensures no Magus falls prey to pure chaos." He gestured to the row of unlit candles. "Mastery of an element circumvents the paths of Chaomancy and Necromancy."

Digesting the information, Maria lifted a candle. She lit it and moved to the next. The flames grew.

THE BUILDING SAT AS a toad among the dead leaves, blending in enough to be unnoticed, yet uglier than its peers when taken as an individual. It had the impression of disuse though Drom couldn't put a finger on why that was the case. It wasn't as though there was anything specific he could say was the cause.

"Home sweet home." Ries ran his finger through brown locks of hair and leaned against the door frame. "Everything as I remember it. I wonder if they ever burned the upstairs bed with all the lice. Oh the stories I could tell you about this place."

"Lice?" Arasha wore a mortified expression.

"I will ward the beds to drive out any vermin." Cellis tapped his foot. Taking the queue, Ries produced a key to open the door. The lock was a cheap one, but based on the standard occupant, the lock might be for show anyway.

"Whatever happened to all of your fretting over quota usage?" Ries asked as the door swung open. Drom wondered the same thing now that he heard it spoken.

"Quota is for those abiding by empty rules set forth through the Order's ignorance. It is a means of control in our era. Anyone of sufficient skill can tell you the source of power has never faltered. It is access to it that was cut off for a time." He spoke this revelation as though it were common knowledge! "If Laethem and the Order wish to play games with me, I'm done playing by their rules. No more holding back. It isn't as though I've held back when there was need anyway. I didn't want to tip my hand about knowing how to manufacture my own quota crystals, however. As long as I can make them, the Order can't find me by scanning for rogue castings or massive quota spends by a single Magus."

"Eh... right. So it was all an act?" Ries sounded less than convinced.

"Mind your own affairs thief." Cellis seemed less than pleased by the response. "Arasha, come with me. Droya, set the door on a wall here in the great room. Thief," He didn't use the man's name, emphasizing 'thief' as he stepped deeper into the building. "Disrobe in another room."

"My first boost? About time. I was feeling twitchy." Ries nodded and moved towards one of the side doors of the great room.

"Master, how long will you keep him human?" Drom had been hoping Cellis had forgotten about the need to renew Ries' spell. Unwrapping the door and setting it flush with a wall to the left, he waited for a response. It was still strange seeing the illusionary forms these two wore.

"Until he betrays us. If he upholds his word, he can remain human and be free."

"Of course Master." Drom forced his expression to neutrality.

"It must take a lot of strength on his part to show such a calm face realizing he could spend the rest of his life as a rat." Arasha stared in the direction Ries had gone. "I can't imagine being able to joke with the weight of one's losses sitting so heavy on your shoulders." Was she talking about Ries or herself? It wasn't obvious from her glazed expression.

"No, he bides his time and hides from his fear in sarcasm." Cellis' eyes shifted to Drom for the shortest of moments. "Real strength is facing the inevitable with the quiet acceptance of what you can't alter and making the best of what remains."

"What?" Arasha didn't appear to recognize the reference. How could she? Cellis hesitated.

"I knew your husband a short time before his disappearance. He did everything in his power to save you from his mistake and when it became clear he could not, he made a deal to protect you." Again Cellis hesitated.

Arasha's eyes glistened with tears and she stared at the Magus unbelieving.

"Master!" Something about Arasha finding out this way terrified Drom. "Not like this. Not now. Drom made the deal to protect her. This is hurting her!"

"Your husband..." Cellis seemed puzzled at Drom's reaction. "He went somewhere far from this world. He left to fulfill a task for me in exchange for my protection over you. If he could have stayed and still been able to save you, he would have."

"He didn't abandon me?" Her expression made Drom want to jump with joy, cry and scream all at once. "I don't understand. When is he coming back? Where can I find him?

"No, he didn't abandon you. Regardless, you may never see him again. There's no way to bring him back and no way for me to send you to where he went. Take consolation in the fact you two would have been separated anyway. He'd have informed you, but didn't have a way to send word to you after making the deal. When this is all over, I'll see to it you'll be with your family again. Until then, you are a slave. That's all the more I can say about the matter. Stop focusing on self pity or the thief and focus instead on the tasks I set before you. Now come along, we have a spell to cast."

"Yes sir." Spoken in a daze as she followed Cellis into the mystic door. It shut behind them.

Alone now, Drom released the tension, trembling overtaking him. Cellis had almost told her the truth and Drom had stopped him. Why? She could live her life believing he met a noble end this way. She would know he loved her enough to sacrifice everything for her. She would never find how low he'd sunk, or that he was now the creature of her nightmares. Drom was gone to her forever. That's all there was to it. It was enough to expect she would move on without being hurt.

Drom went to join Ries to wait for the casting to begin. The man was speaking, but the words didn't register.

THE SAFE HOUSE WAS larger than he'd have guessed. There were more than enough rooms for everyone to have their own. Each room was sparse but livable. Drom had chosen to forgo the comfort of a straw mattress in favor of the hard ground outside of Arasha's door, though he waited long enough to feel no one would be coming out.

He couldn't say if it was a desire to be closer to her or worry about what Ries might do that led him to do so. Whatever the truth, there was a sense of rightness in sleeping there. When he arrived at the door, the faint sound of crying inside came clear in his acute ears. He settled down to listen in helpless silence as she wept.

"Oh Drom." Her voice speaking his name startled him. For the briefest of moments, it seemed she'd discovered the truth. The door remained closed however.

"Why did you leave? Why did you feel like you couldn't trust me to help us through it?" There was a soft thud against the door as of a pillow flung there.

"We could have done something about it together. Instead you had to try protecting me again. Gods, I love you, but you're an utter fool sometimes. How'm I supposed to do this without you? Gone. Forever." She burst into tears again, the sound so ragged it must have stripped her throat raw.

Drom leaned into the door. There was nothing he could do but dwell on the mistakes he'd made. He'd sacrificed them both because of stupid pride and fool notions of what a woman of noble birth would need to remain content. He'd known better and fallen into the trap anyway. Tracing his fingers over the wooden door, he cried as well.

It took everything he had not to make a sound as he did. His body trembled, both from the tears and from the effort. For a moment, he was himself again, lost in the agony he had created for them both. When he regained control, it was with the miserable knowledge that the door between them might as well be an ocean. He'd never be able to apologize.

Making things better was out of the question. At best he could make them less miserable by fulfilling his oath to Cellis so she could be returned to her family. Maybe one day he'd be able to find a way to relay an apology too.

Arasha fell asleep only after she'd wept herself to the point of exhaustion. After a long period of silence Drom slept as well, plagued by his thoughts.

DROM AWOKE TO SOMETHING nudging his arm. Opening his eyes revealed the exact person who'd been part of what prompted the decision to sleep outside the door.

"Drom." The fact Ries was using his former name was startling. "Please hear me out." The lack of a scream or strike was answer enough for the man to continue. "You and I are victims. Cellis is lying to you. I know he can transform you back because he spoke of it a year ago. Before you were transformed. He was telling another Magus about the spell and counterspell."

"Why should I believe you?"

"You shouldn't, but it doesn't make it any less true."

"Get out of my face rat or I'll tell Cellis you were planting lies and you return to being a rodent."

"Look, when the time comes, all you have to do is nothing and we can all be free. I promise you this."

Drom hissed and arched his fingers like they were claws. It wasn't a sincere threat, so no pain chased the motion.

"My apologies for my behavior and for your wife, but I have to keep playing the expected part. Misdirection. As long as Cellis assumes my focus is on being annoying to you, I can keep him from realizing we're aware of the truth. Don't take any of it personal. I'm not your enemy." With that, he slipped away down the hall.

Drom's apron-dress had ridden up some in his sleep. Adjusting it across his now-familiar curves, Drom mulled over the strange behavior of Ries. Another ploy no doubt, but it was unnerving how convincing the man was.

How effortless would it be to believe him? It meant hope in a hopeless situation. Damn Ries and his lies! They had him questioning Cellis' actions. Sleep was slow to return and fitful the rest of the night.

THREE DAYS PASSED BEFORE the meeting could be arranged. The others didn't leave the safe house at all, but Drom had been told twice to journey on minor shopping errands. It wasn't for a lack of supplies as there were an impressive number of nonperishable goods inside the mystic door's room. The real reason seemed to be the barrage of questions Cellis would ask upon his return. What had he heard?

Drom had heard much in fact. It was apparent almost everyone ignored his presence when spreading the latest gossip. He'd be taken aback if no one used Ill'ln as spies! They were the perfect agents, often ignored by everyone after an initial glance. At most, uncomfortable looks were quick to come and depart again.

The lesser Houses and the Order had been unable to locate the two missing leaders. Lines were being drawn between those who believed the accusations were true and those who thought them false. It was said the leader of House Shingu was moving among those loyal to the Prince and the High Council, sewing seeds of unrest. No one knew at all what Lord Kirk was doing or where he was.

Confusion abounded and crime was on the rise in the growing turmoil. Between the loyalist Guardsmen and a growing workload, the Order, and the new High Council who'd moved to replace the ruling Houses had made an unprecedented agreement to send out joint patrols! It was a violation of both civic and mystic law. The breech of legal separation only helped fuel the chaos.

"Most troubling." Strong emotion didn't make it into Cellis' voice, much as was usually the case when Drom returned with news. This time he added, "We have no time to waste. See that everyone is ready for the meeting, we have two hours."

"Yes Master." Drom hesitated to say something more.

"Fellow citizens," A woman's voice boomed from outside before Drom could move to act. Cellis whipped aside a thick curtain and pushed open the shutters. Light flooded the room, causing Drom to flinch at the sudden brightness. "The Circle of the Order of Magi stand before you today, expending a great amount of quota so you may hear our words directly."

His vision returned as his eyes readjusted. Drom's jaw fell open when they did. In the sky above the city, four images of people loomed huge. Their bodies faded away below the waist, but above they were like manifest giants standing over the city. The color and cut of their robes marked them as powerful elemental Magi. Drom didn't recognize the speaker or two of the others, but the last was Laethem.

"Tradition holds that a separation of mystic and mundane centers of power should be maintained for the sake of fair and proper dealings among the people. The former Prince and High Council strove to undermine this balance and frame the Order of Magi for actions we had no part in. It was their intent to circumvent the laws of separation of power. To destroy the barrier in civil and mystic power that helped maintain peace ever since the return of magic to the world. It's unfortunate that while we have apprehended most of the culprits, their actions have forced their intended goals on us all."

"Pfft!" Cellis might spit fire for his expression. "They're going to try adding weight to their position through sheer awe." By now Arasha had come from another room and was gazing out the open window. Her expression implied their plan might be working.

"As you're aware, the plot was revealed and the lower houses have stepped in to bring about justice. We of the Circle are grateful for the swift actions on our behalf. It seems, however, many still believe the lies of the former Prince over the truth."

Arasha was oblivious to anything but the four figures in the sky, so Drom took the opportunity to study at her. The illusionary form might have made her appear as someone else, but her mannerisms were all the same. Watching her fidget with her thumb and forefinger as she always did while deep in thought brought memories of all the times he'd seen it before.

"No doubt you have seen Council patrols and Order patrols working as a single unit. It was our hope to avoid this, but it has proven impossible. While the false accusations were preempted, it grows ever more apparent this situation is forcing aside the tradition of separation. We must face the challenges before us united as a people. As of this day, by consensus of the new High Council and the four seats of the Circle of the Order of Magi, henceforth, the division of power and justice is abolished. A new Prince will soon be chosen from the Houses of the Council and he shall have the aid of the Circle to restore order in Fairmar." The image faded away.

"So this is the fruition of your plans Laethem? I can't say I am elated about the dissolving of the separation or your methods. If we're all lucky, you won't manage to obtain a puppet Prince, but I doubt it." Cellis drew the shutters closed, drowning out the growing din of voices. The silence of those listening had broken against abrupt waves of discussion over what citizens had seen.

"The Kingdom's system always seemed flawed, but this might be even worse." Arasha let her eyes leave the window only after the curtain was drawn. "What's going to keep Magi warlords from rising to power like before the loss of magic?"

"The system of power division was acceptable, it is a few of the leaders on either side who were dragging things down. As to warlords, I can't say. It's a bridge to cross down the road." Cellis returned to his preparations for the meeting.

Arasha wandered back to her room, leaving Drom by the window watching Cellis absently. If the Magi and the lesser Houses combined forces, they might have enough combined power to overtake the loyalists. Could the two remaining High Lords keep their freedom, let alone have a chance of returning to power? It was a foregone conclusion the original High Council would be executed. Among them would be Arasha's father. Any hope of returning her to her family would be gone.

"Master, you have to counter the Circle's ploy."

"Do I?" Despite the illusion of youth, Cellis' eyes took on the hard edge of a man who had seen over a century of life.

"If they succeed, you'll never be able to return or to keep your promise of returning my..." Lancing pain brought a gasp and a hasty refashioning of his intended words, "Arasha."

Cellis was silent. Ries' words returned. Was Cellis lying about all of it? If not, why wasn't he responding? Was he working out a new lie?

"We can't escape without the two Lords remaining free. If the merged forces of the Council and the Circle are accepted by the city, they won't be able to resist. It means both forces will be free to turn their full attention on us!"

Cellis remained silent, but moved away. Drom followed, desperation growing stronger. Cellis opened the door to the storage room and stepped in, snatching items from shelves and handing them to Drom.

"Master?" He couldn't keep the pleading tone out of his voice.

"Don't distract me. I have to make preparations in less than two hours that should require a minimum of three. I'll be lucky if the spell only fails instead of burning me into a cinder. Distractions won't raise my odds in the least.

Drom took what was handed to him. Was this how Cellis agreed or something else entirely?

"How do I help Master?"

THE TIME FOR THE MEETING was near and Drom's whole body was numb. The power levels being drawn through him must have been tremendous, though how he knew wasn't something he could have put a finger on.

Cellis was chanting and making signs with his hands. To the left, smoke rose from a hammered brass bowl. It was pungent and foul, making Drom want to crinkle his nose. A jagged shard of what seemed to be quartz rested on the ground between them. Drom couldn't imagine speaking the tongue twisting sounds Cellis was speaking. Even if he could, he'd never have managed them with the speed they poured from Cellis.

The rumbling flow of words grew into a crescendo. As the final word was spoken in the strange and precise language, Cellis fell to his knees. He was breathing in heavy gasps and looked more vulnerable than Drom had ever seen him. Even frozen in place by the spells of the Red Machtha, he'd seemed to have more dignity, if not control. Right now he could be any person on the street and Drom wouldn't have been surprised. Drom hadn't realized spellcasting could be so draining.

The crystal on the floor now had a faint glow. Cellis reached for it, his voice sore and strained. "It's done. We must take this somewhere along the way to the meeting so they can't follow the source back to us. When it strikes a hard surface, it will activate." He rose. "Keep it secure until I tell you to activate it."

It was warm to the touch and tingled in his hand. It seemed peculiar to Drom since he was otherwise numb. He looked down at the pocketless apron-dress. No belt purse either. There was the option to hold it, but that might draw attention. Hiding it in one of the few secure locations he had turned his stomach, given the warm tingle and intimate nature. Ruling it out left only one acceptable option.

Trying not to make a face, he slid it between his breasts where the dress puckered to form a natural pocket between itself and the cleavage. It stayed put and was out of sight though the tingle kept part of his attention on its new home.

It proved impossible to ignore. That it was mildly pleasant only made him more uncomfortable. The magic of it seemed to interact with his body and led to something he couldn't fully define. An arousal of sorts was the only way he could describe the sensation. Not exactly sexual per se, but he lacked a better word. It didn't sit well with his male ego, so he chose to pretend it was all illusion with only limited success.

The other two were already gathered to leave, so they set out as soon as Cellis could walk steadily. They moved slower than Drom would have liked, drawing out his discomfort. When they came to the junction of Dock Street and Peddler's Lane, they turned east and straight into a group of soldiers stopping random passers. The unit was composed of both Guardsmen and Red Machtha. Seeing the latter brought a moment of panic in Drom. Memories of the men drawing he and Arasha towards the back room flashed in his mind.

"Hog cock," Ries cursed under his breath. "So much for my humanity."

"Silence fool." Cellis muttered back and didn't pause his step in the least. Arasha however balked at the sight of Red Machtha. Her hesitation was enough to draw the attention of several soldiers.

"You there, identify yourselves."

"Run?" Ries whispered without moving his lips though Drom couldn't understand how.

A tiny head movement of negation from Cellis as he stopped. "Greetings, I am Landrin. This is my brother Eli and his wife Riana."

Pain pulsed in warning from the collar as Cellis introduced his wife and Ries as a married couple. It was a ruse, he consoled himself, but the jealous anger didn't leave him.

No one seemed concerned Drom hadn't been introduced, but it wasn't uncommon to ignore Ill'ln when not ordering them about. Drom cast his eyes at the ground in a submissive gesture lest his anger show.

"What business are you about?"

"We were heading to a friend's house on the invitation to dinner."

"Let me see your ID crystal." One was wearing the same insignia as the slain leader from the group at the store. He drew close, eying the low rank Magus robes formed by Cellis' illusion. The way his sharp green eyes focused on it, Drom worried he'd see through the illusion.

Cellis drew out a thumb-sized pink crystal from his belt purse and handed it over in silence. Drom's heart was racing, making the tingle between his breasts more noticeable to him. He stopped trying to watch events unfold. Instead he focused on the crystal in his bosom. peering down from above, it was barely visible there, peaking out of the cleft of flesh. From any other angle it wouldn't be visible.

A quick flicker of his eyes told him no one watched him or was even looking in the vague direction. The questions directed at Cellis were getting more probing. Did they suspect?

Weighing the risks and calculating his new strength, Drom took a few steps to the left where he would be obscured by a horseman's wagon which had also been stopped. Careful to avoid any sudden or noteworthy motions, Drom fished out the pulsing crystal. No one seemed to notice, so he put his hands behind his back and gave a quick prayer to Apuro.

The underhand swing of his arm sidelong flashed in a blur and the crystal was airborne. Drom finished the motion as though swatting an insect away. He moved away from the cart with a frown as though disdainful of the insects its horse was drawing. Hazarding a glance at Cellis, he noted the Sargent of the Guardsmen and the leader of the Red Machtha were now discussing something. Cellis himself wore a deep frown.

The faint clink of crystal on stone told Drom he'd struck a building or pavement somewhere down the lane. Confirmation came in the form of Cellis' true form floating as a half-transparent giant over the city. All eyes were drawn skyward save for Cellis' as the image spoke. Cellis himself shot Drom a peculiar expression that merged relief with irritation.

"My fellow citizens, you have heard by now of events transpiring among the Council, the Order and myself." The image above thundered.

Guardsmen and Red Machtha members moved as the Machtha leader made a series of hand motions. "The source is faint, but it is to the north. Move!"

"Aside from rumors, you have only one side of the story. All the events of the last few days have been orchestrated by the Circle itself! Prior to the coup, one of the Order's leadership was directly involved in an elaborate plan. A plan which set all of this into motion. My own activities were misinterpreted and they believed I was going to expose them. When movement against me failed, they were forced to accuse me of being involved in their conspiracy to circumvent the separation of power. They acted before they were ready. Why else would they assault the Council for breaking tradition, then dissolve those traditions themselves?"

"I beseech you to support and protect those members of the true Council who have thus far eluded the usurpers. Should they make ready to execute any of the captive Councilmen or the Prince, rise up in protest. You're not the blind fools they take you for."

The image faded out though Drom knew there should have been more. A forceful grip and tug of his wrist drew Drom's attention from where it had lingered on the sky.

"We mustn't be here when they return." Cellis' attention was focused ahead as he drew both Arasha and Drom into a lurch forward. "I'm uncertain if I should be seething at you Droya or kiss you. If they had seen you toss it, they wouldn't have needed further reason to debate the merits of taking us into custody." He released their wrists once they were moving. Ries had needed no prompting.

"Still, they were sufficiently distracted to leave us out of their eyesight and it relayed the vital information, so it seems the risk paid off."

"Sorry Master. It occurred to me they were too focused on us for some reason and since no one watches what a Nymph is doing without having some specific reason to do so..." Drom trailed off.

Cellis glanced back, his expression unreadable. "What is done is done." He fell silent afterward and the four of them pressed toward the meeting place. It was slow going to press through the crowd who were ablaze with sudden gossip. Hardly a single person on the streets wasn't engaged in vigorous debate. What had they witnessed? Was it true? No one paid attention to them, so they wove through the crowd like a maze of bodies.

The tone of the crowd was anxious. With every passing moment, a growing sense of unease seemed to linger ever closer. It was a tremendous relief when they arrived at their destination. Late, but whole and unidentified.

The destination turned out to be in the roughest part of town. With the entire town buzzing with the recent events, this area felt more foreboding than usual. They stood before the door of this building nestled into the Dreg District, knocking.

Chapter Nine
The Payment of a Debt

The water in the bowl shimmered, but no image manifested itself to Llwanna. Scrying came natural for her only when it was somewhere close. This wasn't close.

"Not bad for a first try." Her mentor had an expression not unlike a proud parent.

"It feels like trying to push a bolder with willpower alone."

"Not an inaccurate analogy. Keep trying. If you can master advanced scrying as part of your hydromancy, you'll have the option to work with the Circle's navy."

"Wouldn't they have more need of Neomancers? Or at least Hydromancers who're focused on calming waters and stilling storms?" Llwanna tried again to channel power into the water. Again it only shimmered.

"The oceans are vast. Right now, there's a limited range available to be traveled without great risk. It isn't public knowledge yet, but there's an ongoing special project with the Circle's navy. I have it on notable authority there's high quota scrying currently ongoing. Mapping the entire ocean. It may take a few lifetimes to complete, but already they've discovered several new islands. I imagine expeditions to those islands will include Hydromancers to scry even farther afield. You could help in discovering this new frontier.

"If they're seeking land, why not scry for the leylines and other Magi?"

"There's no guarantee a bit of land will hold a nexus of magic, let alone if someone would be there using it. As far as we know, there are no people living more than fifty miles from the mainland."

Llwanna recognized the wisdom of it. If a powerful nexus like Godsaddle Mountain was rare on the mainland, how much rarer would it be at sea? They might even be underwater. She chastised herself for not realizing it.

"Even if such things were there to be found, it would be dangerous to use strong ley-tap spells over such a distance. We don't want to draw the wellspring of magic dry again."

"So they haven't found much land yet?" It was rhetorical. "I'll have to give the navy careful consideration."

"You'll not consider anything if you don't practice. Return to your efforts." Roseline was able to make chastising sound warm.

IT TOOK KNOCKING TWICE before the panel in the door slid open to reveal a pair of icy gray eyes and bushy white brows without open skin between them at all. No word was spoken by the owner of the eyes. Instead, only a flickering glance over the group occurred before the panel slid shut again.

"Wonderful hospitality on the part of your lord friend." Ries glanced around as though expecting the joined armies of the Council and Order to descend on them. Did he believe they had been set up? A better question was: had they?

"Caution saves the wary mouse from the midnight owl." Cellis showed no outward signs of concern. "We come to speak with the master of the house by appointment. If there needs to be a verification of my identity, he had a recent run in with my Ill'ln."

There was no response from within though the last bit had been directed at the door. The curve of Drom's spine tingled from sweat trickling there. He glanced around in much the same way Ries was doing. Was this a meeting or a trap?

The sudden lurch of the door brought a flinch of readiness from everyone but Arasha, who didn't seem concerned at all. Perhaps something from her noble upbringing regarding the meeting of other nobles. He hadn't expected Cellis to tense, however. Before them stood a man looking further past his prime than he had ever seen for anyone but a Magus. He was wearing the clothing one might expect to find on a churl. Where skin was exposed, it was covered by dark spotting and moles and it hung loose over a skeletal frame. Circling a shiny patch of bald was a ring of bushy white. Despite his age, those eyes remained piercing and cool gray. The same eyes they'd seen a moment before.

"Enter and remove any disguises you might be wearing." The uncomfortable worry still hung in the air between them. Drom's sweating lessened though, thanks to no trap springing yet. They would have taken them on the street right? If it was a trap why bother having them remove the disguises first? They stepped deeper into the dim room.

Cellis drew out the two poppets, snapping them in half. In the same moment, the figures lost the appearance of anything beyond dolls with clay smeared on them and the Magus and Drom's wife reverted. Tension lifted as Cellis and Arasha returned to their true forms. He'd not even realized the tension was there. It was odd though perhaps it was a relief to have his wife back to her lovely self again.

The attendant nodded to no one in particular, stating, "His Lordship will see you presently. Until he does, please have a seat in the common room." The others were still squinting, but Drom's eyes had already adjusted to the flickering candle sconces and their minimal illumination. Common room? Indeed! Scanning the room revealed a wooden platform for performers now laid in a dry-rotted heap to one end. There were no tables present, but there were a few seats strewn about. Across one wall were the remains of a serving area and an archway behind it. No doubt it led to a kitchen. Something about the archway made him uncomfortable, though Drom couldn't put his finger on why.

Inspecting the direction the aged man had gone, there were the rotting bones of a staircase which had at one time led up to the second floor. They didn't appear safe to use. Drom was thankful the majority of the building was stone so there was little chance of it collapsing on their heads. Below the stairs were several more openings though only one still clung to the rusty hinges of a half-shattered door.

Anywhere else in the city, buildings in this state would be unheard of, but this was the oldest and worst part of town. The docks had crime, but this area made even the average criminal hesitate. Those traveling with a Magus might be ignored, but anyone else was fair game. This was the first time Drom had been to these few blocks, but it was obvious why decent folk didn't come here. There was nothing here worth the trouble.

"I can finally see more than outlines." Ries broke the silence. "And I have to say this is below even my standards. 'His Lordship' picked a festering anus of a location to meet at."

Something tickled Drom's senses, a stirring of air. The others didn't seem to sense it, but of course they lacked Elf senses. It no longer surprised him when he noticed something others didn't. He tried to decide where the source of the stirring originated.

"You aren't the one who picked the location Ries?" Arasha looked as uncomfortable as the rest of them with these surroundings. Drom wished he could offer her some form of comfort.

"Are you joking? I am a liberator of goods, not a bandit, assassin, or criminal lord! Why would I pick the dreg district?"

A man stepped out from behind a pillar supporting the second floor's stone walkway. Having sensed it, Drom was the only one not to startle as Lord Kirk spoke. In an instant, Cellis had a hand posed in an intricate shape. Ries had drawn two throwing daggers from somewhere. Where he'd had them hidden wasn't obvious. Arasha took a step to keep Ries between herself and the shadowed figure. The last bothered Drom on several levels despite it likely being a coincidence. Ries happened to be the easiest person to put between them.

"Would you hunt for the leader of House Apsuru in a location like this?" The rhetorical question was directed at the conversation of Ries and Arasha, but the man's eyes were focused on Drom. "Superb to see you again Cellis. Your pet seems different, or is it a new Ill'ln from the rude one in the market?"

"She is the same." The Magus glanced at Drom. "I hadn't noticed anything different about her. Regardless, it's not a topic for right now. Did the thief explain to your messenger as I had instructed him to?"

"As I'm unaware of his instructions, I can't say. I was told you were calling in your debt from me. I find your timing somewhat less than ideal. I must say I'm curious how this thief of yours even found one of my loyal men considering they're all supposed to be staying low for now."

Ries beamed with pride, a smug silence settling over him for a few moments.

"You would have to ask him. We need assistance in exiting the city undetected. At least across the river though better to exit the other direction." Cellis was blunt as ever.

"I could imagine why, after your little speech in the sky a few minutes ago. Don't imagine I fail to appreciate the assistance there. I believe I now owe you two debts."

"That was for my own benefit, so call it even. Is it possible to secure your help with leaving the city?"

"Well," Kirk began. He was interrupted by Arasha.

"You do have plans to rescue my father don't you Kirk?" her worried voice sounded on the verge of tears.

"Yes child, I have every intention of saving all the council members and restoring their Houses. Shall I tell him you are in first-rate health when I see him?"

"Please do and tell him also not to worry over me. I made my choices and will live with the consequences."

"As you wish." the man seemed content with the answer. "Now, as I was saying Cellis, the number of loyalists willing to take up arms is seeing rapid growth. I believe in a few more days I will be able to take open actions. When I strike at the council fortification, it should divert their attention away from the gates. You'll be able to pass unnoticed at that time.

"That should be sufficient." He dug into the same pouch where the poppets had been, drawing out a glass marble. Drom recognized it as one of several items Cellis had made the last few days using Drom himself as a focus aid. He extended it to Kirk. "I need you to mark this with a drop of blood and a drop of saliva."

"What is it?"

"A beacon. When I focus the proper spell on it, I will be able to sense your condition and location. It will let me track when the assault happens or meet for a last minute conversation. Only I can use it, so there isn't a risk of someone else finding you."

"Smart, though I would expect no less from you." Kirk drew his eating dagger, pricking the tip against his finger. He licked away the first drop of blood welling up before touching his finger to the marble. Blood and saliva at the same time. "There, three days. Shall we meet again at this same time prior to the assault?"

A furious pounding erupted from the door before Cellis could agree. He scowled towards it and everyone else went tense. The old Magus' reaction to the recent string of unexpected door knocking made Drom wonder if it was a common annoyance in his life. For some reason, Drom remained calm.

Kirk motioned everyone to return behind the archways as the balding manservant returned and opened the slot in the door. Drom had to strain despite his keen ears to hear what was said. There was no chance the others had heard it.

"Quick, let me in. There is no time to waste. The enemy mobilizes against us."

There was no reply. Instead, the panel slid shut, and the door was unbarred to allow a man with the colors of House Unicorn showing beneath his cloak to enter. At the same time, the man at the door spoke loud enough to carry to where they were "Earl, a messenger requires your ear." Kirk stepped forward and the others came out from the dark room beyond the archway again.

"Marcus, what news?"

"Sir," the man bent to one knee. "The false council and the Order troops have begun to capture and imprison anyone from the true ruling houses on charges of conspiracy. Every man, woman, and child! Fighting's broken out across the city. My lord says he will be striking when the sun touches the dusk spire and wishes for your own allies to also move at that time."

"Damn them! They would violate the laws of accountability? It seems they aren't fool enough to provide us the required time for a proper assault either. Go. Tell him I will move too."

Marcus rushed back out and the door was rebarred behind him. Lord Kirk grumbled to himself. "They have to have gone mad with power. The whole city is in a troox of trouble." Lord Kirk strode towards the archway Drom had suspected was the kitchen, bellowing. "You heard him, move. We need every warm body we have armed and equipped within twenty minutes."

Seven men in leather armor came out, surging out of the archway and into a heavy-doored room set off to one side. The churl at the front door once again slid the bar latch out of place. When the men had all armed themselves with weapons and packs, they were let out the front. As the last of them left, Lord Kirk spoke to Cellis.

"I should have expected this. The fact the false council is composed of lesser Houses doesn't mean they would be fool enough to risk giving me time. They may have no sense of honor or respect of any laws, but they do understand battle tactics. I will need to be cautious."

Cellis' scowl remained. Ries wore a sneering grin for some reason and Arasha was biting her lip, close to tears again despite a forced stance of dignity.

"Looks like our plan is out of the question now." Ries went so far as to chuckle.

"Not entirely." Lord Kirk moved to the withered manservant. "Tayon here can see to securing an enclosed wagon, unmarked. I keep one for when I want to travel unnoticed. You four can take it to the gates and hope the majority of their forces are drawn into the conflict. They have to realize this will bait us out, so I can expect the majority of their forces will be waiting to spring the trap."

"Your men will be slaughtered." Cellis kept frowning.

"Some, but it will keep their attention off the real prize. I'm going to lead a unit into the fortification."

"You don't expect them to close the central gates?" Arasha bit her lip deeper.

"Oh, I do. That's why the unit I plan to lead is already inside. A number of loyal guardsmen, a few jailers and several 'drunks' locked up each day will be waiting in the upper dungeon." Kirk grinned and gave her a wink.

Tayon retrieved a dull tan riding cloak from the same room the men had gathered the packs and blades from. He also brought along an unnoteworthy sword. Why wasn't he also wearing armor for extra measure? For that matter, why had they seemed ready for betrayal or attack, yet had to move into another room to obtain weapons. He was missing something here.

"Wait here. My man will knock three times and flash a parchment with the picture of a dragon on it when the slot is opened. I will see he takes you out of town to a nearby village. One of my loyal vassals is there and he will see to it you're supplied with proper equipment for travel." Kirk made a whistle and clicked his tongue twice.

From upstairs, a heavy thumping sounded in irregular patterns along with scraping clicks. The source stuck their heads out a moment later, peering down between broken rails before scrambling toward those unstable, dry-rotted stairs. Two apsu-hounds, great lizards like miniature apruru, were at the man's beck and call. The gray-green creatures rotated their narrow heads a moment before scrambling down the stairs. One went right down the center while the other chose to climb the distance down on the wall itself instead. They were rare battle beasts these days though it made sense the leader of house Apsuru would raise and train them. It explained why the men hadn't bothered to be armed. Two of these could have made short work for any patrol trying to force its way in.

Kirk donned the cloak and sword, taking care to hide his house colors. The gesture seemed odd since the two reptiles would mark him as noteworthy anyway. Perhaps he intended to have them climb to the rooftops and follow along above. The man didn't wait for further conversation. He and Tayon slipped through the door, trailed by two massive lizards. After a moment, Ries moved forward to bar the door once again.

"Do you believe he'll succeed?" Arasha's lip was trickling blood from her absent, worried chewing.

"I have yet to see him proven wrong in tactics." It wasn't a yes from Cellis, but it did seem to calm her somewhat.

On reflex, Drom gathered the hem of his dress and brought it up to Arasha's lip. Cellis averted his attention and Ries ogled the sudden exposure of flesh. Gentle fingers blotted away the blood as she stared at the door after Kirk. The glazed and distant expression faded, and she followed the source of the gesture. Their eyes locked and Drom's heart leaped. She was so beautiful. She wasn't screaming, did she recognize the emotions in his eyes?

No. She regained herself enough to yelp and shove Drom away with all her might. The force was enough to drive him back several steps and should have hurt considering the sensitivity of his new skin. Instead, the sharp slap of palms on his collar bone only sent shivers of pleasure. He was no masochist, so brushed it off as the joy of her touch. It had been too much to hope she would recognize who he was behind these Elf eyes. Still, it was a microscopic victory she'd only yelped instead of screaming or fainting. He made a passive withdraw further away and cast his eyes downward.

"Droya," Ries sneered. "You're aware the lady slave isn't comfortable with your kind."

"I fear the thief is correct." Cellis was shaking his head.

"Can we stop calling me that?" Ries grumbled. "I am a person, not a profession." Whatever else was said was lost as Drom's attention shifted.

Arasha moved to the far end of the room, crouching against the wall. The simple cream chemise rode up some, but the tan supertunic over it kept the position decent. It was a relief to Drom at least since it wouldn't provide Ries any more excuses to focus on her.

Still, her wary eyes never left Drom. It was enough to make him want to cry.

THERE WAS NO WAY TO recreate the illusion with the poppets broken and the room holding all the supplies back at the safe house. It was an oversight thanks to the rush of their hasty projection spell that had Cellis cursing to himself in a steady mumble. Time passed. It seemed like hours though Drom didn't expect it had even been one. There was no talking aside from the muttered curses from the Magus. When the three knocks came, Cellis had taken to pacing and Ries had one shoe off picking caked mud from the bottom.

The parchment was shown when they opened the port and the door was unlatched. They slipped out and into the carriage at as brisk a pace as they could muster without drawing attention. How had a carriage traveled through the Dreg district without being set upon? Cellis was the last one in, pausing to argue with the driver about their need to detour to the location of the safe house. He didn't explain it was to collect a door, no doubt for obvious reasons. In the end, the old Magus won, though Drom suspected he might have used subtle spellcasting to influence the driver. With how dead-set both parties had been on the opposite point at the start, it seemed possible.

Once there, the door was loaded atop the carriage. Voices yelling and the clash of blades on a nearby street came in the distance. If the fighting in the streets had reached this far into the city, he could only imagine how fierce it must be at the center where the high Houses resided.

With the door secured, they moved towards the Northern gate. More than once, the sound of metal on metal was loud enough to penetrate the heavy curtains. It was enough the others would shoot concerned glances in the direction of the source. These conflicts never came close enough to interfere with their travel, however.

After some time had passed, Drom imagined they were close to the Northern gate. Had his parents managed to close their shop down when the fighting broke out or had they been caught off guard.

Their mercantile wouldn't be a target, but who knew what might happen. Quick prayers to several deities he knew his parents put trust in were silently offered and a special prayer to Whiccup, the patron god of his mother.

"Why are we slowing?" Cellis pulled the curtain back with a hooked finger, his voice impatient. A frown crossed his features, bordering on an outright scowl. "This will be trouble." Cellis motioned negation when Ries and Arasha tried to peek out as well.

"What is it?" Ries complied with the motion, but didn't seem willing to stay in the dark.

"There are a number of travelers and townspeople trying to leave the city. I can see at least one Magus involved with several Guardsmen asking questions or speaking with groups. It also appears the Guardsmen are checking carts and wagons for anything or anyone hidden away."

The carriage lurched to a complete stop. The voice of the driver, directed at some unseen person, came through the heavy carriage curtains. "Is this delay necessary?"

"Yes, but we will try to be brief." The second voice sounded younger than Drom had been expecting.

"Does this have something to do with the fighting we passed or the Magus in the sky?"

"In part. Stay seated please." There was a pause. "Marc, please check the cabin."

"Yes sir." Presumably Marc, again a young voice.

"This could become ugly." Cellis grumped. Drom felt a growing tension in himself. It intensified as he directed his attention in a certain direction. The spot was shifting though, meaning either it was his imagination or it was mobile. Whatever it was, it was moving towards the carriage door!

At the moment it crossed the door, the handle turned. It eased open to reveal a young man, no more than 20. He was wearing a long gray robe cut in the manner of an apprentice Magus. Dusty blond hair was cut short and his blue-green eyes shifting to each of them in turn.

"Sorry to be a bother. We'll be quick, I promise." Marc's eyes fell on Cellis and grew wide. Surprised recognition blossomed across his features and crossed to a fearful awe. The young man's jaw worked without a sound for a moment before he drew in a deep breath.

Whatever he had been about to scream was replaced with a wet gurgle forced around the dagger that sprouted from his throat. Even as the first struck, Ries was already drawing a second from what seemed like thin air.

"Stop wasting seconds." Ries shifted towards the door of the carriage, reaching out.

The tension in Drom was fading though he couldn't imagine why given the situation. Outside, his ears picked up an odd twang and whistle. Ries was halfway through the door and the Cellis was starting to move when Drom perceived a solid thunking sound at the termination of the whistle.

It all played out in an instant, but seemed to stretch out as though events were flowing across molasses. Something was bellowed out by someone beyond the carriage. Everything felt wrong. Tension returned, but not because of whatever was going on outside. It was centered on Ries. The farther out the door he inched, the stronger the tension. What did it mean?

He needed time to figure it out, but there wasn't time. He wanted to puzzle it out, but something in him insisted action was required. Half out of this new peculiar instinct, Drom's hand lashed out to catch Ries' wrist before he disappeared out the door. There was a glint of metal as Ries swung his other arm back on reflex.

Drom followed the odd instinct again since logic didn't have anything to offer at the moment. His other hand rose to meet a blade so it drove into the flat of his hand and protruded out the other side. Was he in shock? It didn't seem to hurt much at all. His fingers closed around Ries' own still wrapped at the hilt of the dagger. Time seemed to lurch forward again, no longer dragging out. All the tension slipped away, though pain did not blossom in his hand as he was expecting.

The body of the young Magus collapsed backwards away from the door. Arasha yelped, only now reacting, curling her knees up into her chest and wrapping her arms around them. Cellis looked startled while Ries wore no expression at all. He studied his captured hand and the blade extending through Drom's own. A thin flow of blood tickled, but there wasn't any real pain there.

"If we wait, we die." Ries tried to jerk his hand free, but Drom's grip was like iron. He had no more success than an ant encased in sap.

"We must wait." Drom wasn't sure how he knew it, but now that he'd said it, he knew it was true.

"You'll kill us all."

There was an unexpected jolt of movement that put everyone off balance. The carriage had lurched into motion. Drom and Ries fell hard onto the rear bench beside Cellis who lunged to pull the jostling door shut. Before it closed, Drom caught a glimpse of an arrow striking a Guardsman as people were running about.

"Kirk's men?" Ries was scowling at Drom as he pulled the freed blade and drew a cloth from a pouch to wipe blood from its surface.

"He must have sent a modest number of troops set to take the gate after we had time to pass through. Our delaying for the doorway was a stroke of marvelous fortune." Cellis studied Drom, fingers pulling in thoughtful tugs of his beard.

Chapter Ten
The Illusion of a Human

The tawny mouse peered out at Laethem from Maria's hands. It hid as if he were a snake. She couldn't help but beam. "Old one-eye decided I've advanced enough to have a familiar."

"And you chose some timid vermin?"

"He's not vermin. He's smart and already improving my control. His name is Whiskers."

"Of course it is. You won't catch me with such a common creature as my familiar." Laethem puffed up in the way he had when soapboxing. "Maybe a fierce beast like a hippogriff. Strong, smart and serves as a mount in addition to a familiar."

"No!" That idiot. She loosened her grip as Whiskers squeaked in protest. "Your master still hasn't taught you about that yet?"

"About what?" He seemed genuine in his confusion at the outburst.

"There are two types of creature you never make a familiar. Those with natural intelligence, for one, because they aren't bound to the Magus' will. The other are homunculi since the two magics interact in unpredictable ways. A homunculus familiar would be horrific. Mingled magic shaping the familiar instead of your nature." It sent a chill down her spine.

"Oh." Laethem's reaction failed to capture the proper level of concern. It annoyed her. "That's unfortunate."

"I swear you're reacting with as little emotion as Erica." Which brought up something she'd been wondering for a while. "Why do you still spend time with her anyway?"

"I don't know. She's always been useful backup when there's trouble."

"I'd venture half of the trouble you find yourself in is thanks to her presence. That woman's twisted and dangerous." She didn't bother explaining and Laethem didn't ask. Just as well. Maria didn't like to remember what she'd seen Erica doing.

She clutched Whiskers closer at the memory. No animal deserved to be stomped to death. Especially not to the obvious pleasure of the culprit. Erica scared her more than the possibility of a hippogriff familiar.

THE BLOOD WAS CLOTTING before Cellis moved to do anything, but by then Drom's apron-dress was stained with heavy bands of crimson. He'd been using a portion to staunch the bleeding. Ries was all but pouting that he'd been wrong and Arasha remained curled in the corner. She was watching Drom as though he'd lash out at her any moment.

"I didn't realize Ill'ln senses were that acute." Cellis pulled some dried leaves from his rear belt purse and crushed them. These were pressed into the puncture on either side. The flow of blood renewed, but was staunched again right away by the herb. "Did you hear one of the Guardsmen by the carriage say they were under attack? Was it a Guardsman who couldn't see the poor apprentice?"

"Well," Drom struggled to explain it. "I did hear arrows loose and hit, though I can't say I recognized the sound at the time. I sensed Ries shouldn't exit the door and we couldn't follow him out if he did."

"Apsuru shit! Not even an Elf could hear arrows being loosed at such a distance over the sound of so many people around the gate." Ries wore a snarl.

"I am no mere Elf, I am a Nymph and I can't lie to my owner." Drom couldn't help being insulted at the title of Elf. This wasn't the life he would choose, but there was a strange sense of pride at being more than a common Ill'ln. It felt as though the complete and willing submission of being a Nymph put him into a category above others. His reaction weighed uncomfortable in his mind, but was true none the less.

That reaction was also enough to catch both Ries and Cellis off guard as both now gawked at him. Drom blushed and shifted his eyes away in an attempt to seem irritated rather than embarrassed. Ries let it slide for now, thankfully.

"Ries is right. An Ill'ln's senses are stronger than a human, but you shouldn't have been able to distinguish such a subtle sound from the other noises at that sort of distance. Even so, I would not believe you had such instincts to recognize the danger in actions without at least first understanding why those actions were a threat. Peculiar." Cellis' eyes gave Drom the sensation he was in a specimen jar.

"I would explain it better if I could Master."

"I understand." Cellis drew out a loosely woven strip of cloth and wrapped Drom's hand. "Everyone get rest. This is going to be a long day's travel. More so for having to recast the spell on Ries every time we stop."

"You could always make it permanent." Ries offered.

Cellis' only response was, "Get some rest."

KIRK HAD NEVER MENTIONED the distance of the 'nearby village', but it turned out Cellis was more or less correct about the time. They did not stop to camp at night, so made it there by the first light of dawn. Had it not been for the bright moon, the trip would have taken the better part of two days.

The horses had worked up a heavy lather from pulling their burden with only half an hour of rest at a time. They'd have to be removed from service for a time to recover from the journey.

Drom was unfamiliar with the manor house before them. He'd never once been outside of the city proper in fact. He knew of things only from reading, travelers and customers.

"Rosewood Keep?" Arasha was the last to exit the stable, following the carriage driver. "I never knew Lord Nephtin was a vassal to Kirk."

"I suspect it's not accidental. Known vassals will be watched or arrested." Cellis kept glancing at Drom, who pretended not to notice. The expression of careful study was a touch uncomfortable.

"How do you hide a vassal?" Arasha seemed a bit more composed than she had been. The long trip had allowed her time to calm down.

"I wouldn't know enough about mundane affairs to answer the question."

"I am more interested in what they have to eat," Ries interrupted, "Than how you serve someone 'off the books.'"

The five of them, counting the carriage driver, reached the front entrance. Cellis prepared to pull the bell cord, but the heavy door swung open before he could. A near-skeletal woman stood before them. She pushed aside an errant lock of graying brown hair with a finger like bone wrapped in parchment and eyed them with open suspicion.

"The runner already brought your note last night." She made an odd curl of her lip that reminded Drom of a snarling canine. "His Lordship will see to you after breakfast. Until then, I was directed to see to you."

"Thank you. That is most kind." Cellis managed to say it without a hint of sarcasm. Could he have done the same in the man's place?

"Well, come in." The woman's brown eyes moved to regard each person as they entered, stopping between Drom and Arasha. "Oh my. Of course." She sounded put off.

"Is something wrong?" Cellis looked between Drom and the woman. "Is there a rule in the keep against Ill'ln?"

"No, but the message stated the two women with you would be a Lady and a servant. It was assumed there would be a Lady and her maidservant. I see a woman who might be a Lady hiding in rags, but for certain an Ill'ln is no maidservant."

"Arasha is noble-born and Droya is a unique case." Cellis frowned, "Why is it an issue?"

"His lordship keeps no slaves, and we didn't see to obtaining clothing befitting an Elf. Not that you've granted us enough advanced warning if we had realized." The woman made an exasperated sound. Drom gritted his teeth at being called Elf in that tone yet again. "I suppose we might be able to fashion something out of a flour sack."

"I can wear my current dress." Drom offered, dreading the rough texture a flour sack was sure to have, even compared to the dress he wore. It was uncomfortable enough already.

"Nonsense," Ries interjected. "The dress is soiled with blood and will draw attention we don't need." The toothy expression he wore unsettled Drom a bit, even as it annoyed him.

"I must agree. Droya, we will need to replace your clothing even if we do not do so for anyone else." Cellis was almost apologetic.

"But please fine woman," Ries bent at the waist and kissed the hand of their hostess. "Don't inconvenience any of your people. Droya will wear whatever you might have on hand that fits and is prepared."

"Mmm Hmmm." She looked unimpressed. "I will see you each to a room. Baths have been drawn and clothing set out to pick from.

If you are in luck, some of it may even fit. Breakfast will be served in an hour."

Drom wasn't sure what to make of Ries. What was he plotting with his words? The moment he was starting to gain a sense of some control over his life again, things were once again out of Drom's hands.

DROM WAS THE LAST TO be seen to a room, adjacent to Arasha's. It was odd since Arasha had been the first to be bestowed a room. Drom wondered if this was the elder woman's way of showing her frustration that he wasn't a maidservant as expected.

The room itself was 'humble', containing few pieces of furniture. To one side, a wash basin rested on a stand with a pitcher of water. Centered in the room was a simple straw bed. On one side was a modest armoire and to the other side was a bedpan built into a seatless chair. Against one wall was a large bathing basin half filled with steaming water. The only other items of note were a mirror against the wall near the room's only window and a tiny bell set into the wall he shared with Arasha's room.

He untied the blood-stained apron-dress and folded it neatly. It would need thrown away, but by now it had become a habit to be careful with the only possession he'd been granted. Unclothed, he gazed at the steaming water. The idea of bathing was almost too much to have hoped for. It was the first time since the change he'd been able to do more than wash with a rag. He'd never cared for soaking baths in his prior life. Then again, he'd never had to wait days at a time to wash off before any of this either.

Still, he didn't move to it right away. He'd had no chance to review his reflection since his transformation. The mirror drew him, but also scared him. All he knew of his form was what he could tell from looking down or the vague reflections in glass and water.

A quality mirror meant for the first time he could perceive how he looked now.

His steps were timid, edging forward until the new form moved into view. He was met with the full form of a beautiful woman. Ill'ln were always attractive by human standards of course, but she was a diamond among rubies. Even with the patched hand and dust from countless days on her honey brown skin, she seemed to shine. He peered down at himself. It didn't seem that way from this angle. Again he lifted his eyes to the mirror.

Waves of vibrant red hair framed a delicate oval face before flowing over her shoulders in light waves. Her large gray eyes were a shade shy of being silver. Those eyes had a way of making the slight upturn of her nose seem a bit more petite than it actually was. Though he knew he was holding a neutral expression, the natural shape of the lips in the reflection formed a demure curve, flushed red with the natural blood flow rather than paints and pigments as some richer women wore. He'd have taken her to be a noblewoman if not for the platinum chain around her thin neck or the long ears jutting at angles from either side of her head inches beyond the hair.

Her breasts were larger than he'd thought. He knew they were there, but never put it together, thanks in part to the unique angle of view. They were the sort he'd heard women saying caused them back pain. He'd remained unburdened, so it never clicked. Though he wanted to, he couldn't turn his eyes away. Those breasts remained firm and round in a way which would have been unnatural if they'd seen more than a few months of existence, but gravity hadn't yet had its way with them. A woman without a bodice to support them would have long ago seen them hanging low when unfettered like this.

In contrast, the woman before him had wide hips with a narrow waist which seemed like it had spent years in a corset. Twisting his hips, her bottom was well-rounded and her sex was hidden in a tuft of light red that hinted at the folds below. Her arms were thin, as were her legs, but well-toned revealing the slight oddities of musculature common to Ill'ln. Her hands and feet were delicate and without callous, seeming out of place on a creature with such physical power.

Drom's body reacted, skin tightening in places and a flush of heat in his blood. There was a faint tingle between his legs along with the sense of moisture. The woman in the mirror took on an expression of sudden horror and he diverted his eyes. By all the gods above, it was horrible. The image of his new form aroused him despite himself. What effect was it having on men unaware of the truth? "Cellis you bastard, how dare you do this to me?!"

"So we finally meet, Droya." Drom whispered to himself after he'd recovered. Had Cellis made him like this intentionally? Maybe Ries was right and Cellis had no intentions of returning him to his former self. Was there in fact a cure, but the Magus wanted to keep him as a servile, oversexualized work of art?

Drom removed the bandage from his hand and slipped into the bath. He tried to push those thoughts aside. Images of his new self kept plaguing him, made worse by the need to rub sensitive skin to wash. To push it back, he tried to picture himself as he had been before. The image was vague and fleeting at best. Every time the water shifted or washcloth touched skin, the vision of Droya transposed itself instead. Eventually he gave up and wept. Whether it was the magic, some aspect of the piercer, or his own mind betraying him, the only physical image that came into his mind when he tried to imagine himself was the body he wore now.

CLEANED, DRIED AND with self-control of his emotions again, Drom wrapped his hair up in the way he had seen Arasha do many times before to draw extra moisture away. After rewrapping his hand, he walked to the Armoire and opened it. A faint gasp escaped him.

It was full of silk finery, with blouses, skirts, and dresses of highest quality hanging within. He'd assumed their belief that he would be a maidservant meant he would be offered clothing consistent with the plain clothing he'd seen on the woman who'd shown them in. Instead, they seemed to be prepared for a maidservant who was also a Baroness.

"Damn you Ries." He cursed. "I should have sensed you were trying to make sure they put me in silk and lace." The anger was half-hearted though. Drom should have realized anyway. His wife had been a Countess with maidservants when he'd first met her by chance at his store in the market. Those girls had dressed like ladies in their own right.

Sifting through the selection, only about a third of the clothing had any chance of fitting his new proportions. All of them were absolutely feminine. The blouses were frilled and would hang oddly. The skirts were sown for a corsetless waist, so had slim hope of finding purchase on his unnaturally narrow midsection. Drom wouldn't care if they hung awkward and loose, but a skirt that sat too low might trip him or prevent him from fulfilling his duties.

That left several dresses designed for a woman wearing a corset and with room for an ample chest. The first he ruled out since it tied in the back. The other two were side-laced, the first being saffron-yellow with white lace trim. Its upper portion had a high and tight collar and detached sleeves. Composition of the lower skirting was billowing folds of cloth with pleating designed to rest over a dress-frame. One which was nowhere to be seen. How in the world did they expect it to be used? The more important question was if it had the wire frame, how did they expect a maidservant to complete her tasks while wearing it?

That left him with only one choice. The last dress bore a dipping neckline which squared off and appeared to be designed to display the wearer's ample bosom. A rich blue in color with pale blue trim accenting it and a distinct lack of lace made it far less frilly than the others before it. Its sleeves were attached and there was a wide sash for the waist to hide the side lacing. The lower skirting was sleek and strait, divided on both sides where the laces ended. He guessed it might have been sewn this way to allow for riding horses. Many freewomen skirts were divided in this manner, but since the material was satin, he couldn't imagine someone riding in it much. Still, it would allow freedom of movement.

"Blue it is." He grumbled. If he hadn't seen his wife dress and helped her once or twice, he would have been at a loss for how to don it. As it was, he nearly forgot to put one of the silk chemise on under it first. The smooth flow of the cloth brought a tingle where it brushed skin and he couldn't help but revel in the softness. He'd grown accustomed to the rough cotton dress on his hypersensitive skin, but that didn't mean it had been comfortable. This was a wonderful replacement. It didn't irritate his skin at all. He knew he should hate it, but there was so little positive about this new life that the modest touch of comfort was enough not to care. Still, the fact he found himself eager to wear it did make him blush in shame.

The dress slipped on with ease and fit well. Surprisingly well in fact. The laces were tricky, but after a while he managed to tie it snug without obvious puckering or pinching. He tied the sash in place and though it was still damp, unbound his hair. With a sigh of resignation he stepped before the mirror again so he could adjust the dress as needed.

Freezing stock still, disbelief at what he was seeing held him fixed. Aside from the long ears perked at an upward angle, she might have been a woman of high birth. Not just any woman, but one whose beauty might easily compared to descriptions a goddess such as Erosana or Agopaydin. Even the platinum piercer chain could have been a simple necklace on her delicate throat.

Drom wanted to cry again and Droya in his reflection wore a pout on her face. Her ears wilted downward until they were flat against her hair. He reached up, touching them. Doing so, he realized he could cover them with hair and the loose curls would hide them! This revelation caused them to push against his hand, trying to rise again with his emotion.

He tried taking conscious control the muscles of his ears with marginal success. While he strained, they would stay down, but if he relaxed even a little, they would rise again. Ill'ln endurance or not, keeping them down grew painful over time. Still, to look human again, even if it was as a woman, it was worth the strain!

Despite having them hidden, something didn't feel right in the refection. Studying the woman in the mirror revealed the reason. It was the lack of shoes. Ill'ln walked about barefoot, but no maiden in clothing such as these ever would. He wanted to say it was part of the disguise, but deep down a part of him was being a bit vain about his new appearance. To feel human again would be a lone pleasure he might never have a chance at again. He wanted to do it as perfectly as he could. After some digging in the bottom drawer, he found a pair of silky blue slippers that would fit him and still match the dress. They had sturdy enough soles to handle a bit of walking.

Slipping them on, he rushed out the door. Already, he was late for the meal and the bouquet of delicious scents wafted all the way to his room.

"ONLY ABOUT FIVE DAYS travel that way." Cellis was in the middle of a conversation. "I should be able to cast something to shield us from the effects as we pass through."

"Enough for yourselves, the pack animals and the seven armed men I will be providing?" The voice came from a well-dressed man of thirty five at most. The food before him remained untouched.

"I believe so, yes. It isn't a matter of being able to encompass us. It is a matter of not attracting attention doing so. Once I arrive I will have a better idea. Worst case, I send the porters back to you."

"You could free me from the geas and have one less person to worry about." Ries put on a charming expression. His clothing was now a gray silk doublet and matching pants. All of it was trimmed with black.

"Not yet."

"No, of course not."

"What about me sir?" Arasha was dressed as regal as any noble woman should be. She was even smiling again though her next statement proved it had nothing to do with the finery. "My father is sure to be free by now and if I was to join him..."

"You might distract him from his goals or be taken captive and used against him." Cellis finished for her. "Perhaps after his efforts are concluded.

Drom stepped from the shadows of the hall. His legs were unrestricted thanks to the open sides of the dress, but he took tight steps anyway. The illusion afforded him by the clothing would be broken if he didn't at least act the part. His ears burned from the exertion of holding them down for so long, but he kept the muscles tensed.

"Come now Cellis, the lady slave deserves more than a 'later' from you." Ries cast a glance at Drom with unmasked appraisal and froze. He blinked rapidly as though trying to wash away dust from his eyes.

The others noticed and shifted to seek the cause. Arasha's brow knit with uncertainty at the reactions of those around her. Was the small modification so drastic she didn't recognize him? Cellis frowned his bushy brows shot up as realization dawned on him. The host studied Drom with a soft smile.

"Ah, the last of your friends has arrived. My dear servant Kalliah's eyes must have deceived her. By the way she talked, Arasha was of peasant stock and your companion was the lowest of creatures. Come, join us."

"Your servant wasn't speaking false regarding myself Sir." Drom spoke only because the others were still too stunned to do so. The slow realization and horror dawning on Arasha's face was heartbreaking. He tried instead to focus on being the docile Nymph he was emulating. "Arasha is of noble birth, but due to circumstances beyond her control, is now a slave."

Taking a deep breath, he let his ears lift from beneath his hair. It was a physical relief, but an emotional struggle. It stung to lose having someone believe he was human again. "I however, am a mere Nymph. To wear such clothing as these is above the limit of my station, but there was no other option. I didn't want Master accused of dressing me in this manner or to draw extra attention while we travel, so hid my ears."

Their host, there could be no doubt at this point he was Lord Nephtin, took his turn being speechless. Drom blushed and cast his eyes down.

"A wise decision Droya." Even so, Cellis continued to stare. "Illegal if you are found out, but all things considered, what is one more charge against me?"

"She's beautiful." Ries mumbled to himself. He wasn't speaking loud enough for the others to overhear. With Drom's keen ears exposed again, it might as well whisper into Drom's ear. Ries sneered and spoke aloud in his smooth tones. "So Droya, about the use of your services."

"She looked absolutely human." Arasha's voice was strained between a tone of horror and of awe.

"Indeed, you had me fooled. A moment ago, I might have asked if you were being courted by anyone." Lord Nephtin's voice wavered only a fraction. "I may have to ask every Lady I encounter to lift her hair for me, to be certain."

"We can muse over the implications later. Right now, there is a more pressing issue at hand." Cellis' words indicated he was past it, but his eyes never wavered from Drom. No one else noticed it, being themselves fixated as well. "I believe the direction we were discussing would be the wisest. No one goes that way, so why would they scan it? They shouldn't believe I learned of a spell to aid our survival there."

"The Circlers aren't fools, even if they act like it. They'll watch for such things regardless of location for sure. I don't grasp magic, but I do understand tactics." Nephtin glanced away from Drom long enough to emphasize his words. "Why not detour the extra six days around it?"

"Because it's the obvious choice."

"Master," Drom was a bit confused from missing the earlier portion of this conversation. "I have a question if you'll allow."

"Oh? Be out with it then."

"Can armed men turn aside a troop of Magi?"

"No, but they will dissuade bandits while they are with us."

"Are there bandits where 'no living being goes?'"

Silence filled the room as everyone renewed their stares at him. Drom's ears wilted.

"She has an exceptional point." Ries was the one to break the silence. "I can't recall of any group who works near the area. There's no plunder to be had where there aren't travelers and every traveler gives it wide berth."

"From the mouths of slaves." Nephtin mused. "Perhaps I must reconsider my stance on owning Ill'ln."

"Alright. I would still need at least one man to handle the mules, but as there would be fewer mouths to feed, I wouldn't need as many of those either. With a bit of rearranging, I might even fit most of the extra supplies I am bringing into the spare room." At the puzzled glance Nephtin gave Cellis, he added, "The door we brought along."

"And it would be enough to ensure your spell didn't draw attention?" Nepthin sounded uncertain.

"There are no guarantees even on the most minor of spells, but with such a limited scope, I believe it might."

"Then so be it. We will make preparations today and you can be off tomorrow morning."

"One more question if I may?" Drom wasn't sure he wanted to learn the answer, but Cellis nodded. "What is our path?"

"Godsaddle Mountain, on the far side of the creeping wastes." Spoken as though the creeping wastes weren't certain death.

Chapter Eleven
The Aid of a Vassal

Cellis clapped his hands down in frustration. "I know what we were taught. I can't blindly believe it. Magic is like a plugged river and the dam broke."

"I'm sorry, but how can so many other Magi be wrong?" Llwanna kept her nose scrunched. "If they say it is a deplete-able resource, they have a reason."

"If it was like felling trees, we'd see a gradual return. It was a sudden, full resurgence. Observe how strong magic is these days. There are Magi alive who were among the first to tap into it again."

"Maybe it was gradual, but we couldn't recognize it until someone relearned how to tap in."

"Okay, so why didn't magical beings revive slowly?"

"They were all dead." The certainty left her voice.

"Not all of them. Many were laying dormant at sites of lingering power. Embers of magic waiting to be fanned back into a flame. Why did they spill back into the world all at once?"

"So let's say y'er right. Why not talk to the Circle about yer idea? Show them the information backing it." Llwanna put a hand on his arm, but it did nothing to calm his ire.

"I did. They don't want me prying into things I 'don't understand.'" He mocked a pompous tone. There wasn't humor in his words.

"They didn't believe ya made a solid case?"

"No. I suspect they did. It seems to be something they aren't willing to accept."

"That doesn't make sense." She was frowning now. "Magi are seekers of hidden truths. Why wouldn't they accept a sound hypothesis? At the least they should'a looked inta it."

And there was the source of his anger. The foolishness had shattered his idealism and burned away all respect for the Circle. "I'm guessing they already knew I was right. If I'm correct, there's no need for quota. They use it to keep tight control of us. They care more about holding on to power than the truth."

DROM ONLY HAD VAGUE memories of the lessons of his youth. The details he could recall about Godsaddle Mountain were sketchy at best. He knew it in terms of geography, but not much about its history and nature. As the name implied, there was a legend about the origin of the mountain everyone had heard, but other than that he didn't know much. It was the only mountain in this area, rising as a tiny pair of bumps on the horizon from the city wall. It was also important to Magi, but he couldn't recall why. Whatever else he might have been taught about it had long been forgotten.

"It's a stretch of ground covered by a layer of what looks like a grassy plain. It's actually a unique species of plant." Nephtin must have mistook Drom's thoughtful expression for trying to work out what the Creeping Waste was. "Other living things within it's expanse don't survive more than a minute, so it's the only living thing to exist where it grows."

"It's not a whole species," Cellis wore an expression which might have been what he'd show if he were correcting a child. "Rather, it's a single entity. A plant-based homunculus left behind from an ancient war."

"Technical details. True plant or not, it's still a death sentence cross."

"True." Cellis sighed. "Droya, you eat. Everyone else finish so we can make preparations to leave. I want to be mobile at sunrise, so if you expect to sleep tonight, we should rush to handle everything today."

After a night sleeping in a carriage, no one needed prompting to want things done quick enough for a full night of bed rest. Except Lord Nephtin, everyone rushed to finish and left. Drom walked to the unused place setting and browsed for a tray to fill his plate from. As he was about to ask where they were, the answer came in the form of house servants entering from a side door. Drom tucked his ears, wanting to avoid having more people aware of his shame than already knew.

The delicious fragrance of the meal had been in the back of his mind, but now they had his full attention. As the members of his group rose from the table, maids removed their plates and glasses. A manservant carried a tray of food while a second placed items from it onto Drom's plate. Fresh baked berry danishes, thin-sliced fruits stewed in syrup, thick slices of cured meats fried to perfection. More still beyond. Each was like ambrosia after the simple foods he'd been eating most of his life.

When the servants with the food left, a woman came and filled his glass with a weak wine. Lord Nephtin watched with an amused expression through this flurry of motion. Perhaps it was Drom's expression and rapid consumption which drew the expression more than the swift actions of his servants.

Once finished, the remaining servants departed leaving only the two of them. Drom tried to ignore it as he ate in silence, but the man's deep brown eyes stayed on him the whole time. It didn't set off the sort of tension he'd experienced dealing with the inspection of the carriage, but it did make him uncomfortable. It wasn't like the looks he'd grown familiar with. Not lust, discomfort, disgust, or any number of expressions directed at him since taking this form.

What was the man waiting for? Did he expect something? No answer came. Instead, Drom finished the meal in silence.

"I must assist Master in his preparations now." He rose from the table.

Lord Nephtin made a dismissing gesture with his hand, but the corners of his lips were curved upward. Drom gave an awkward curtsy. Bowing would have been more proper as a Nymph, but with his current appearance, the curtsy felt like a better fit.

He rushed off, glad to be away from the nobleman's gaze.

THE DAY WAS UNEVENTFUL, broken only by a late lunch and the castings to keep Ries from returning to rat form. Everyone but Drom was exhausted by the end of the day. There'd been much to do, including a complete rearrangement of the contents of the 'spare room'. The amount of supplies they had packed into it was more than the four of them could have used in a year. That wasn't even counting the prepared saddle bags. When asked, Cellis had indicated it would be a five-day journey, so why did they need so much? Drom wanted to ask, but feared he would like the answer less than the suspense.

The final task was a quick check of the beacon to find out how Lord Kirk was before eating. He was in excellent health and mobile, so nothing to draw concern yet. Casual conversation filled the table, though the men all kept shooting sidelong glances at him. Lord Nephtin and Ries both had expressions that were uncomfortable and direct in their assessment of Drom's form. Cellis' gaze was a blend of hard and thoughtful. Arasha paid almost no attention to Drom once the conversation began, but he took it as an improvement. Anything was better than the fearful glances he was becoming accustomed to.

"It will be sorrowful to see you all off so soon, but I'm glad to have had you here." Nephtin offered as he finished the last of the slow-roasted venison left on his plate. "Runners have informed me that I might be joining the conflict soon, so perhaps I will be of aid to the Earl in concluding this ugly business. I do trust you will feel welcome to return in the future?"

"Perhaps." Cellis was noncommittal.

"Stupendous." As though it had been a warm and whole-hearted agreement. "I have prepared two rooms for you. I am told, the young lady is not comfortable alone with Ill'ln, so it will be up to you to determine your sleeping arrangements."

"Two! Not four?" Drom let it slip casting his eyes downward to add, "I would have thought each person had a room as was the case when we arrived."

"Those previous arrangements had assumed Cellis traveled with nobility. I need the extra rooms for those runners to rest before they return to the city. You're free to keep the clothing, as I find them fetching on you, but I don't want to supply the servants with any ideas.

"It's suitable." Cellis spoke before Drom could respond. "Droya, you will share a room with myself."

"Oh, well then." Nephtin seemed amused though Drom couldn't imagine why. "I will assume that means Ries and Arasha will be sharing the other room?"

The whisper in Drom's mind he'd become so used to ignoring went silent for a moment in the wake of his own venomous thoughts. It soon redoubled as though encouraged by his joining in. Of course his thoughts came with pain. He ground his teeth to keep from screaming out, yet the notion of Ries and Arasha alone together kept his consciousness present. The pain was terrible, yet distant, keeping his body from crumpling. It was like a faint wall of numbness formed between his mind and the pain, buffering the effect.

"No." Cellis was firm, "Arasha will have her own room. Ries will sleep with the stable hands."

The shock of Cellis' statement drove his dark thoughts away. The pain was slower to dissipate. As the numbness trickled away, he noted the last hints of pain brought a pleasant sensation hard to describe, let alone reconcile. Like the burn of a first-rate pepper stew. Perhaps it was that he'd managed to keep the pain from overwhelming him. Despite now being pain-free, Drom was left weaker, trembling.

Slumping into the chair to keep it from showing, Cellis stared at Drom's hand. Glancing down, the soup spoon he'd been holding was now bent into the shape of his closed fist and blood was soaking through the bandage again.

"As you wish." Nephtin followed Cellis' gaze. Drom folded his free hand over it and sat as he'd seen proper ladies do.

"Just wonderful." Ries tossed his own spoon into his bowl, the clatter suiting his visible irritation.

"Thank you sir." Arasha focused her eyes on the spot where her own bowl had been resting. Maids were now gathering the dining-ware from the table. Thankfully they didn't ask for the spoon in Drom's hand.

Slipping it under the table, Drom dropped it and caught it on a slippered foot. Hoping there wouldn't be much obvious blood on the footwear, he gently slid the spoon off and gave it a light shove towards where Ries had been sitting. As the others rose, he did as well. It was a struggle not to inspect his slippers.

"My men will show you to your quarters. Rest well and I will see you off in the morning." Two house soldiers entered the hall as Nephtin spoke. Had they been waiting outside the room, prepared for their queue? "Abel, please see the young man is shown to the stable. He'll be sleeping in the loft with the stable hands."

One of the men nodded and led Ries off towards the entry. The other led the rest of them to the two rooms. Arasha's was first with a far step down from the room she'd been led to earlier. He and Cellis were taken to an unfamiliar but well-attended room. It had two beds and enough comforts to verify it was a guest bedroom for visiting nobility. The beds even had down batting rather than straw. It would seem Cellis was to be treated as a noble still.

"How is it you didn't collapse out there?"

"Master?"

"Don't act as though the violence in your mind wasn't written in your features. The piercer chain should have lit up your senses like a pyre. You didn't make a sound, let alone collapse."

"Oh," Drom tried to find the right words, "Nymphs don't consider violent thoughts, so I couldn't react. If I'd let it happen, it would have violated my word."

"Festering wounds!" It was an uncommon curse these days. Its rarity said something about Cellis' age. The only reason Drom recognized it was from one of the rare books from his shop's collection. "You weren't fending off that sort of pain on my behalf. The gods alone could save us if every Ill'ln had someone or something they cared about as much as you do for her!"

Drom wasn't sure how to respond. It didn't have the tone of a compliment, but wasn't focused into a reprimand either. All he could find to say was, "She is worth more than life."

"Perhaps that's it." Cellis spoke in a distant tone as though focused on some far point beyond the horizon. "Temper your wrath. Outbursts like that could get us all killed. Including her."

"Yes Master." Drom refused to be the source of peril for his wife. He had already ruined her life enough as it was. "May I express some thoughts I had while we were working today?"

"Why not?" Cellis rubbed his temple with his thumb, remaining distant. "Do so."

"The Order of Magi and Lesser Houses have combined forces and are overturning long-standing traditions. Even freed, what's the likelihood the Prince and High Council's men can win as things stand?"

"It is not impossible, but seems unlikely. There's no doubt the Circle will coax permission from the usurper council to take over civil control thanks to the split in Guardsmen loyalties. One well-trained Magus is worth an elite. A Master Magus is worth at least a troox or more." Meaning they were a match for between a hundred and a thousand men per Magus. Worse odds than Drom expected.

"Do you care which side wins?"

"Honestly?" Cellis stopped his distant staring, a cold blue gaze settling on Drom. "Many things about how the Order of Magi is run irritate me, but I believe the separation of power was one of the wisest rules they ever put in place. I suppose it means I favor the side of the Prince. There are surely other Magi who would feel the same way."

"Do you favor him enough you'd be willing to create mistrust in the power and responsibility of Magi and their magics?"

"Power unchecked or a return to ancient bias, some choice. Still, I already committed myself to bringing their use of power into question with the projection. I'm listening, what is it you have in mind?"

"Use the extra men who would have been with us to spread the truth about the origin of Ill'ln. They could do far more damage to the Order with the information than they could ever hope to do through fighting."

"Assuming I could provide those men with proof to back the claim, Order justice would have them suffer the same transformation as yourself if caught."

"I didn't realize." Drom had thought it was such a smart idea, "It would have been an excellent way to keep the Order from gaining allies; but I wouldn't want anyone else to suffer being made into such..." It didn't seem right calling them creatures knowing the truth as he did now. "Into this."

"Oh, it is still a wonderful plan, but it has its risks. Do you believe you could withstand two powerful spells channeled through you and only a third of your typical sleep time? Or rather, could you manage despite the long journey ahead tomorrow?"

"If it will help Arasha's father, I'm willing to do whatever is required."

"I hope you also understand this alters nothing in your own situation."

"Yes, I know. We won't be returning for a long period."

"Observant." The aged Magus' brows lifted a bit. "Perhaps by the time we return, I will have worked out a cure."

"Perhaps." Ries' words about the existence of a counterspell came back to mind. "Do you believe you'll be able?"

"With enough time. The issue is one of you living long enough to do so in a time frame where it would matter. Historically, it took around twenty years to develop the first generation of Ill'ln. In general, counter spells can be worked out in the same period as developing the original spell. In this case, I will have to reverse engineer the spell without being able to do direct experiments. I have no idea how it will influence the time required."

Cellis' shoulders lowered. "I'm not a young man any more. I doubt I can pull off a miracle of speed developing the counter spell. Ill'ln are slow to age, but I'd prefer you not return to yourself so late. I recognize your wife is already at least half of the average lifespan for a non-Magus."

That someone who appeared as seasoned as Cellis might still have another half a lifetime of years before they peaked and began to decline was mind boggling. How old could a Magus grow? Worse, Drom had almost no chance of returning to a human before Arasha had long since passed away. At least if Cellis was telling the truth about the counter spell.

"It's all speculation at this point. I'm hoping I can use my vast knowledge to accelerate the development of a cure. For now, fetch the spare room door. I'll need to pry a few items from the shelves."

"What are we going to do Master?"

"I'm going to craft a delayed spell in the form of a potion and you are going to become an image in the sky."

"Me? Why?"

"Because they can't turn you into something you already are."

"Drinking a potion will project my image like the crystal?"

"No, breaking the potion at the feet of Red Machtha members will cause an accelerated transformation into an Ill'In. Your message is going to be through one crystal while another is projecting events as they happen."

"Won't those spells use a lot of energy? Isn't that supposed to let them find us?"

"Must I explain everything?" Cellis was terse. "Casting the spells over an extended period will thin out the power draw. Also, by using a potion, some energy will be drawn from the elements at the moment of discharge. Now, are there any more questions or do you want to save the explanations for our days of travel and instead focus on the long task ahead?"

"Sorry Master, we can start."

"No, we can't. Not until you retrieve the doorway."

Blushing at his own failing, Drom slipped out of the room and down the hall to where the door was being stored.

DROM WOKE MORE EASILY than he had expected. The castings of the previous night were still fresh in his mind along with the words he'd had to speak for the recording.

'Observe, all citizens of Fairmar, the works of the Order of Magi. Witness how your trust in the Order is rewarded. The Ill'ln you despise with such venom are in truth, your own people. The Order has lied to you for centuries now. Ill'ln were not created from animals as other Homunculi are. They are men and women transformed against their will into a blend of monster and slave.' It was here in the recording he'd let his ears rise from their hiding place beneath his hair. 'Gaze upon new-formed Ill'ln and realize this could be the wages of your loyalty.'

It sounded dramatic to Drom, though he wasn't a quality actor by any stretch of the imagination. Cellis had been pleased enough not to bother a second try. It made Drom thankful since the magic-induced numbness had already been making things difficult. The message being shorter than the one Cellis had done before also helped.

Everyone was quick to eat that morning. It was a shame since it was the last chance to enjoy such rich foods for a long while. Lord Nephtin nodded and chuckled when Drom made the timid request if he might take a loaf of the delicious bread served that morning. It was filled with a mixture of fruit and nuts.

The mules were ready by the time the sun crested the horizon. The numbness must have still been lingering in places since Drom's ears weren't sore while holding them down like yesterday. Shouldn't they have been more painful today rather than less? If this was because of the numbing effect, at least there was something about the awful sensation he could say he liked. It made the act of keeping his ears down for part of the message much easier. Having them more comfortable today was a blessing.

Aside from Cellis, everyone seemed well-rested. The Magus was little better today than he'd been when he'd gone to sleep. Seeing the bloodshot weariness of the man, Drom found himself thankful for Ill'ln resilience. He helped Cellis onto a Mule, then went to Lord Nephtin as he'd been instructed to do last night.

"Lord Nephtin?"

"Yes?" The man's eyes roamed over Drom's form, but only for a moment.

"Master has instructed me to entrust this note, crystals, and vial to you." He produced all four, the loss of the warm pulsing of the crystals being both a relief and a regret.

"He needed to send you with a letter when he's fewer than twenty paces away?" Lord Nephtin's eyes shifted from the Magus onto the revealing front of Drom's dress where he'd had pulled the items from his bosom. The man's amused grin had returned. Drom wished he had a belt and belt purse for this outfit to avoid such situations.

"He's worn out." Drom chose to ignore the expression from Nephtin and what it was caused by. "The note contains instructions on who to target and how to use the items. He also instructs whoever takes on this task does so understanding it might come at a severe price if they are caught by the Order of Magi. However, it will help ensure a victory for your side if it is done properly."

"What do they do?"

"I was told I could not reveal that information to anyone." Not last night. It was the standing order against revealing his own origin which still affected what he could say. "It will be clear when they are used." Drom couldn't help but add, "I suggest you yourself be within Fairmar City at the time it is done if it is safe for you to do so. It should be an enlightening experience."

"Earl Kirk picks unusual allies." Lord Nephtin's amusement waned a bit, but he nodded and let it drop. "Oh, and I saw to it several of those loaves you so enjoyed were packed in the supplies."

"Thank you." Drom couldn't help the curve of his lips at hearing.. He didn't dwell on it, instead joining the others again.

No one else aside from Cellis was provided with a mule to ride, but the pace wasn't harsh once they were moving. No one would need to ride them anyway and they were better used for carrying supplies. Two alone were dedicated to the door Drom had been carrying by himself. He suspected the only reason Cellis rode was because sleep deprivation had taken too strong of a toll on him. It offered him a chance to rest if not actual sleep.

Lord Nephtin's farewell was to raise his hand, open palm, before returning to the manor. Drom's keen eyes picked up on him studying the items he'd been handed. One of Nephtin's men had come along to lead the mules, using a rope chain to keep them spaced in an even row as they walked. The animals weren't balking the way he had seen mules do in the market square so many times before. It wasn't clear if this was due to the skill of their handler or the lack of city bustle.

No one spoke, but Arasha kept shooting glances at Drom. It could only be described as moments of uncomfortable curiosity, followed by sharp avoidance of eye contact. She wore an ill expression every time she glanced away again. Ahead, Cellis seemed to be asleep despite remaining upright. Drom supposed he'd been wrong on that count. Ries didn't bother to feign any activity to hide the fact his eyes were fixed on Drom's backside from where he walked a step back and to the side. Drom scowled, but it only made Ries grin, so he shifted his attention forward again.

Minutes stretched into hours and the dirt path forked several times. Each time the sign of human travel faded a bit more until at last the path was so overgrown from disuse it might have been a deer path. It didn't have the feel of a civilized trail. The location they stopped at wasn't cleared, but didn't have much brush thanks to the dense forest canopy above. It also had the advantage of several larger rocks to sit on.

Dried meat, fruits, and a travel loaf were shared along with water to wash it down. After the opulent meals with Lord Nephtin, it was like chewing shoe leather. At least it was filling if not enjoyable. The fancier loaves were saved for another day. Only Ries and the man who led the mules spoke, and not anything of consequence. Their conversation revealed the man's name was Raymond, and that Ries wove lies like a spider weaves its web. Despite knowing some facts, Drom still found the lies sounding almost believable. One more reason to mistrust the man.

They were soon moving again. Somewhere between the morning and now, the whisper in his mind had transitioned. It seemed less feral and more pleading. Urges to violence had morphed into urgings to escape into the forest. Demands had become pitiable begging. What had prompted the alteration? The shift had been so slow and subtle, it had gone unnoticed until now. Drom turned the mystery over in his mind for another hour until the constant glances from Arasha once more drew his attention, bothering him. Fear was rough enough, but the expressions of disgust were too much.

"Pardon my asking Lady Arasha," He chose the formal title she had worn when they first met. "But is there something specific about myself you find offensive? If so, I will do what I can to remedy it."

"You?" Arasha's eyes shifted away, as if it would deny her previous glances. "Why would I care enough about a beast to be offended?"

Drom hesitated, trying to decide what to say that would help. "I realize you dislike me and find me frightening. I accept there isn't anything I can say or do to alter this fact." He wanted to scowl at Ries who was smirking as though he were watching a farce. The fact such an expression would be counterproductive at the moment kept him restrained. "There must be some way I can be less offensive to your senses."

"Give it up Elf, you aren't going to change her mind." Ries' tone held the same subdued humor as his expression.

"Nymph, not Elf. Get your terms strait rat." It was difficult to keep his tone level. "You do not speak for Lady Arasha. Her voice is her own to use."

Arasha stared back for a long moment. When she at last spoke, the tone reminded Drom of the strong-willed woman he'd fallen in love with. For a few seconds she was back to the person who used to rail for hours in debate with him about why station was unimportant or why slavery was unethical. She was a woman with strong opinions and unafraid to express them.

"The Ill'ln is correct. I do speak for myself. If you want to ease my mind, go kill yourself monster. I am not going to feel safe with you anywhere near me. Since Cellis isn't going to let that happen," It was the first time since being bought she called the Magus by his name. "Why don't you stop trying to play human. It's a disgusting parody of reality that should never have been allowed in the first place."

The viciousness made his ears want to wilt though they were already laying flat against his skull. With a sigh, Drom let his ears return to their natural position, brushing a few stray strands from where they still clung. "As the Lady wishes." At least for a short time, he had been able to feel almost human again. If only she knew the truth. "It was not done to offend you. I apologize."

Silence fell across the group, aside from a stray snicker from Ries who seemed delighted in the irony. Cellis could have explained the humanity of Ill'ln, but didn't. Why wasn't he explaining? It wasn't as though all of Fairmar wouldn't recognize it soon enough. Despite all of it, a part of Drom was elated. Arasha wasn't shuffling along or sneaking glances any more. She was taking firm strides and looking others in the eye again. Glaring if truth be told. Something about their interactions had rekindled the spark of who he knew her to be. For that, he would endure her lashings, both figurative or literal if need be. Her happiness was what mattered to him.

IT WAS THE EVENING of their second day traveling before anything more than a brief conversation occurred. The forest was thinning some and a warm breeze had leaves rustling when Drom noticed what looked like an unusually large butterfly perched on a limb above. No one else seemed to notice, but Drom watched it open and close its wings. It was better than studying at the backside of the mules.

His keen eyes drew into tight focus. It astounded him at how much detail he was able to pick up at this distance. It wasn't a butterfly at all! The wings might have been similar to a butterfly, but were composed of six parts rather than four. More noteworthy was the fact the body wasn't a slender insect. Instead, the form was strikingly human. Its limbs were abnormal in length when compared to the rest of its body and it had two thick antenna extended well over its head. More like short, fleshy catfish whiskers than insect antenna as one might expect from the wings. Flesh toned rods curving forward in gentle arcs from under a mane of curly black hair. Those traits aside, the body resembled a child's. Like a miniature seven or eight-year-old, minuscule enough to fit in a single hand. What was it?

The tiny being was leaning hard over the edge of the limb to stare at the group. Its wings would close and open again in slow movements, but it didn't seem to be a particularly useful motion. Before Drom could examine further, it burst into a flurry of motion, zig zagging through the air towards them.

Arasha glanced up, a pleasant expression forming as she took note of the burst of colorful motion. She must have taken it for a butterfly as well and lost interest after a moment. No one else took note of it at all. Drom sensed a slight rise in tension. Was the tiny creature dangerous? He tried to find the source of tension as they traveled forward through the ever-thinning forest. It seemed to surround them. The tiny creature was fluttering closer, and he struggled to decide how he should react.

In a fluid motion, he dipped to scoop up a stone. Were there more of them? Were they surrounded? It couldn't be a threat, but the tension built as it neared. They stepped past the last of the trees into an area of only grass and dirt. He could see both Arasha and Ries watching his behavior with open curiosity. He wasn't sure what he would even do with such an undersized stone, but kept it in his hand.

Drom only avoided crashing into the back of a mule by a narrow margin. His attention had been on the approaching creature, so failed to notice when Cellis stopped the caravan. He braced, ready to throw the stone. He released his tension though as the sense of danger stopped growing. This, despite the little winged creature now being close. Whatever the creature was, it wasn't the source.

"Stop!" the miniature girl squeaked. "Bad place!"

"We have arrived." Cellis' voice boomed compared to the creature's. None of them seemed to have even heard it yet. The others shifted their attention from Drom's peculiar behavior to the expanse ahead.

"Bad place sister. No go."

Drom studied the 'bad place' along with the others. Ahead of them, the grass thinned out to bare dirt. Scattered across the dusty band of ground were tiny bones and dead insects. Ten feet farther, the dirt gave way to what seemed to be a thick mat of low growing grass blades. They sprung up and spread like a lime-green sea. Several large lumps rose from farther into the mass of plants. The nearest of these was close enough to recognize the rotting carcass of a deer, antlers jutting from the festering mass.

"Bad place indeed." Drom muttered.

"Stay back." The miniature winged girl reached them at last and landed on Drom's head. She grabbed a handful of hair and flapped with all of her might.

"It's alright." Drom tried to keep his voice soft so as not to overpower the tiny being.

"Ack!" Arasha jumped away from Drom. "What is it?"

Everyone's attention shifted, searching for what she was referring to. With a roll of his eyes, Cellis spoke like a man who'd had his picnic rained on.

"That, my dear, is one of the more annoying of the non-lethal sub-elementals known to exist." He let out an annoyed breath. "We seem to have the 'helpful' attention of a fairy." The word 'helpful' dripped with enough sarcasm to drown a giant.

"Are they dangerous?" Ries was touching something inside of his sleeve.

"Only to your sanity and peace of mind."

"Shall I kill it?"

"No. It's dreadful luck to kill an innocent fae without provocation. Try to ignore it and it might clear out on its own." Cellis walked to one of the mules loaded with his personal supplies and opened the flap. "Right now, I need to focus on this casting to keep us alive through the wastes."

Chapter Twelve
The Echos of a Trauma

Laethem swallowed his frustration. Maria, now Maria of the Embers, had been asked to join the Circle before him. His time would come. Best to focus on the task before him. To that end, he was going to prove his worth. He suspected their friendship was the only reason he'd been granted an audience.

"So you believe a base on this newest island is vital. Please elaborate." The seat of Air seemed decrepit enough he might crumble. How much longer before he died or retired and the seat would be free for Laethem to assume?

"It is the farthest land mass ever scried. Far enough that teleportation isn't an option and ship travel would take months. It's a long way to travel every time further scrying exploration needs to happen. A base there would mean exploration could occur full time."

"Seasonal Storms in that area of the ocean are already well documented." Maria didn't hint at any sense of friendship in her tone. "What if there was an emergency? How would we rescue such valuable Magi without teleportation?"

"Simple," The genius of his plan made him beam even as he laid it out. "We would expand the Circle navy with additional ships. Set a route between the island and the mainland. We have ships rotate out along the route. In moments of urgent need, the magi can teleport from ship to ship."

Several eyebrows rose. Circle members exchanged glances. There was a pause as the Elder seat of Air dismissed him. "We will consider your proposal Magus Laethem."

Confident, Laethem nodded and strode out. Soon he'd be hailed as a hero. He was certain he'd be at the front of the list of Neomancers when the seat of Air opened.

DROM DIDN'T RESPOND to the fairy and when she realized he wasn't going into the wastes she settled down. She contented herself giggling and playing in his hair. Why the little creature was so focused on him wasn't clear, but she seemed to have no interest in anyone else.

Ries had returned to the shelter of the trees and was reclining there chatting with Raymond about rope quality and other pointless things. Arasha was close at hand, but only because of her interest in what Cellis was doing to prepare for the spell. Why was it every spell had to involve such pungent aromas? How did Magi like the Red Machtha ever cast anything on the spur of the moment if everything involved such lengthy preparations and obvious scents? Did they cast many things ahead of time and hold them inside like an arrow drawn taut?

Magic was such a headache. Each question answered only led to more questions. Drom was thankful he'd not shown a talent or he might have had to train for magic. Life was complicated enough without all of that.

Both Cellis and Arasha eyed him as he laughed with a snort.

"Sorry. I had some stray thoughts I found ironic."

Cellis went back to work. Arasha however kept staring. Drom tried to keep his eyes in a humble downcast. The urge to look back was making it difficult.

"I've never heard an Ill'ln laugh before." She ventured to herself. Her eyes glistened and the first tear fell as she turned away.

"Lady Arasha?" Drom's tone sounded tiny to him. "Have I offended you again in some way?"

"Go away." Arasha snapped in a voice wracked with sorrow. Her hand waved in a shooing motion.

"Yes Ma'am." He stepped away despite the burning desire to hold her close and make it better.

"Drom..." spoken to herself, but his keen ears heard it as if Arasha had spoken it aloud. "I miss you."

"I," pain flared. He would have violated a rule to say what he'd started to. Instead he followed it with, "Am sorry to have upset you." He tried to decide what he'd done or said to cause the reaction. His laugh! He always laughed in a snort despite his best efforts not to. It wasn't a conscious choice, just a immutable aspect of himself he wished wasn't there. In laughing, he'd reminded her of himself. This time, the irony made him want to cry.

"Sad girl." The fairy piped up.

"Yes. Comfort her?" Drom kept his voice low, hoping only the fairy would hear.

"Comfort humans?"

"Only that one."

"Why? Humans mean."

"That one is kind."

"Oh."

The fairy appeared to take his word as true and accepted them without question. She released Drom's hair and fluttered over to Arasha. Landing on her shoulder, she stroked and nuzzled at the giant cheek beside her.

Arasha paused, smiled, then wiped her eyes. "Hello little fairy." She brought a finger up to brush the tiny girl's shoulder. There was a musical giggle, causing Arasha to laugh in return. The tears were soon forgotten, and she returned to watching Cellis prepare as she idly played with the fairy.

Drom was surprised they weren't talking to one another, but given the giggles, the fairy didn't have much breath left to talk with. Things continued this way until Cellis was ready. At that point, Drom was made to play the part of a familiar again. Arasha and the fairy both grew quiet to watch.

The spell seemed more intricate than normal, which spoke volumes indeed. Some aspects Drom had come to consider standard were there: a circle marked this time in salt, something emitting a foul scent, droning words chanted in a guttural language, and several dried herbs smoldering in a cup. At least the scent of the herbs helped cut the pungency of the other component.

Other aspects were new. For example, a glass globe with no apparent opening, filled with water. It seemed to be the target of the spell rather than anyone in particular. Cellis was also not making the typical hand gestures, but was instead doing a bizarre hop-step dance around the globe within the salt circle. Whatever it was, the intense power it was channeling into the orb tingled at Drom's senses. It was another oddity. Until now, all the spells he had acted as a familiar for required Cellis to be in physical contact with him. At least in passing if not continuously.

No answers were forthcoming. Hour after hour of numbing magic rushed through him. He now thought of it as being plunged into cold water. At first it was a shock, but over time it robbed you of the sense of touch. It seemed it might shut your body down with enough time. Imagining it made Drom shiver.

When the spell concluded, the sun was resting along the horizon. Drom's skin prickled like goose flesh. Cellis seemed weak enough it took an effort to stand, but wore a pleased expression. The fairy had fallen asleep on Arasha's shoulder, though Arasha herself remained awake if not alert. Somewhere along the way Ries and

Raymond had set up camp. Both were already eating bowls of stew beside a large pot over a warm fire. Everyone devoured the meal. After a brief and tired renewal spell to keep Ries human, they slept. Cellis fell to snoring the moment he laid down. The fairy disappeared somewhere when Drom wasn't watching.

In the morning, they ate a simple meal of cooked grains before setting off. Drom's skin didn't seem right. It almost felt tight though it flexed as much as it ever had. He dismissed it as residual numbness from the long casting the night prior.

"Everyone stay within ten feet of the center mule and myself. It's where the focus of the spell is centered. The range of safe travel extends from that point." Cellis hefted himself onto the only animal without heavy saddlebags.

"Isn't it a bit close for all the animals and ourselves?" Ries shot glances towards the waste.

"Walking, we'll remain well within. Sleep will prove a bit tricky though. I do have a plan for that point, however."

"I should be able to keep the mules close together." Raymond seemed more concerned for the animals than the group. "Keeping them in one spot at night without a tether bar is beyond me though."

"Already taken into account."

No one else objected, so they worked out a travel formation. Drom thought the fairy had left them in the night, but as they moved, she returned. She squeezed out from a saddle bag and fluttered back to Drom.

"No! Danger! Bad place!"

"It's alright. We have a protection spell."

Cellis stopped and studied Drom. The others stopped as well lest they break formation. Even though they weren't yet in the wastes, everyone was on edge.

"It kills!" Every word the fairy spoke seemed to come in an exaggerated scream which barely managed to be audible beyond four feet.

"Yes, but not as long as we are near him." Drom pointed to Cellis.

"Droya," The old Magus now wore a frown. "I was unaware you knew Fae."

"Fae, Master?"

"Yes. Fae. The language you were just using. I wasn't aware you were educated in such a rare language prior to coming to serve with me.

Drom was confused. His curiosity grew more intense about why the fairy hadn't spoken to Arasha yesterday. Not directly. He studied the tiny girl fluttering in front of him with her arms stretched in a 'stop' position.

"Why don't you talk with the others?" Drom asked it.

"Humans can't talk."

"On a contrary." Cellis' voice took on a strange musical tone as he spoke and the use of 'a' instead of 'the' was peculiar.

"A talking human?" The fairy sounded frightened and in awe. She zipped to put Drom's head between the Magus and herself.

"They've been talking this whole time, you only noticed now?" Were fairies so oblivious beings?

"No Droya." The musical tone was gone from Cellis' voice. "She only speaks Fae. She can't understand Fairmarian."

"I don't understand. I've been speaking Fairmarian."

"Curious." Cellis studied Drom as though it was the first time. The tiny fairy was now hiding behind Drom's shoulder, fluttering so the top of her head peeked out to keep a weary eye on Cellis. Everyone else was rapt in their following of the exchange.

"Bad place. Scary humans. We go?"

"No, I must stay with them. The 'bad place' isn't dangerous if I am with them."

The little fairy shook her head and fluttered back from Drom. "You won't stay?"

"I can't. You stay away to warn others?"

The tiny being's expression was a struggle between fear and resistance. It bore a touch of uncertainty to round it out. "Please?" she whimpered, but accepted the futility and was already fluttering back away. "Will warn others. Sister have luck." It rose into the canopy behind them. Only after it was out of hearing range did Cellis speak again.

"You were not at all aware you were speaking Fae?"

"I swear Master. I don't grasp what you are talking about."

"This creates some fascinating historical implications. Not to mention how it may influence future homunculi design. However, we have more pressing concerns at the moment. The sooner we are beyond the Creeping Wastes, the better. Two days is enough time skirting death for me." He was moving even before he finished speaking. Everyone fell into pace with him.

It was another day passed in near-silence. After half an hour, the stillness of death seemed to close in on them. The only signs of animal life beyond their group was an occasional bird carcass. No doubt from flying too low and succumbing to the effect of the plants crunching under foot

Drom found himself unsettled and the others all seemed subdued in the presence of this seemingly innocent flora. Even Ries and Raymond stopped trying to banter by the time lunch and a renewal of Ries' form was at hand. So the day passed until it was almost time to make camp for the evening.

TWO HOURS BEFORE SUNSET, a shape became visible to the East. Without a word, Cellis corrected their path towards it. At first, no one commented, but as it resolved into a crumbling wall, Ries broke the silence.

"I don't imagine the inn is still in business."

Arasha startled, drawn out of whatever had been on her mind and blinked to peer ahead of them for the first time. Raymond chuckled. Cellis didn't react at all.

"What is it?" Drom's keen eyes picked up on other less obvious rubble in the same area.

"Benzaian. It translates from ancient Farmarian into 'Greenhill'. Dead and gone four centuries, give a decade or so.

"Because of the Creeping Wastes?" Drom ventured.

"After a fashion." Cellis didn't clarify.

"Did we need something here you doddering windbag or were you sating a desire to study ancient history?" Ries didn't appear as irritated as his voice implied. "I think we'd have done well to keep on our original course.

"This is where we need to be." Leading them around the wall to reveal numerous lesser walls, half crumbled into piles of loose stone, Cellis ignored the tone. "It is a fair bit more worn down than I had expected, but will serve our purpose."

"And that is?"

"Keeping the mule team from wandering beyond our protection."

"How did you realize we would find it?" Arasha was peering back the way they had come at the near-featureless open expanse. "Magic?"

"No. Basic knowledge of history, a memory of maps, and remembering how to walk north against the sun."

"Luck." Ries was scowling now. "If we had been angled a single degree too far to one side..."

"Then we would have been no worse off than expected." Cellis finished.

Silence returned as they circled the structure, seeking a dip or opening into one of the piles. One appeared soon enough, but a sense of urgency was creeping in. The sun laid against the horizon now. Plants sprung up everywhere among what could have been cobbled paths long ago. Now it resembled little more than shattered clay and cracked stone. A semicircle of waist high stones was found to serve for a camp site and the mules were hobbled opposite to the only break in the wall. A modest fire was built and wood from where it had been packed into one of the saddle bags was used to fuel it. The renewal spell was cast one final time on Ries for the day.

"I LOVE YOU ALWAYS." Arasha's fingers played across the swell of Drom's chest, sending a tingle of pleasure.

"As I love you my dove" he returned in his new voice. For some reason, it seemed natural. Arasha's fingers slid over his flat stomach and brushed over the soft fuzz of his new womanhood.

"We are together again." She cooed. "As it was always meant to be."

"I never meant for any of this. I'm..." He cut off with a slender finger of her hand pressed to his lips.

"Shh. What is done is in the past. Kiss me Droya. Kiss your wife."

He might have paused at the use of his Ill'ln name if not for the invitation. Drawing her in close, their lips met and all the fire of his passion and her own mingled. It was ecstasy.

The moment was broken as she writhed away from his grip. He woke to see her eyes open as the kiss broke and she tried to push away with all of her might. Her face filled with terror and her scream split the night.

IT STARTLED DROM OUT of the dream as the real Arasha began screaming. Shocking him more was that she was held against him. How had they ended up laying together?

Arasha was on her feet the instant he let go, running blind into the darkness. The fire had died down to coals, so the waxing face of the moon Nodel was the only light to navigate by. Fopei was still in a state of new moon. Drom was sure he was the only one with a clear view by the way the others were all stumbling to their feet and moving in blind confusion.

Arasha was clambering up a mound of stones past the braying group of agitated mules. Drom's mind lurched in fits and starts. Had he been sleepwalking?

Arasha made it to the top of the mound.

When she woke, it must have seemed like his arm on her and the grip of his hand was an attempt to grab. An attack.

She disappeared over the top of the pile.

"What's going on?" Ries' voice was the first to gain coherency.

"Arasha," Drom started before the shock of realization hit him. She was outside of the protective circle!

Drom was on his feet and in pursuit in an instant, heedless of the questioning cries after him. How long did Arasha have outside of the circle? It couldn't be long based on the bodies they'd seen on entering.

As he reached the wall of stones, the air seemed to grow thicker. Like a smithy while the dampers were all closed and smoke was filling the room. He ignored it. Taking a running jump, he expected to gain a limited distance up the pile. Instead he was launched over it. He landed off balance on the other side. How had that happened? Ill'ln strength? There wasn't time to dwell on it. Drom cast keen eyes about while regaining equilibrium.

There was no sign of her. "Arasha!" His piercing voice was shrill in his own ears. She must have already collapsed.

He rushed to find her path. Time wasn't on his side. Had she run strait or turned after the wall. Drawing air stung now, but not as much as he expected it should. How much time before this new body's endurance faltered?

There. The vegetation of the waste was parted by her passing. Moving as swift as he could without losing the trail, Drom found her laying face down among the foliage. She was obscured by the plants and was breathing in shallow gasps. Drom's chest was beginning to burn. Faint now but growing sharper.

He scooped her into his arms and ran with all his might. This frail-appearing body continued to impress him. He covered the distance between the wall and himself swifter than any human could have hoped for. For once, he was thankful to be Ill'ln.

Another leap brought him among the others who were arguing about what should be done.

"... stay here. If not, Droya won't see where to return." Cellis was calm voiced as he stoked the fire back to life.

"What are the odds?" Ries broke off as Drom landed in view from the firelight. "Apparently, strong odds."

"She's dying. Save her." Drom laid his wife before Cellis.

"How did you survive that?" Raymond didn't hide his shock.

"She's an Ill'ln." Ries acted as though it should explain everything.

Cellis made a soft clicking sound with his tongue. "She is indeed dying." A deep frown curved the corners of his lips. "I am not sure my knowledge of healing arts runs deep enough."

"You have to try." Drom left no room for debate.

"Casting a spell here would tip our hand if the Order is watching this direction.

"Save her." Drom's voice cracked in tones between demand and begging. His face was wet with tears.

"Such a tone with the Mage. Now, now Droya." Ries was about to taunt more until he caught the expression in Drom's eyes. Whatever he'd intended to say was choked back, and he eyed Drom's wounded hand as if weighing the chances of surviving a fight, let alone winning one. His eyes fell on Drom's piercer chain with further calculating looks. Drom didn't bother keeping eyes on him.

"It isn't that simple." Cellis brought his ear close to her mouth to listen and feel the shallow puffs of air if present.

"It is."

"I can keep her from dying, but I might not be able to fix the damage already done."

Drom remained silent. He waited now in a crouch. He might have spoken if the pain of breathing hadn't caught up to him. Dizziness setting in wasn't helping either.

"No promises." Cellis hesitated. The flow of magical energy trickled through Drom. There was no visible ritual except a mumbling chant from the old Magus.

The numbness of channeling energy crept over him, but this time the tingling also left a sensation as if it was entering his lungs. His palm itched and tingled as well, standing in stark contrast to the rest of his body's growing numbness.

The mules pawed the ground and strained at their ropes, sensing something in the casting that made them nervous. Raymond made tisking sounds to calm them though he seemed almost as nervous as they were. Ries frowned.

Despite how little action the casting seemed to require, the swell of power flowing through Drom steadily increased to match several of the more powerful castings Cellis had done so far. He didn't care.

That it was strong didn't matter. That he imagined it must be necromancy, healing variations or not, was irrelevant. He didn't even worry when it was doing more than numbing him this time. All that mattered was it could save his wife.

Arasha's breathing grew so shallow even Drom's keen senses had difficulty recognizing the slight rise and fall of her chest. His heart might seize if this went much longer. Before he could react, a wisp of yellow smoke rolled from the corner of her lips. It dispersed into the air. As the last trace faded, she drew in a coughing gasp.

Convulsing, each draw of air was drawn between fits of heavy coughing. It sounded painful and labored, but she was alive. The tingle of magic ceased though the numbness remained everywhere except Drom's hand and chest. Those bore intense itching.

The convulsions ended and Arasha laid still. The rise and fall of her chest was steady now.

"Swell work there." Ries eyed the small flames that sprang up among the coals, but lacked tone or expression.

"Necessary work, but it may return to haunt us later." Cellis was scowling.

Without looking at anyone, Drom let out his breath. He hadn't realized he'd been holding it. Pale yellow mist expelled from his own mouth. Weakness overtook him and his vision dimmed. The last sound he heard was Ries' voice.

"Great, I'm not carrying both of them out of here." Anything else spoken was lost to unconsciousness.

Chapter Thirteen
The Wrath of the Dryads

They would all rot. Erica would see to it if time itself didn't first. She might have looked smug, but that would require her to care what they thought.

"Do you have anything to say in your defense?" The stuffy seat of Water sounded like he didn't intend to be swayed.

"As fearful as you are of death, why not borrow a bit of life from those who'll never live beyond their middle age anyway?" Erica humored them, but kept her hand on the smooth bottle hidden in a fold of her robes. "We are in possession of the power of gods, but squander it with our restraint. Take what we need from the world around us. Why worry about disturbing the limited pools of magic in the face of such plentiful abundance?"

She studied their expressions. Laethem's brow furrowed in a way that spoke of devastation. Feeling betrayed. Fool. Maria and the others wore expressions of horror and disgust. They were fools too.

"Borrow?" The seat of Earth spoke now. "Stolen. Your limited quota is no excuse for Necromancy. We needn't discuss this. The verdict is clear. You don't even show the slightest sign you care. You're unrepentant."

They were correct. She didn't care she'd done it. She wasn't afraid, enraged or even concerned. It was another puzzle she'd already solved before she'd even been called here.

"In keeping with the law of sympathetic symbolism, the years ripped from your victims will be drawn away from you." Was Laethem's voice wavering? Pathetic. "You will die."

"You'll not have the chance." She flicked the cork from the bottle in her hand and drew it from her robe. She'd drunk the dram before they could act, the bitter fluid stinging her tongue where it had touched. For the first time, she showed an emotion. A thin sneer as she spoke. "I rob you of your justice by completing the act myself." She quoted, "Death, he watches with slotted eyes." It was fitting her final words would be the first from Heralds of Tayvon.

The Circle scrambled, but the effect was quicker than their impromptu castings could undo. She swayed and fell. Grinning still, she knew she'd won. Darkness overtook her.

HAZY AWARENESS RETURNED to Drom's senses. First was a cool dampness and the kiss of a light drizzle on his skin. Next came voices.

"You have my gratitude." The first voice belonged to Ries.

"It's no bother. As long as you don't need the letter there sooner than a week or so." Raymond was replying.

"Sooner is better than later, but I am in no position to complain. It will arrive whenever you can make it there."

"Indeed."

Speaking ended briefly before he heard footsteps move closer against the backdrop of the rainfall pattering.

"And?" Ries again.

"No clear ground to set up a tent, but there's an overhang which should fit us all." Cellis' voice dripped irritation. "I guess we'll have to press on to the base of the mountain. There'll be acceptable shelter there."

Drom opened heavy eyes. It was impossible to determine what time it was from the light, as the heavy clouds dimmed everything and shut away the sun. Though the storm had darkened everything, for him at least, there was more than enough light to observe his surroundings. He was on the ground under a few sparse trees. In the direction he was facing, the broad expanse of the creeping wastes was visible.

"Would you like them on the mules again?" Raymond was off somewhere to his left. "If it is far, we can make a litter now that there's wood to work with."

"It isn't far. We could carry them ourselves instead of bothering with the effort to keep them on the mules."

"Dibs on Arasha." Ries spoke.

"No." Drom pushed up on weak limbs. His movements were sluggish despite his efforts. "I'll do it."

"You recovered faster than expected." Cellis' voice bore clear surprise. A glance confirmed his bushy white brows were lifted to match the tone.

"I'm tougher than I look." True enough these days.

"Wonderful to have you with us again, girl." Ries sneered as he spoke the final word.

"Must you antagonize her?" Cellis' irritable mood had returned it seemed. "If you are strong enough, carry her yourself Droya. If she stirs, we'll stop so you can set her down and step away before she wakes."

"Yes Master." Drom studied where Arasha had been laid under a protective pine bough. The branch had been diverting most of the light drizzle.

"The options for fun in my life right now are limited. Antagonize Droya or flirt with the lady slave. Those are it." Ries' eyes flickered to where Drom was now lifting Arasha's unconscious form. "And since the fair lady is still under the weather,..."

"Stow it thief." Cellis wore a harsh scowl. "Your only a few days away from being free of your curse. Don't test my resolve to do so."

That brought silence from Ries. Raymond now eyed Cellis as though the Magus might draw down lightning on them all. In silence, they followed Cellis as he made his way through the increasing trees and brush. The shadowy form of Godsaddle Mountain loomed in the distance above the canopy ahead. Much of it was obscured through the haze of rain.

The 'pulse' of the mountain's magic was overwhelming now. Impossible to ignore. Drom expected even if he were blind, he'd sense the exact location where the heart of the mountain lay. Judging by the obscured silhouette ahead, it seemed like they were aiming for the point between the peak and plateau.

WHEN THEY REACHED THE bottom of the mountain, true darkness had overtaken them. The rain hadn't stopped the whole time, making everyone miserable and damp. It wasn't helped by the chill of the rain. The only light they had to work with was a lone hooded lantern. The lack of strong light slowed their travel.

Arasha remained unconscious, but had managed to stay warm despite the drizzle. Near the base, they'd followed the contour instead of climbing upward. Walking so far around the side the plateau was obscured by the peak, they'd slowed down following the stone cliff rising to their left.

The light beyond that of the lantern had grown so dim even Drom's eyes found it difficult to make out details. He was about to inquire about how Cellis was sure of his path, but the question was answered before he could.

"That would be the end of my ethereal thread. We are here." Cellis reached ahead, groping blindly.

"Some shelter. I'm still getting wet." Ries' voice came from an inky shape to Drom's left.

"It is only a short way ahead. I set the thread short of it to avoid banging my head on the low opening."

Drom strained and tried to make out the supposed opening. "Why don't we use magical light Master?"

"I can't cast effectively when it is both raining and dark. A torch is out of the question when it is this wet and we only have the one lantern."

"Maybe," Ries couldn't seem to contain his frustration. "You could have brought extra lanterns among the piles of junk you crammed into that room of yours."

"I have one, but we've no way to set up the door at the moment to access it." Cellis' tone grew more irritable. "Do you ever manage silence for more than ten minutes?"

"I haven't had a voice for the last few years. I need the practice to ensure it's back into top shape as soon as possible."

Cellis let it drop. After a few moments of his silhouette casting the lantern about, he stopped. "Here it is. Finally some relief from this rain. It should be around twelve steps in my direction." Stepping forward, the lantern illuminated the overhanging walls which formed a cavern set into the cliff. It hadn't been visible from where they'd stood even at this near range until he'd stepped in. "Mind your head."

Thirteen steps from Drom's position. Who was counting though? On the final step, a blessed relief from the endless rain came.

"I'm going to have to tether the mules once I can see again. Would anyone mind bringing me the lantern?" Raymond's voice was still far enough away to imply he remained outside the overhang. Ries took the lantern back out to aid Raymond and Cellis tried start a fire. They were left in darkness again.

As the sound of blind rummaging filled the cramped space there was a gradual restoration of Drom's vision. It took a moment to discover why. There was a faint light source here. He cast about and found there was a pale glow coming from a natural stone shelf.

Placing Arasha on a sandy portion of ground free of stones, he took a moment to study the others. Cellis gathered what would be needed for a fire from a saddle bag he'd brought in with him. Weakness from the journey showed through in his slow movements. The other two were outside working with the mules. They weren't paying enough attention or their eyes weren't keen enough to notice the faint glow. Now able to make out his surroundings, Drom shifted and peered over the lip of the stone shelf where the glow originated.

He was met by the eyes of a tiny creature, similar to the fairy. The dainty creature squeaked in surprise and flew back from his face. Where the fairy had seemed childlike, this being wore the sleek femininity of a woman. It's wings were different as well.

As she hovered, her dragonfly wings caught hints of the glow coming from her skin. The light broke into a rainbow of colors where it struck them. So close, the hum of them filled his ears. Shifting in the air to the side, she peered past him. Drom ventured a glance too. There was an ember now and Cellis was blowing the flame into life.

"You're Ill'ln?" The tiny glowing creature whispered in a voice already meager enough it would have been hard to hear at a shout.

"Yes." The complicated truth seemed like too long of an answer.

"Don't worry. I will send word to the dryads."

"You speak better than another fairy I met." It gave him a scowl that implied he'd heaped a great insult on it. His ears wilted a bit, and he shifted subjects. "Dryads?"

"Mmm Hmm."

"Why are you sending them word? About what?"

"To help save you of course."

Drom tried to respond, but she gasped and flitted off into the night. Behind him Raymond's heavy breath preceded his words.

"Find another fairy did ya?"

"I'm not sure. She seemed different."

"How?"

"Her wings were long like a mayfly and she was glowing. She also spoke with greater clarity."

"A sprite or pixie then." Cellis came over now while Ries remained behind to feed the fire.

"What's the difference." Raymond faced the aged Magus.

"Size and intelligence. It's academic." He pulled at his beard. "What did this one say Droya?"

"Something about talking to dryads to save me."

"Wonderful." Cellis rolled his eyes. "I had hoped they might remain dormant until we were at least up past the tree line."

"What's a dryad?" Raymond looked lost. Drom stared at the man a moment. Didn't everyone learn the term? Anyone with even a moderate education should. Had the man been raised a serf or churl? Cellis seemed less phased.

"They are the most common variety of nymph." When Raymond eyed Drom sidelong, Cellis clarified, "They are the human-like form of an ancient oak tree's spirit."

"Oh, a tree spirit. I guess city folk use a special term."

"An accurate term. It is what they call their own kind."

"How can those be a problem? We ain't cutting down any trees."

"We don't have to. Someone else did. Our only advantage is dead dryads can't become corporeal."

"Wait," Drom interjected, "Why would we be dealing with dead dryads?"

"Because we're going to be climbing the lost staircase." Cellis raised a hand to cut off the obvious question. "It was built before magic failed. Three fourths of the way complete at the time. The stair had wards to prevent the dryads from haunting the path. Every step was hewn from a dryad's oak to ensure it would withstand centuries without the need for repairs. When magic failed, construction stopped. There was no way to detect the remaining dryad oaks needed. When magic returned, the wards were all gone, but the dryads were not. They had only been dormant."

"Without magic," He continued, "The logs rotted as their natural counterparts would, leaving the spirits as shadows of their former selves and all of them eager for revenge."

"But they can't touch us right? They're only spirits yeah?" Raymond's voice trembled.

"That is what incorporeal means. No physical forms. You needn't worry anyway since you'll head home in the morning." He shook his head. "But no, they can't touch us."

Raymond nodded and walked to join Ries by the safety of the firelight. Drom wasn't satisfied with the answer.

"Why worry about them staying asleep until we are past the tree line Master?" The last word no longer required an effort to add.

"Dead and weakened or not, they still have some of the glamor they held in life. They will try to trick us and lure us into danger."

"So, even though this time it's indirect, I'm putting Arasha at risk again."

"Life is risky. At least if you are trying to live a life of value anyway."

"So says the man who owns me thanks to taking a risk." The piercer caused a faint tingle. It seemed it was too close to the truth with Raymond nearby.

"It could have gone far worse. Rest for now. We'll have a long day tomorrow." Cellis was right, but his tone made Drom want to argue. His assent was grudging as he walked to where the bedrolls were being unpacked. It was too much like an order to risk hesitating long.

Seeing to Arasha first, Drom hoped she would wake soon. It worried him she still hadn't risen. Once Arasha was somewhat dried off and in blankets, Drom studied the rumpled wet dress he wore. Sleeping in it each night, along with his time draped over a mule and a drizzle had done it no favors. It bothered his sense of male identity he cared about the dress. Still, it had made him feel human again. It bothered him more to have it in shabby shape.

Sighing, Drom went to pull the spare dress from the saddlebag it had been packed into. It wasn't as ornate, but of a similar cut. This one was pale green satin.

He disrobed in a rush, blushing despite himself at the leers of Ries and sidelong glances from Raymond. He quickly pulled on the spare dress and laced up the leather midsection. None of it mattered. The only thing that mattered was Arasha. He hoped she would wake up soon. The guilt of being at fault for her condition was eating at him.

DROM ATTAINED HIS WISH though it cost them half a night of sleep. Arasha woke in a panic and almost ran again. It took Cellis and Ries both to keep her from doing so. Raymond focused on reassuring his mules. It took hours to convince her Droya had been protective of her and hadn't been attacking that night. Even after, there was still a weariness of Drom that kept him in Arasha's line of sight at all times.

When the morning broke, everyone but Arasha was suffering from a lack of quality sleep. The rain had become a faint mist adding a haze to the surrounding morning. The hazy forms of trees could be seen for a few yards before all was lost to the gray mists. Something out there was making a low drawn-out whistle. Drom found the effect unsettling after the conversation about dead dryads.

Could the dryads stray from the path? The words of the sprite implied they could. Was this morning fog natural? Second guessing didn't help, but Drom found it unavoidable.

Supplies were transferred from several saddlebags into three rucksacks and the door was unbound from its litter. Everyone but Arasha, who watched from the back of the overhang, worked in silence. When finished, Raymond and Ries shared a friendly conversation before parting ways.

Raymond went southwest with the miles and was lost to the fog. When the last mule had faded from view, Cellis spoke.

"It is going to be a tough climb. Keep your wits about you. We will take a break at the fork and should be at the top before nightfall."

"And what is it we are going to find there?" Ries shouldered one of the packs, handing another to Arasha who donned it.

"Ancient magic reborn." Cellis lifted the last pack, motioning Drom to pick up the door. "Strong enough to mask a large casting unless they already suspect our location."

"And if they do?"

"Then at least they will have to reach the mountain and run a trace. It buys us time."

"Is the spell you plan to cast going to finalize my transformation? I desire to be done with this curse and your miserable rabble." Ries paused, "The sweet Lady slave notwithstanding."

"No, but soon enough after."

"I'll believe it when I see it."

Drom hefted the door and followed as they moved. Everyone fell in behind Cellis. Arasha kept Ries between Drom and herself.

"I haven't let you revert to a rat have I?"

"You haven't ended the curse either."

"As I said before, it must wait until we are no longer at risk of you going to the Council."

"I could offer you my word of honor." Ries grinned with more charm than he should have been able to manage. Even recognizing him for what he was, Drom understood the persuasive pull of the man's charisma.

"Honor among thieves perhaps? I am under no illusions about the likelihood of you showing me any honors."

"What do you think Droya? Shouldn't a Magus honor his promises?" The double meaning struck home, feeding doubts. "Even if it is one who's betrayed his oaths in the past?"

"He never gave you a time line on it. Only a promise to make it happen sometime after you'd helped." Drom wanted to lash out, writhing fears driving his tone perhaps a bit less level than he'd intended. Would his own deal be honored? The strange whisper was jarring in it's startling resurgence. It had been subdued for a long while now. It was still there, but more mellow. It didn't beg to attack or whine to run. Instead it was singing as though it was already free.

"Can you please stop prompting it to talk Ries?" Arasha's voice was laced with pain and discomfort. "If not for you making it talk, I could almost forget the monster for all the other troubles."

"My apologies Lady slave."

Silence filled the air. As they sought the base of the stairs, Drom's cheeks grew wet with tears. His ears hung limp, a feat which now came as second nature, and his eyes never lifted from the ground. In a moment of anger, his thoughts screamed for the inner voice to be silent. It was an aimless cry of despair, trying to control anything at all about his situation. For a wonder, it listened the first time. Under the circumstances, he might have marveled at the sudden silence. Instead, his mind was elsewhere.

MORNING HAZE HAD CLEARED by the time they arrived at the base of the stairs, warm light beginning to lift the chill from the air with it. Leaves obscured the view of the larger mountain, but near at hand the stairs rose at a shallow angle, following the side of the steep mountainside. The 'steps' were crude, not even or well-spaced. It was far more rough than Drom had expected.

Each was constructed in the same manner. A hewn oak log extended across the path. Each was half-buried and backfilled with stones, gravel, and dirt. Aside from the oak timbers, nothing about the 'step' was what could be considered level. Drom doubted the slippers would last long and resolved to remove them. His new form had proven adept at withstanding all but the sharpest of points. At least as far as the soles of his feet were concerned.

The logs had also seen better days. Most were in one state of decomposition or another. Many had wormy holes with fine brown powder piled under the openings. Most had moss spreading over at least part of their length. A few even had mushrooms sprouting from thin veins of white lacing their surfaces.

The entire length seemed almost lost to antiquity. It appeared as though the lightest foot travel might break it down. The four of them stood before it, none moving. It was Ries who broke the silence.

"That's some praise-worthy craftsmanship there."

"Let's see anything you do stand up to a few centuries of weather." Cellis added no inflection to his voice.

"You don't envision a few of my witty phrases withstanding the ravages of time?"

"You've had witty phrases?" Drom couldn't resist the jab, but kept his voice as innocent as he could manage.

Cellis chuckled and even Arasha smirked. Almost as soon as it appeared, she chased the expression away. Drom counted it as a victory to have anything more than a scowl.

"You still owe me a debt note on physical services." Ries' lip curled in anger towards Drom. "Should I assume you want me to call that debt due today?"

"I owe you nothing." It was Cellis who spoke as he placed a foot on the stairs with gingerness that spoke of testing his weight. "Therefor, what I own owes you nothing either."

"One day, you will wish you'd been kinder you senile bastard."

"We all have regrets."

"All too true." This time it was Arasha who spoke. She fell silent again, but her eyes glistened with unshed tears. She followed Cellis.

"Yes, I regret I didn't kill him before trying to lift his goods." Ries fell in behind Arasha. "My mistake for showing restraint."

"I'm beginning to wonder," Cellis didn't bother glancing back. "If you have some reason you want to convince me to reconsider my word about restoring you."

That silenced Ries. Drom took a place at the end of the slow procession. The stairs made a slow ascent, leaving Drom to wonder if they would spiral around the mountain a few hundred times before reaching the top. Strait up the steep sides wasn't a realistic option, but this low angle felt sure to take forever.

They reached a bend in the trail and Drom noticed it was reversing back on itself. After a short distance, the mountainside rose steeply to the left. It formed a sheer cliff on the side of the stairs. The incline increased a little, but the open air and loose stones to the right of the path were unnerving.

Passing around a bolder where the stairs skirted close, the path came to an abrupt stop. Soil and stone rose up in evidence of a rock slide. The stairs were absent and jagged stone extended out at angles so continuing strait was impossible.

Someone or something seemed to have been using this route since the landslide, however. A precarious path snaked over the blockage at an angle out from the sheer cliff. There was a clear dip in the loose material as of many feet passing along that way. Something about it nagged at Drom's mind.

"This could be a problem." Cellis drew to a stop, studying.

"Your powers of observation never fail to amaze us." Ries took his pack off and set it on the ground. He looked as though he expected to be waiting a while.

"Something is odd about this." Drom offered to no one in particular.

"Odd in what way?"

"I'm not certain Master. It doesn't seem right."

"I don't imagine anyone did this because of us. It doesn't seem recent."

"What about the dryads?"

"They can't interact with the physical world in such a direct way.

Drom nodded, but something still played havoc with his mind. Something was wrong about this. He listened inward, but the voice was only humming a bright tune. No help there. He scanned the pile, keen eyes taking in every patch of muddy earth and each jagged stone. The only thing aside from these were slimy black mushroom caps poking out here and there in a line amid the jagged debris where their path timbers should have been. Delicate things which had an appearance reminiscent of rotting marrow.

"No help but to skirt around it."

"On that?" Arasha eyed the narrow path over the steep pile of loose stones. She leaned ever so little, eying the spot where it arched around the right of what had once been the path.

"It's firm enough something else has managed to make a modest path." Cellis made a motion for Ries to put his pack back on.

"Master?" Something kept nagging at Drom's thoughts. "What type of mushrooms are those?" It was a strange thing to fix on, but it might delay them until he could ferret out the source of his caution.

"Jelly caps." Cellis remained distracted. "Black Ratbane if I am not mistaken."

"Are they typical to this area?"

"Yes." Cellis sounded annoyed at the diversion of his attention. He was focusing on the loose path skirting out where there should have been a sheer drop. "Inedible and unnoteworthy outside of use in a few minor spells. You can find them anywhere in the kingdom where hardwoods grow."

"Oh." The answer didn't help.

"Ries. You're nimble. Please take the lead."

"Sacrificial lamb now am I?"

"Do you prefer rat instead of a lamb?"

"Cute. Always with the rat references. I half suspect you are doing this and using the name 'ratbane' on those mushrooms to prod me in some twisted joke."

"The world doesn't center on you."

"Hardwoods?" Drom asked as something dawned on his realization.

"Yes. Oaks, elms and the like. Any further questions or can we focus on something relevant?" Cellis' eyes never left the circumventing path.

"It's a trap."

"What?" Ries was first to respond.

"How is that?" Cellis was reluctant to pull his eyes from the path.

"If the stairs were swept away in a landslide, what are the mushrooms growing on? You said they live on hardwoods. There's nothing here but stone and bare soil."

Shock settled into the faces of the others.

"I'll be Koos' fool!" Cellis exclaimed. "Crafty rotten spirits."

There was a hiss followed by a musical giggling with no clear source. The pile across the path faded away to reveal the slow incline of the stairs once more. What had been the path to the right, was once again a sheer drop of loose stone. 15 feet down onto jagged stones. Not certain death, but lacerations and broken bones would be a minimum result.

Everyone, especially Ries who'd have been the first to cross, was shaken by what had almost happened. Cellis thanked Drom for averting disaster. For a wonder, Ries did as well. Arasha mumbled something which might have been, "Fine job monster."

"Thank you Lady Arasha." The words passed Drom's lips without irony.

Arasha gave him an uncertain expression, but didn't reply. Far more wary of tricks now, they made slow zigzags over switchbacks up the mountain. The grade of the stairs gave the impression they were walking back and forth over the same ground. The plateau and peak took turns looming above them until they reached a fork in the path.

One switched back on itself towards the plateau, the other ascended towards the peak. Cellis studied both with a frown.

"Is everything alright Master?"

"No. It seems we have another trick before us."

"Why do you think it?" Ries let out a huff of air and smiled after dropping his pack for a break. This time Arasha did so as well, dropping to sit beside it on a bed of moss and leaves.

"The split in the path occurs after the tree line in all the accounts I have read. We shouldn't have reached it yet."

"Trees grow." Ries grumbled.

"That answer is too easy." Cellis seemed to be taking his time, so Drom set down the door. He wasn't sore or stiff as he would have expected to be.

"The most obvious and simplest answer is often the right one." Ries grumped. "Complicated solutions get you killed."

"Says the man saved once already today by a complicated answer. It's also too early to be this far along anyway." Cellis wasn't cutting in his tone, too distracted for jabs. Instead, he prepared to cast Ries' booster spell. It wasn't due yet, but they weren't moving forward until the direction was sure.

Chapter Fourteen
The Freedom of the Elves

Lwanna could sense the start of another argument and tried to cut it short. She affected a tone that her answer was unimportant. "I have an ongoing conversation with Cellis about it." She returned to arranging the ship's cabin.

"Him again?" Michael's face reminded her of a building thunderhead.

"He and I have been friends for around a century. If ya and I are to be wed, ya'll have to accept he's a part of my life." Fluttering her eyes, she tried to defuse the frustration she read in his expression. "Besides, jealousy doesn't suit ya handsome."

"Thad's not the poind. We break the law. I have no qualms about thad, bud we do id with restraind." Michael moved to check the door. A force of habit whenever he talked of such matters. She'd long ago grown used to his peculiar accent. "He would see the world plunged indo chaos. He'd abolish the laws endirely."

"So? A little anarchy could be fun."

"Hoo are you the educaded one of us? Thad would be a disasder. Anarchy is only fun if id's peaceful. Even when id is, id's bad for business."

"Ya expect it would mean war?"

"As sure as a blood dawn brings a sdorm." Her fiance didn't make eye contact as he spoke the thickly accented words. "Hisdory dalks abood the Magi of old and their wars. Hoo desdrucdive those evends could

be. Hoo sdrong does one have do be do resisd when holding so much pooer? Hoo simple would id be do see jusdifiable excuses do unleash thad pulsing pooer?"

"Is that how ya see me? Or is it Cellis alone who ya don't trust?"

"Even if both of you have iron wills, there are many others who would be dempded do led loose. Men who'd make the world dremble."

"However the world feels, I don't fear." She put her hands on his arm. "Love, if the world trembles before men who'd make themselves gods. The gods themselves tremble before those who have the strength of heart ta resist for the greater good. If the system ever fails, I trust Cellis ta make the gods tremble."

Michael still looked unconvinced, but let it drop. He brushed back a strand of her hair and cradled her cheek. "I hope we never have do find oud love."

AN HOUR LATER, THEY were no closer to an acceptable answer. The switchback trail seemed the obvious choice, but that made it seem like a trap. Arasha had ventured they might use the mushrooms again, but both directions had several varieties of expected mushrooms visible. The dryads had learned their lesson it seemed.

Time was slipping away and there seemed to be no way to resolve the matter. No way aside from picking a path and hoping. When Cellis rose, it was with an air of preparation about him.

"I suppose there is no help for it but to cast a divination spell."

"Why wouldn't it be acceptable Master? If it's a tiny one." A sudden and omnipresent sense of danger struck him. A tickle in Drom's brain which bordered on paranoia. He shook it off as being fear of being traced.

"Casting spells leaves a trail. I've already had to do them enough to leave an arrow pointed right at us. Doing it twice in a single spot means an exponential increase in the residue."

"So why are we bothering with this long trek again?" Ries pushed up to his feet and stretched.

"They may not have noticed us since I have been using new crystals each time. I..." Cellis froze, eyes down on the spear tip pressed to his chest.

A group of three elves and six Ill'ln had appeared from nowhere. How he'd failed to hear their approach with his sensitive ears was beyond him. Ill'ln were familiar enough in form, but Drom had never seen a real elf in person. He knew them only from tapestries and illustrations. They were the height of toddlers, but proportional to an adult. Unlike the Ill'ln who were so often their namesakes, their ears were similar to those of a human. Only the slight point at the tips differed. Each wore the same long black hair tied back in a length of braid which bore a green cast when the light struck it. All three elves were male and armed with spears.

The Ill'ln were unarmed, but seemed far more imposing. Between their comparative size and known strength, they were intimidating enough. Four women and two men, none of them wore a collar. Both the elves and the Ill'ln wore clothing crafted from woven fibers dyed in yellows, browns, and burgundy.

Drom was the only one without a spear pointed at him. What had his attention instead was Arasha, frozen in horror. There was a shift in her tension, implying she might try to run at any moment. What would they do if she tried?

"Cruel monsters." One of the elves spoke in musical tones, similar to those of the fairy and the sprite. "Sasha, release her."

The Ill'ln woman nearest to Drom stepped forward and reached for his piercer chain. He remembered Cellis' comments about Ill'ln who had their chains removed without first being Nymphs. Even if he didn't remember, Arasha's expression was enough. He drew back. That these uncollared Ill'ln weren't tearing everyone apart didn't register in his reaction.

"The poor girl must be under compulsion to avoid its removal." Sasha offered to the elf who'd made the order.

"We have do nothing to you." The awkward syntax and musical tone from Cellis verified they were speaking Fae.

"Be silent monster or die where you stand." Spoken by the elf in front of the Magus. "Barthus, Melbron. You'll have to restrain her to assist Sasha."

The two male Ill'ln moved forward on either side of Drom. Both shot their arms forward to secure Drom's own. Sasha's hands were equally quick. She was working the clasp even as Drom was trying to pull away from the two men. That loud whisper cried out with joy for its freedom and for vengeance.

"No! You can't!" Panic swept Drom up. With all of his might he managed to free an arm, but not in time. The chain fell away, and the voice went from a whisper to a loud demand.

"Give her space." The first elf directed to the three Ill'ln who'd been 'helping'. They complied.

Drom fell to his knees, holding his head. The light hearted sense the voice had had the prior day was gone. It had been replaced by a feral anger again. This time no whisper, but a raging torrent. His own thoughts were weak shadows before them. It was torn between anger at 'the humans' and elation at freedom.

"Kill the humans so they don't try to follow us. We'll take her to safety." Drom had no idea which of them had spoken, but he lifted his eyes. All three elves were tensing to strike. Ries wore a confused expression. Cellis was chanting under his breath. Possibly an attempt to craft a quick spell in time to matter. Then there was his wife.

Arasha wore wide-eyed terror, but had no way of grasping what was coming. She was all he cared about in the world. Despite this, the voice was eager spill her blood as freely as these others were. It had control of him and would kill her with glee if he couldn't stop it.

OTHER BEINGS APPEARED. They slipped into visibility as one might step from behind a veil. All were women with gray-brown skin and hair of varying shades of green, red, and orange. None wore clothing and each could have been called beautiful if not for the marred aspects of their forms.

Some were missing limbs. Others bore deep scars. Bits of moss and ugly fungus sprouted from the skin of most. A number of them were pocked by holes as though something had borrowed through them. These had to be the dryad spirits. They wore expressions which mirrored the voice gripping Drom's mind.

"It's alright now. They'll die and you'll at last be free sister." Sasha had a gentle hand on Drom's shoulder.

The elves drew back to strike. Arasha was going to die and there was nothing he could do.

No!

Drom had to stop them. Fighting against the inner voice was like swimming against a strong current but he refused to become swept up.

"Stop." Each word had to be forced as though it was its own sentence. "Don't. Harm. Them." It was exhausting. He struggled to rise. His muscles giving grudging ground.

"What?" The elves and Ill'ln shared startled glances. A dark haired Ill'ln was the first to recover and speak.

"She is right. They had control of her. It is her right alone to strike the killing blows." A whisper rose among the dryads and their captors nodded in agreement.

Drom's body lurched forward against his own control. It was only with a supreme effort he stopped himself. Was the inner voice able to control his actions? "You. Must." It was too hard to speak like this. Drom cast his eyes to where the piercer chain had fallen. Sensing his intention, the voice screamed in protest. He ignored it. Arasha had to be saved.

Jerky steps brought Drom to the string of platinum links. With the speed of molasses in winter, he reached for it. The fae stood in confusion and shock as his fingers wrapped around its length.

"What's she doing?"

"Does she assume it affects humans?"

"Please sister, don't. Why touch the vile thing?"

Drom couldn't respond. Every ounce of his strength was locked in a struggle. The chain rose, inch by painful inch, towards his throat. Horror swept over the faces of the fae. Revulsion filled their eyes.

"Don't!" Barthus, still close at hand, reached to stop him. So did Melbron.

"Stop her!" The elf who had first spoken cried out.

Countless words from the dryads tumbled over one another so none was distinct. The remaining elves and Ill'ln cried out as well. Drom tuned them out. He only had seconds before those two Ill'ln men would catch his hands and stop him. He shoved the voice inside his head down with all his willpower. The clasp caught.

Raging though it was, the inner voice dimmed once more to a whisper. The first warning tingles of pain rose up and Drom dropped his hands from the chain. Firm hands grabbed an arm on either side, gaining purchase to trap him again.

"Not this time." Drom's face twisted into an involuntary snarl. The two men's grips were like iron and he didn't have an advantage as Ill'ln here. Even so, he fought with rare determination they couldn't match.

One foot came down hard, griding along Melbron's shin and into his foot. Heel met upper arch with a loud crack that spoke of breaking bones. Melbron released his grip at the sudden lance of pain, freeing one of Drom's hands. Balling it into a fist, he took Barthus in the stomach with all the force he could manage.

Barthus didn't let go, so Drom brought a knee to the groin with enough power to lift the man's feet from the ground. It worked.

Barthus dropped to the ground, clutching at the tender injury and Drom dove away, coming up near a startled elf. The expected pain from the piercer chain never came. It seemed harming other Ill'ln didn't count.

"Let them go."

"Why would you fight us sister?" a female Ill'ln who hadn't had her name spoken asked. "We're trying to help."

"She has gone mad from extended captivity." The elf near Ries said.

"You chose freedom. I chose to serve my Master and protect those with him." Drom shot scowls in every direction making sure none of the living fae would catch him off guard. "You're threatening to kill someone who means more to me than my own life. More than my freedom. Harm them and you will have to kill me too. Otherwise I will kill every one of you."

Every fae wore wide eyes and expressions of disbelief. Only Cellis could follow the conversation and he said nothing. Arasha's eyes were closed tight. She trembled, but must have had her eyes closed since before the fight or would have already moved to run. Seeing her like this added fuel to his anger.

"You are certain you will not join our tribe in freedom?" The first elf was speaking again. He had to be the leader.

"My place is with them. Release us and we'll be gone from this place soon enough."

Several Ill'ln were helping the two injured men to their feet. Sasha stepped towards Drom, but lifted her hands in a show of no threat when he tensed.

"She should be allowed to depart with them. We gave her the freedom to choose and she did. We should respect the choice she made."

"She doesn't know any better." One of the Ill'ln women who wore her hair in a long honey braid countered. Her long deer-like ears were tilted down and back as she spoke. Not in the sharp manner Drom could manage now, but enough to convey greater expression.

"That wasn't fear or madness in her voice. It was love. I knew it once myself for a kind master long gone."

"If that is the case," The Elven leader hesitated before he lowered his spear. The other two followed suit. "Far be it from me to destroy something so rare and precious."

"We could kill them all." Barthus leaned hard on the Ill'ln helping him. His voice was still a wheeze.

"We could, but we will not." The leader raised his hand to forestall further debate. "Unless my position is being drawn into question." No one spoke, so he continued. "Continue in peace, but do not remain here for long or the decision to let you live might be withdrawn. Harm this land in any way and none will be spared."

The elves were the first to walk away, disappearing into the underbrush in utter silence. The Ill'ln left one by one next. Sasha and Barthus lingered, each for their own reasons. Only the dryads remained. None looked pleased, but they too faded away until the group was again alone.

As they did, their illusion was replaced with reality. The path strait uphill extended only a few dozen paces up the hill before terminating in a pit. The switchback remained unchanged.

"What just happened?" Ries scratched his chin in confusion.

"Droya did the impossible and in so doing, saved us all." Cellis openly stared. His scrutiny was uncomfortable.

"Okay. So no more deathtraps I take it?" Ries glanced to where Arasha remained trembling. Her eyes were still closed tight. "Or pointy sticks to the chest."

"No. They will leave us be as long as we don't dawdle." Cellis moved to gather his things. "We should be moving. So much for making camp."

Arasha cracked opened her violet eyes, seeking signs of the fae and Ill'ln in darting flickers. Drom moved to gather up the door while Ries leveled further protests.

"We should rest. Night has drawn near."

"I suspect sitting down after a firm warning to be quick would be unwise." Cellis grabbed his bag and started up the switchback.

"You realize they're about. Can't you magic them away?" Ries pressed.

"The world isn't so simple. Magic requires preparation and knowledge to execute. If I was prepared with spells for dissuading fae, I would have cast it the moment we heard the dryad's warning. I came close to casting a spell on the fly, risky or not."

Drom had been confused about that himself, but assumed the answer would be something of that nature. Travel was slow, but the golden light of Nodel was strong and Fopei cast a red hue from its slivered crescent playing counterpoint. The moons provided more than enough light at this elevation.

As they pressed on, Arasha asked about all she'd missed.

"Why did they let us go? I don't understand what you mean about Droya."

"She is a Nymph." Cellis kept his eyes forward as he answered. "Removal of her collar didn't change her mind about us. She pled on our behalf and they accepted her plea."

Arasha glanced back at Drom, confusion painted in her expression.

"You told me she was a chain-broken Nymph." She returned her attention to Cellis, "How true is it? What about the way she was acting when they took the chain off?" When had she opened her eyes to see it?

"The removal of the chain affected her briefly. That's all. Regarding her other behavior, she does as she is told because she is a chain-broken Nymph, but she plead on our behalf by her own choice." Cellis was choosing his words with care. Drom was sure of it.

"I did not wish for them to bring you harm." Drom left the 'you' of his statement ambiguous as he spoke up.

"I see." Arasha's face remained facing forward, but Drom knew the tone of uncertainty wavering there.

For a wonder, Ries didn't try to say anything pointed or snarky. It allowed silence to settle around them as they continued to climb.

Nothing else rose to bar their path, so by morning light they were able to rest at the peak. Across the yawning span of the 'saddle', Drom studied the distant plateau. The flat surface was dotted with stone ruins of some sort.

Arasha and Ries dropped their burdens and took the opportunity to rest. Drom was not so lucky. Cellis needed assistance in setting up for the spell. Even if he hadn't, Drom wouldn't have gotten any rest. The pulse of the mountain's magic was intense here. It drove at him more like the surf crashing against him than the distant throb from the day or two past. Twice while arranging many components and drawing the complex lines on the ground a flare surged strong enough to send Drom reeling. Cellis would pause when these hit, but seemed otherwise unaffected.

When the work was complete, the pattern was the most intricate Drom had yet witnessed.

"Now what do we do Master?"

"We wake those two and have them stand in the center." Cellis opened the bag where his counterfeit quota crystals were kept. He poured them out. "Then I begin casting as if I were twelve people to avoid any single flow being too strong."

"You can do that?"

"We are going to find out. I've never split the flow of magic more than six ways, but it should be possible, if difficult. Having a familiar like yourself should help."

"What happens if it doesn't work?"

"The worst case scenario? We die."

"Oh." Drom hoped the casual way Cellis spoke of it meant he was joking. He doubted it.

"Don't worry about this. I have the greatest chance to succeed of any Magi alive."

"Because the others who have tried already killed themselves in other glorious ways Master?"

"Sarcastic and respectful at the same time. Impressive."

Drom ignored the remark. "I'll wake Arasha and the rat." He moved to do so. It wasn't easy to wake Arasha without terrifying her, but Drom succeeded with the aid of a long stick laying near the path that had led them up the mountain. Ries woke at a simple touch. The man was on his feet in an instant as if being attacked. When it was clear there was none, he fell into a more relaxed stance.

"Time for my spell again?" Ries spoke with his teeth gritted.

"After we arrive." Cellis crouched to light a few candles. They emitted a foul odor. "You should still be fine until then. I need everyone to stand within the circle please."

Arasha was quick to step over the lines. Drom suspected it was to better observe the casting rather than eagerness to comply. Ries was slower, almost defiant, but did enter the circle. Cellis didn't wait for them to grow comfortable before starting. Crackles of mystic energy tingled through Drom. Cellis chanted as the power rose.

Drom could almost feel the separate flows along with a sense of what the magic was doing. Invisible threads were plucked and strung through him. He dismissed it as his imagination. As if he would have any clue about how the magic worked.

Arasha stared enraptured as Cellis made intricate movements around the inner ring of the markings. Maybe it would be best if she stayed with Cellis, assuming Ries had been lying. Cellis seemed open and was proving to be a decent person. It was obvious Arasha enjoyed the chance to be so close to magic.

Still, what if Ries had been telling the truth? Of course it was to his own benefit, but sometimes liars told the truth. If it was something that gave them what they wanted. How could he be sure? More important, what could he do even if he was sure?"

The flow of energy grew stronger, but erratic. A glance at Cellis showed the man was struggling with this casting. Sweat poured from the Magus' brow already. Each time the magic swelled in sync with the pulse of the mountain, Drom sensed the lines of power waver within himself.

The only way he could describe the sensation was the image of an out of tune lyre having the strings plucked by a drunken minstrel. Worse was he himself was the instrument being played. Dressed as he was and having the tingle of magic numbing his senses would have made him useless, regardless.

His mind wasn't numb however, so perhaps he might at least try. The magic had to flow through him which allowed for more powerful castings. With this fact established, it was a question of what changed in the flow. Drom imagined it was one of three things: he was a filter, a stabilizer or an amplifier of the energy. It didn't seem like filtering, but could be either or both of the remaining two.

The one who might be able to answer was preoccupied, so he had to assume for now it was stabilization. Honestly that was the only thing that seemed like it would help anyway. Drom wished he knew what other familiars did when their masters were casting. Another of many wishes he didn't expect to be fulfilled. 'You don't have any idea how to help do you?' he asked the feral whisper in his head. To his surprise, it paused. It offered nothing helpful of course, opting instead to return to ranting. His only option was to experiment.

Closing his eyes, Drom tried to focus on the sensations flowing through him. Where did it start? Where was it flowing to? A visual came to mind. A series of cords which rose from the ground through him and into Cellis. Drom imagined them then flowing into the quota crystals laid around the circle.

It was something to work with, so Drom decided to stick with the image for now. Probing inward, he felt the inflow was tangled and unsteady. He knew the improvement was marginal flowing out. Fixing the image in his mind, he opened his eyes. As a blacksmith's puzzle, so too was this. He only had to find the trick to the tangle.

Out of habit, he moved his hands as though working such a puzzle. It did help with the visualization in his mind. He worked at twisting and bending the lines of power as they flowed through him. It wasn't until he pulled one free and it snapped taunt he knew the truth. It wasn't a delusion. He could make himself useful. Cellis must have felt it too as his bushy white eyebrows threatened to climb to his hairline. The Magus couldn't stop casting without ruining the spell, but he was studying Drom with great intensity as the chanting continued.

Drom stood for a moment, trying to decide if the adjustment to the flow was positive or not. The singular line of power flowing in now was far more stable, but only made a slight difference in the whole of the other lines flowing out. He decided it was a positive shift and set about working even harder to unravel the tangle and steady the flows. One by one, they pulled free from one another and stabilized. As each did, the outflow grew more steady, but also more powerful than before.

By the time the last two were freed from one another, Cellis no longer seemed to be struggling. Drom's mind was left as numb as his body for the effort. The power flowing through him was tremendous, threatening to consume him now that it was in such a narrow focus. The numbness made it hard to concentrate and form a cohesive thought. Because of this, it took longer than it should have for the magnitude of what had happened to sink in. He'd not only acted as the conduit of magic, but had manipulated the raw essence of it's power.

How far could he manipulate the flows? Could other familiars do this? Many questions came to mind, but there was no way to ask for the answers. The swell of power from the mountain grew. One of the stronger pulses was about to release. The surge of power through Drom redoubled and threatened to burn him away.

Cellis spoke the last word of his chant before stomping a glass marble so it shattered against the stones. A strange rush of air, both inward and outward all at once billowed. For a moment, the world was transposed. Visions of the mountain overlapped with the vision of a ship's deck. In the span of a blink, the mountain was gone, leaving only the deck. Their arrival was marked by a thunderclap. It drew every eye on the ship. Several crewmen tensed and drew their knives. Ries drew two blades of his own, ready for the fight.

Chapter Fifteen
The Revelation of a Nymph

"When you capture him, it would be child's play to alter his memory so he would confess guilt in all that's happened." The words of Laethem's thin confidant were tempting. Still, he remained uncertain.

"Accessing memories is difficult enough, but altering them? It's never a simple matter. Besides, I've used far too many void spells these last few months. You're wise beyond your years and I do trust your strategic analysis. Even so, I believe you're underplaying the risks and hurdles. It's anything but straightforward."

"Bah. We all must walk the line 'tween life and death." The words were taken in part from a poem called the Heralds of Tayvon. Something about that nagged at Laethem as the angular young man spoke it. Something half-forgotten. The feeling passed as the red-haired youth continued. "Every Magi in the city draws on the void to stay young and attractive. You're pulling no more than they. If you overdraw a bit more than most, who'll notice in the recent turmoil?"

"It would be far too easy to siphon too much power. I'd risk those around me growing sick." The young man put a reassuring hand on his arm. It was cold. He had another pang of familiarity wash over him he couldn't place. Something about the gesture.

"You aren't going to be using enough Necromancy for that." The young man's tone had a soothing effect.

"I suppose. Now how do I take both Llwanna and Cellis? I'm strong, but not that strong."

"Ask Maria." Was the young man aware of their friendship outside of the council? "You trust her to help don't you?"

"Yes, but she'd certainly discover what we've been doing."

"Ask to interrogate the prisoners first while returning with them. I believe you can modify their minds with enough subtlety to remain unnoticed. Didn't the spell I researched for you work perfectly on the store owner?"

"Yes Erin, it did." Something seemed wrong. The moment again passed. He would do it, despite hesitations. What was he missing? What was it that kept trying to nag at his consciousness? "I'll have to hurry."

JUST WHEN CONFLICT seemed a forgone conclusion, a familiar voice came from the far end of the deck. "Cellis!"

"Llwanna. Wonderful to see you again." They remained cautious as Cellis responded.

"Sdand doon," The harsh voice with a thick accent belonged to a man who must be the captain because the crew relaxed. "These are the ones we were expecding." Several crewmen hesitated to relax, given the sharp scowl their captain was giving Cellis. Perhaps they believed he might change his mind.

Ries put away his blades while Drom and Arasha simply watched. Llwanna wore a youthful appearance in person. She crossed the deck in bold barefooted steps to pull Cellis into a warm embrace. The affection was returned, drawing a dark glare from the captain.

"Llwanna, this is Ries, Arasha and of course you already know Droya."

While the two exchanged pleasantries, Drom made a quick study of those around him. The captain was the only one wearing anything on his feet in the form of black leather boots. Aside from Llwanna' in a loose blouse, the captain was also the only one with his chest covered. Even then, covered was a relative word. His loose vest left most of his broad chest in clear view.

Llwanna's face was as pretty as ever, but her body was more boyish than Drom would have expected. The unmistakable streak of platinum was evident despite a ponytail and tricorn hat both interfering with the view. Unlike the captain and crew, she was a pleasant and social.

Speaking of the crew, they were a varied lot with several nationalities. All were clad only in short-legged trousers and bore scowls. Unlike their captain, who was focused on Cellis, the majority of their attention was on Drom and Arasha. For a surprise, the expressions weren't lustful. Instead they bore varied forms of aggression and anger.

Drom almost folded his ears under his hair, but thought the better of it. Averting his eyes, the warm flush of a blush rose at all the attention. Those keen ears caught many murmurs about the group. Most were against the presence of the women. He wasn't sure why women would be an issue when they had no visible quarrel with Llwanna's presence.

"Droya is shy, is she?" Llwanna furrowed her brow and clicked her tongue a few times before continuing. "That's a rare trait in an Ill'ln. I'm guessing there's a story ta that."

"There's a story to everything. You understand it as well as anyone." Cellis might have gone on if not for the interruption of the captain.

"Noo thad you've arrived, we can be durning back dowards dry land insdead of ood do sea." The accent sounded Karmenian to Drom. He'd only had rare dealings with them, but the 'oo' sound replacing 'ow' in worlds like now and difficulty pronouncing the 't' sound were both typical of native speakers. Many of the man's crew were grumbling in agreement with the captain.

"We aren't turning back. We're continuing forward." Cellis didn't even acknowledge the captain despite responding to his words.

"Are we noo?" The captain's voice was calm, but there was an edge to his tone and body language that caused Drom's ears to wilt by reflex. "And on whad supplies do you indend for us do manage this fead?"

"Droya, the door if you please."

Drom had all but forgotten it. The door had been transported with them despite not being in direct contact with anyone. It seemed being within one of the circles was enough though this raised questions of its own. Now wasn't the time to seek answers. Instead he cast his eyes in the direction where the door had been in relation to them before the teleportation.

There it was on the ground before several crewmen. Ignoring their stares as best he could, Drom moved to pick it up. He walked towards the only upright surface large enough to set it against. Pressing it into place alongside the two existing doors, he looked to Cellis for confirmation. A nod, so Drom opened it.

"These supplies Michael." Cellis acknowledged the man directly now. "There's enough here to see us the rest of the way." Surprised murmurs rippled through the crew.

"Supplies or nod, we aren'd aboud do sail indo empdy wader." Michael remained firm.

"No, we aren't." Cellis signaled Drom to shut the door. "We're heading for a recently discovered continent." The crew fell silent. "No one in the public's been told of its existence yet, but it is spoken of among Magi. Already supply ships have formed a partial chain to the new land mass, but the Circle isn't willing to expend the quota for a long jump. It's made their progress slow."

"Wait. They haven't reached it yet, but they know it's there?" Ries scowled as he voiced what others were no doubt wondering.

"Scrying is far reaching and uses little quota compared to teleportation."

"Did you realize this?" Michael scowled at Llwanna.

"No. When do I interact with other Magi aside from Cellis these days? I haven't had contacts in the Circle navy fer decades."

"The reality is, I'm not supposed to know as much as I do." Cellis watched the setting sun. Drom wondered how far west had they teleported? "But I've never been one to accept things remaining hidden from me. I still have a contact or two."

"Wait a minute," Ries sounded hopeful. "Doesn't this mean my part is done? Send me home you pompous spellslinger." Every eye aboard was on the thief, but his attention was for Cellis alone. "You promised my freedom if I helped and I did."

"Very true. You are free to do as you will. I'll cast a more permanent reversion spell and you may depart as you wish. It might be a long swim, however."

"You double-crossing piece of..."

"A spell powerful enough to return you home would pinpoint our location." Lwanna interjected.

"Some sdradegisd." The word strategist was almost too muddled by his accent to recognize. Michael moved closer. "One more worthless mooth do feed when you could have seddled all of this before arriving. Your slaves can go ged comfordable in the holds below. Cellis, Llwanna and I will speak with you in the cabin."

"Droya will also attend me." Cellis didn't offer room for debate. "Arasha and Ries, head below. I will join you shortly."

Michael scowled, but nodded before striding past Drom into one of the original two doors. Llwanna gave Cellis an apologetic look before following. For his part, Drom scowled at Ries. The last thing he wanted was the untrustworthy man alone with Arasha. Not that he had a choice.

"Master," He ventured as the aged mage drew close. "Was it wise to bring Ries?"

"No, but he's aware of too much and bears us no abundance of loyalty. I'll find a way to send him back when we reach our destination. Come, time to indulge Llwanna's husband in his posturing."

"Why does her husband seem to hate you?"

"He's an exceptional man, but any man would feel threatened by someone whose relationship with his wife extends to a century longer than his own."

Drom considered Cellis' words as he entered and shut the door behind them. The room was well-appointed. He'd had little experience aboard ships, but it seemed odd items weren't bound to the floor in any visible way. How did they stay in place when there was rough water?

"This whole siduadion feels a fore shord of a heighd." His accent made it sound like hide instead of height. "Whad have you godden us involved in?" Michael retained his scowl. "Whad was done thad you expecd a drace?"

"You mean besides the use of more quota than the average person uses in a decade to reach this ship?"

"I have ta say I'm curious about how ya managed the feat with so many people along." Llwanna was leaning against an ornate desk, cleaning her nails with a letter knife.

"I used a powerful familiar." Cellis avoided eye contact with Llwanna.

"Oh yeah?" Llwanna leaned forward. "Did ya kill the poor creature accomplishing the feat?"

"No. She is well."

"Where is id?" Michael scanned over Cellis as he leaned against the desk as well now.

Cellis glanced at Drom, whose eyes flickered among the others. Llwanna followed Cellis' glance. Creeping horror dawned in her expression.

"Oh no. Arquillion help me. Tell me ya didn't!"

"Desperate times."

"IDIOT!" Cellis braced at the strength of Llwanna's outburst. Michael leaned forward with an expression of confused curiosity. His scowl was gone. Llwanna's words tumbled out. "How much did ya channel through her?"

"Assuming quota levels for a Master Magus." He avoided active eye contact with Llwanna now. "Between 16 and 20 years of quota use,.depending on the Magus in question." Drom was flabbergasted by the meekness in Cellis' tone of voice.

"Are ya insane?" Llwanna eyed Drom like he might morph into a flailing monster at any moment. He tried to appear as benign as possible. "That much power channeled through," She cut off to study Drom with greater intensity. "Wait. Why hasn't she evolved?"

"I believe she has."

"I've changed?" Drom was caught off guard enough he blurted the question out.

"Yes." Cellis avoided looking in Drom's direction again. "It hasn't been all physical. A few traits have been, but not all. The reason we don't use hormunculi or sentient beings as familiars is the way it affects them. Magical beings are prone to rapid and extreme transfigurations. Sentient beings tend to develop based on their own wills rather than those of their masters."

"Why are you explaining id do the Elf?" Michael bore shock in his voice if not his face. Llwanna looked as unsettled as Michael sounded.

"She has the right to understand."

"What?" Now anger swelled Llwanna's face. "I don't like the way they are treated, but ya know better than this. How long before she adapts?" Drom had no idea what she meant though it made him nervous.

"Droya. You have permission to speak freely and as yourself to these two as long as we are in private."

Both of the others looked confused. Drom must have worn a similar expression. "Master?"

"Drom." Cellis responded. It took a moment to sink in before Drom's eyes went wide. It was like a weight was lifting. Having his real name directed at him no longer seemed familiar. As foreign as something outside of himself. It was also embarrassing, causing his ears to wilt again. This drew even deeper scrutiny from Michael and Llwanna.

"I..." What was there even to say now that there was someone to listen? "Was a merchant." It was all he could conceive to say.

"Oh Cellis. No." Llwanna's expressions shifted to deep pity.

"I was indignant and following Order law since they've been checking such things of late." Cellis' voice didn't sound defensive so much as regretful.

"Nod all of us are familiar with hoo magi work." Michael shifted his lips to the side in an unfamiliar expression. "This whole conversadion's as useful as a shepsder in a sald mine. Wand to clarify for the only layman in the room?"

"I was human." Drom couldn't meet anyone's eyes. "I was stupid and fell into Laethem's plotting. As far as I understand it, he was going to use my wife to control her father in his coup. Since I wasn't aware of it at the time, I tried following omens. They led me to steal a nymph artifact. Based on a natural nymph I believe, not the Homunculus. Becoming Droya was my punishment."

"I'm so sorry." Llwanna moved to put a hand on Drom's shoulder. Her emotions seemed to shift at a breeze.

"I shouldn't have resorted to theft." He furrowed his brow, trying to put on a positive expression, "Besides, if it hadn't happened I'd be on the auction block anyway. Laethem's plans would have gone smoothly, and I'd never have seen my wife again."

"Your wife?" Michael's brows rose.

"The slave I bought, Arasha." Cellis offered. "She's unaware this is her former husband." Drom bristled at the word 'former', but let it go.

"Cellis, what sort of bastard have ya become? That's crueler than any punishment should ever be." Llwanna seemed as though she wanted to hug Drom.

"He bought her at my request. It saved her from Laethem so now I can at least try to help her." Defending the situation seemed awkward, but it was the truth. "I've also been able to help her several times only because I am a Nymph."

"Elf." Michael interjected. "A Nymph wouldn'd be able do exerd free will or personal desires."

"Technically they can exert a will, just not outside of the degrees set by the one who trained them to it." Cellis interjected

"Nymph." Drom insisted. Elf would have been a demotion in terms. "I gave my word to act as a Nymph and have remained obedient as payment for saving Arasha. A Nymph is compliant with her master's wishes, regardless of anything else." He didn't catch his own wording. "Master asked me to speak freely, so I do." He scowled.

Cellis' bushy brows rose. Michael nodded, accepting the logic. Llwanna retained her concerned expression and spoke in soft tones.

"So what are the alterations ya've noticed?"

"For one, he's able to look more human with an effort. Those ears are able to flex more than any normal Ill'ln. Enhanced reflexes and maybe some sort of advanced sensory ability. Some degree of accelerated healing. Also, her sense of pain seems dulled."

"Dulled?" Michael interrupted. "Kill id noo before the piercer chain fails endirely!"

Drom stepped back at the harshness of the statement. Cellis spoke as he stepped in front of Drom defensively.

"The natural violence of Ill'ln is also being curbed from my observations."

Was it? The voice was less powerful these days, though the whisper was still there. He'd assumed it was a natural part of getting used to this form.

"Cellis, Michael's right." Llwanna appeared pained by the admission. "I'm sorry Drom, but an Ill'ln who can pass for human and is resistant ta the piercer chains is too dangerous."

"Physically chain me for now if you're worried, but let me live at least long enough to make sure Arasha's safe and freed again." He stood his ground. "Kill me afterward if you must."

"You accepd death?" Michael appeared doubtful.

"I don't have much choice in the matter do I? I don't want to die. I want to be human again so things can return to normal." Inside he knew things would never be the same again. "If I have to die though, at least I can do something for Arasha. Something she needs for once."

"I've never seen an Ill'ln who could accept the idea of dying." Llwanna looked thunderstruck.

Drom almost agreed with the sentiment. It had been in the back of his mind this whole time, but without being voiced. He'd not only failed Arasha at the end. He'd been failing her all along. Long before he'd been transformed.

"I intend to see him returned to human." Cellis' voice was casual, but his body remained tense.

"Whad?" Michael shot the question, wide-eyed.

"How?" Llwanna spoke at the same time as her husband. "Creating a counterspell of that level could take decades of dedicated work."

"Every spell and counterspell we have exists because someone dedicated the time to craft them."

The conversation seemed to verify the lie in Ries' words. Could it be an act on the part of Llwanna? It didn't seem like it. Not unless this whole conversation had been fabricated for some reason. He'd be happier about the confirmation if not for the fact that it also confirmed how long it would take and his growing resolve he was stuck this way for an undetermined amount of time.

"I've done things I regretted over the years, but nothing I regret more than what I've done to this man. If I don't at least try to make it right, I'm no better than men like Laethem."

"Alright." Llwanna made a dismissive gesture.

"Are you insane?" Michael addressed Llwanna, his body as taut as a crossbow string.

"I've known Cellis since I was in my teens. This is the third time I've ever heard him admit being wrong without adding some qualifier." Llwanna leaned back against a cabinet built into the wall.

"So you'd led a monsder loose on the ship because your old friend can admid he was wrong? Dwo wrongs don'd make a righd."

"Sometimes there are things a person has ta do ta be able ta live with the weight of their mistakes. We magi live long enough ta make a lot of mistakes."

Michael glared at her, Cellis, and Drom. After a pause, he let out a huff and turned his head away. His arms crossed like a pouting child who knew they wouldn't have their way. Llwanna pushed off of her spot and moved to kiss him on the cheek. He grumbled something, but that was all.

"I'll promise you won't have any trouble from me." Drom tried to reassure them.

"This whole trip is trouble." Llwanna didn't sound upset though. Her arms slipped around Michael's waist in an absent gesture. "But since I'm the one who sold Cellis the stolen platinum piercer yer wearing, it's as much my fault as anyone's.

Silence fell among them thereafter.

DROM'S SLEEP WAS FITFUL. Plagued by atrocious dreams and not helped by having to sleep on the floor of a swaying ship. Ries slept with the crew. Arasha had been allowed to stay in the captain's cabin. Cellis had requested seclusion, which came in the form of the hold, reorganized with haste, at the lowest point of the ship. With only one cot to be spared between them, Cellis was of course the one who slept in it. Regretful or not, he was maintaining appearances.

Maybe it should bother Drom more than it did that it came natural at this point. Other things weighed too heavy on him to worry over it. Decades confirmed. So long between now and a cure Arasha would be an elderly woman before he could be human again. She might not even live that long. It was all but hopeless.

With no way to restore his life, it left Drom in a dark head-space. He couldn't save himself from the path he was on. If it was within his power he would save Arasha, but then what?

He woke with a start. It took a moment to pinpoint what had woken him though. Keen Ill'ln ears picked up on faint footsteps. Dim light from the lone lamp near the entry to the hold was more than enough for his eyes. A scan of the room revealed the source of the footsteps sneaking closer.

"What do you want Ries?" The figure paused. After a moment he dropped the pretense of stealth.

"Shh." The voice confirmed Drom's guess of identity. "You'll wake him up."

"Why should I care?"

"Because this is the moment I told you about. Don't stop me and you and your wife are free."

"I'm aware you lied about the cure." Drom didn't know so much as bear a strong belief. Ries hesitated and sighed.

"Okay. It was a half truth. The cure doesn't exist yet. On one of my 'errands', I made contact with the Circle. I was promised freedom for the three of us and a cure for you if I could kill or bring them Cellis. If we'd not left so suddenly and without warning, they'd have been led to the safe house that evening by a former associate of mine."

"It won't take much to coax this crew into going back." Ries glanced to Cellis. "At least if he's dead. Let me save us."

"Why would you wait until now? If the Circle knew why didn't they strike while we were still in the city?" Drom grew uncertain of whom to trust again. He stood up as Ries drew closer.

"There wasn't a choice. The Circle was supposed to strike the night we left. Originally there was going to be more time. Cellis' redesign in the plans ruined it. This is the first time since then it was safe to do the job."

"They promised to cure me?" Drom's emotions were turbulent. He should have been eager, but mistrust and something else left him balking instead.

"Yes. They'll work on a cure." Ries drew a knife.

"They promised?" The Circle had promised to cure him? If they cured an Ill'ln, it meant accepting and admitting to the truth. By now, they had to be putting out the social fires created by the message crystal left with Lord Nephtin. No doubt they would be denying it. There was no way they'd let Drom live. Let alone cure him.

"They gave their words." Ries inched closer, careful to not rouse Cellis more than the conversation might already be risking. Drom's Ill'ln eyes picked out the glint of the sharp blade despite the lack of strong lighting below deck. He didn't trust the Circle at all, but there was still something else bothering him. Something deeper. Something in his own mind alone he was almost able to pin down.

Something which eluded him, but tickled close enough that he could almost pin it down.

Drom stood frozen, trying to puzzle out why he was resisting what he knew. Even if they agreed, the Circle wouldn't be willing now. They wouldn't release Arasha or let Drom live. The only hope to free himself laid with Cellis. Both offered a way to return to humanity, but Cellis was the one who he trusted.

Why hesitate? Cellis was the path to freedom. There it was.

Freedom.

Freedom was why he balked. Why would he hesitate now by defending the Mage other than some perverse desire to prevent his own freedom? Arasha would need freed, yes, but he'd transitioned in a way. It could have been the magic or it might be from within himself, but he knew it was true with sudden clarity.

Ries lifted the blade high, glancing at Drom with an unclear expression.

Didn't he want to be human again? "No." Drom answered himself as much as he was speaking to Ries. As he spoke, he shot a hand out to catch at Ries' wrist.

"Are you an idiot? Cellis can't cure you!" Ries struggled not to raise his voice. "You only have one chance at being human again."

"I was a selfish fool before. The way I was, I focused on what I wanted and didn't listen to the woman I loved. It ruined her life and there's no fixing the damage I've done."

"Release my hand and you'll have a chance to fix it."

"Either the Circle or her father has to lose. No matter which, things can't return to how they were. As Droya, I see things clearly. I love her. With nothing left of my own, all that remains is the desire to see to her needs. Her real needs, not the imagined ones."

"You're certain I can't change your mind?" Ries was tense, but not pulling his hand away.

"No. Somewhere along the way I've become Droya in truth." Her voice rose. "I accept what I am." She was surprised, both by her own words and even more astonished to find she meant them. Fate or choice, it didn't alter the truth.

A second blade flashed from its unseen hiding spot with such speed Droya was unable to fully evade. She released his wrist and twisted her body to the side. The knife opened a gash between two of her ribs, but missed going deep enough to strike the lung. Shouldn't there have been pain? The raging whisper surged inside her head, demanding an attack.

"You've made a stupid choice." Ries didn't strike as hard as he had before, his blade instead flashing in shallow slashes. Each left only a thin trail of blood, but offered no chance to catch his hands.

"Cellis isn't the source of my problems." She blocked several more strikes with now-bloody arms. "Without him, Arasha would be the victim of Laethem's plot anyway." Droya wouldn't be able to keep this up long.

Cellis stirred at the noise. The sound of footfalls on the narrow stairs outside the dividing wall implied someone on the deck had heard their raised voices as well. Ries didn't speak again, now focusing on disabling Droya to reach at Cellis before it was too late.

Droya was oddly calm. The whisper was there, but she had no urge to follow it. Some cuts were deep, but there wasn't pain. Block. Block. Evade. Light spilled into the store room. Block. Feint. Block. Cellis' eyes opened.

Desperation filled Ries' features, leading to a rushed lunge. This made an opening for Droya to do more than stay defensive and take shallow cuts. A voice from the entry registered in her consciousness though the details were lost, for her focus was elsewhere. Her mind was on the glinting metal alone.

It was the blade on the left as it drove forward. She anticipated and caught his hand by allowing the blade to bury to the hilt in her own palm.

"Not this time Drom." Ries' other blade whipped forward as his left hand yanked back. His hand didn't come free, but it did pull her off balance. Eyes widening, Droya couldn't stop the follow-through. It would strike true.

It didn't strike true. It never landed at all, in fact. Ries' frustrated expression melted into confused pain. The thin blade of a rapier withdrew from his chest, blossoming into a red stain. Cellis was sitting up, looking tense and troubled.

Michael wiped his rapier clean on Ries' sleeve as it dawned on the thief he was already dead. Michael paid no attention to the man he'd impaled. Instead, his focus was on Droya.

"Id's a wise thing for you, Cellis, thad you had a standing order of prodecdion."

"I didn't." Cellis stood, stepping around Ries as the man's body collapsed.

"Whad?" Michael's stare intensified.

"It's true." Droya remained eerily calm and confident. "Ries tried to tempt me with talk of a Circler cure. More silver lies. We can discuss soon if you like, but perhaps we can see to my wounds first? I'm not sure how much longer I'm going to remain conscious." It was becoming hard to keep her eyes focused.

Llwanna and Arasha stepped forward into the lamplight. That Droya had missed their arrival was a testament to how much the struggle had taken out of her. Llwanna's expression was of slight surprise, but the one Arasha wore was more complex.

"Of course." There was a tinge of magic as Cellis chanted. Droya couldn't help but smirk. He was healing her using magic channeled through her.

"She protected you without being ordered?" Arasha spoke, it seemed more to herself than forwarding a real question. Her eyes shone with intensity as they waged a visible war between a lifetime of fear and a burning curiosity. The thumb and index nail of both her hands made faint clicks as she fidgeted them against one another.

"Alrighd," Michael lifted Ries' body. "Maybe she can be drusded." The word 'trusted' gave grudging ground as it was wrestled from his lips.

Chapter Sixteen
The Changing of Ownership

Cellis glanced through the open door he'd set against a bit of the cliff barely flat enough for it to function. He'd worried the space would have been too uneven by a narrow margin. It was useful, but sometimes this artifact unsettled him. His companions were visible, still sleeping outside.

He turned his attention back to see Llwanna's scowl fill the scrying orb.

"How do ya expect ta draw enough power ta transport all of ya and yer supplies?"

"Using the Dragon's Gate to store supplies." The true name of the extra-dimensional room he stood in. It was the first time he'd spoken its name in decades.

"Ya still have that? I expected ya sold it off years ago. I realize ya figured out how it works, but the stories were all wrong."

"It was the first artifact you ever brought me. How could I part with it?" His reply brought a rose-cheeked smile to her face. He added, "The value was in the story anyway. A door which might lead to the hidden land of dragons. The hope of finding where dragons fled to before the failure of magic. People pay well for such stories in an artifact. Truth doesn't factor in. Magic or not, a closet isn't going to draw a high price. For certain, not enough to compensate for the loss of the cherished memory tied to it."

"I figured ya'd tell the story and not mention the reality."

"The sentiment can be worth more than money."

"Okay, so maybe we'll see dragons somewhere here on the ocean. Every cartographer notes them as being out here after all." Her tone was teasing. "Perhaps prove the fables true like ya wanted ta do back in our thirties?"

"The legends? I'm sure they are as valid as the door." He frowned at the prospect of the years wasted hunting myths. He'd been a fool to convince himself they'd been true. "Here be dragons indeed."

THE NEXT FEW DAYS PROVED uneventful, aside from an unnatural and rapid healing. When Cellis and Llwanna thought she couldn't hear them, they spoke with concern over how quick Droya had healed so far. Cellis had only cast a minor spell meant to stabilize her. It had been weak and not meant to do more than a rushed prevention of dying. The rest of the healing was being fueled by some adaptation in Droya's physiology. Even so, they made her stay in a bunk for the full recovery.

Left alone for long stretches, Droya could sense things she'd not been conscious of before. At times there was a tingle similar to Cellis' channeling through her, but outside of herself. It almost always coincided with moments when the ship would lurch forward.

She also knew of Arasha's frequent visits. Though she never came in or spoke, Droya recognized her light breathing beyond the heavy door. These visits were a mystery, but comforting. One such visit was interrupted by Cellis.

"Here again?" Cellis' voice was clear enough regardless of his attempt to be quiet.

Arasha made a startled squeak. "Sorry. Yes."

"Something about her troubles you?"

"Other than being a monster."

"Yes. Other than that."

There was a drawn-out pause.

"If you aren't comfortable," Cellis didn't finish.

"No. I don't grasp how to express it. That Ill'ln. It's watched me ever since the auction. She's supposed to be a nymph, but she seems," She trailed off.

"She's special. An Ill'ln unlike any before her."

"More dangerous?"

"Perhaps." As Cellis spoke, Arasha's breath caught. "But only towards those who would harm the people she's loyal to."

"Ill'ln don't feel loyalty." Two of Arasha's nails clicked together.

"And the situation with Ries?"

"A fluke." Arasha's tone sounded like she was trying to convince herself.

"Droya has saved you. Twice I know of through direct action, several more times indirectly. Whatever your past with Ill'ln may be, don't hold it against Droya."

Silence hung outside the door, broken by her footsteps moving away. The door opened and Cellis stepped in, still watching the direction Arasha had gone.

"I terrify her." Droya spoke unprompted.

"I take it you overheard us?" To Droya's nod, he added, "I suspect it's less a reaction of terror now. You don't act like other Ill'ln.

"I'm not like the others. I wasn't born to this."

"More than that. You've been changing, as all familiars do."

Droya knew this was true, but it didn't help. "It means I'm more dangerous."

"I don't believe you would harm her." He added, "She has a wonderful heart."

"Yes. I'll miss having a place there."

"When we restore you," Cellis didn't finish.

"No." Droya interrupted. "There's no going back."

"I can extend her life while we search for the way. She wants to learn magic anyway. I can speak to her and help her understand."

"That's not what I mean Master." Droya made sure to include the honorific. "Drom doesn't exist anymore. I'm not sure how much of my past existence was real anyway. How much of it was me and how much was an attempt to live up to expectations? In a twist of irony, it's captivity that freed me to find myself. Even if I was restored tomorrow, I'm not that person now."

Cellis frowned. "I did this to you. Not only do I owe you your freedom, now I owe you my life. I always repay my debts."

"Drom was going to lose her one way or the other. This transformation, my massive debt, or some other idiot idea getting in the way of her honest needs. I wasn't a leader, businessman, or husband of any real quality. I did the things I thought I was supposed to, not what I should have done."

"And this is better?"

"This is who I am at peace with being. In the end, all I ever wanted to do was serve Arasha. To love her and focus only on her needs and wants. I was always her Nymph in my heart, but let notions of what I was supposed to be interfere. This change has only brought me to a point where I can express myself unfettered."

"Irony aside, how can you be sure the magical alterations aren't why you feel this way?"

"I can't be certain, but it's how I feel."

"So what would you ask of me instead?"

"Have a spell ready if I lose control."

Cellis' lips curved down in confusion. "Lose control?"

"When you take off my piercer."

"What?" The old man's brow threatened to replace his hairline. "Why would I?"

"It's a platinum piercer. It keys to the owner only. The last human who put it on me."

"You want her to rechain you herself?" Confusion gave way to surprise.

"I'm already hers. I always have been. The only difference now is the lack of trust. We need to restore it."

MOST OF THE CREW WAS above deck, along with Llwanna. Michael and two of his strongest men stood near the door of the hold, trying to pretend the casual hands on their blades were insignificant. Droya remained kneeling as Cellis entered with Arasha. Droya made a point of not raising her head or eyes. Nothing could be allowed to spoil this effort.

"... see how this would be." Cellis spoke with a tone meant to sooth.

"But why do I need to be here?" Arasha trembled.

"Because." He looked uncomfortable. "You're going to be her new owner."

"What?" Familiar terror bloomed on her face. "I don't want to own an Ill'ln!"

"It's more important than you might realize that you do." Hadn't they convinced Arasha before bringing her here?

"No. There's no reason I would ever own a monster."

"You've admitted yourself she's no ordinary Nymph."

"And bile isn't an ordinary scent, but it doesn't mean I want it for my perfume." The analogy didn't help Droya's emotional state.

"And if I told you it was what your husband wanted?"

Vex him! Why would he say that? It would make her ask,...

"What do you mean? Why would you even bring him up?"

"I've overstepped myself." Cellis stepped towards Droya, reaching for the piercer.

"You want me to own it and evoke my husband to persuade me. I deserve a better explanation than that."

Cellis stood motionless. Like a night frog in the lamplight. "I," He looked to Droya in apology. "Your husband, you see... this Ill'ln is," Droya didn't let him finish. Eyes never lifting and head still bowed, she broke in.

"Master. May I speak? It would be best coming from me." Everyone present looked at a loss for words, but Cellis nodded.

"Remove the piercer sir." Droya held out her hands. She tried to ignore as Arasha stepped backwards. There was a hesitation before the clasp released. The whisper she'd grown used to ignoring was now a head-splitting wail. It took every bit of Droya's self-control not to tense up. The cold metal chain met her palms, and she closed them around it.

-Kill them! Run!-

-No.-

-We must be free.-

-Freedom isn't worth losing Arasha.-

-Run!-

-Be silent.-

The voice complied, which caught her off guard. Droya was able to focus outward again. Arasha was wide-eyed in horror. Michael and his men were tense. Even Cellis wore a tight expression. Droya drew in a deep breath and spoke in measured words.

"Master evoked your husbands name because I am linked to him. The task which took him from you is one from which he can never return. His only communication with this world is through me. If you can overcome your fear and collar me, I will serve your needs with everything in me. I will do everything in my power to ensure you are as content and safe as I can. I will do for you everything he wishes he had done." Droya extended the piercer, closing her eyes.

Hesitant footsteps. Timid fingers brushing her palms. The chain slid out of her grasp. The stinging slap across his cheek that followed was unexpected and set the voice off again.

-Kill her!-

"Your husband was trying to save you." Cellis' uncertainty had shifted to sharp concern. Slapping an unchained Ill'ln was insane.

-Kill them all.-

"Drom had no choice. The omens were tied to it and decided his fate." Droya was having difficulty maintaining composure. She tried to ignore the inner voice, hoping the mention of those omens would prove the link. "If he'd stayed, you'd be a pawn of the Circle in hurting your father."

-Rip out their throats and flee.-

"I don't want an Ill'ln." Arasha pled.

-Escape into the wild.-

"Please Mistress." The word felt odd, but Droya pressed on. "Bind me to you so the link to Drom is yours alone. I beg you."

-No! Don't allow it.-

Doubt was broadcast from Arasha's body language. Moving slow, as though expecting to be bitten, her hands moved to place the piercer around Droya's neck.

-Death awaits!- The voice faded out with the click of the clasp. The sudden release of tension was short-lived. Her eyes lifted, the self-loathing in Arasha's expression filling her vision. Droya's former wife stared at her own hands as if they'd betrayed her.

"SO HOW DOES THIS WORK?" They'd returned to the deck. Arasha sat against the railing of the bow, being the furthest point of distance without diving overboard.

Droya considered a moment and closed her eyes. "Speak to me and I'll speak the exact words that are his."

"What was the task?"

"Drom's task?" Droya knew it's what she meant, but wanted time to decide how to answer.

"Yes. Why'd he have to leave me?"

"I was following fate's path and it led me to helping unravel the plots of a man named Laethem."

"The Circler?" Arasha knew him?

"The same. I was stupid and got myself stuck into a situation where there was no way to save both of us. I saw a chance to at least save you. Cellis helped me to do so." All technically true.

"By sending you away from me?" Arasha leaned closer, seeming to forget Droya's form.

"If it hadn't been this way, you'd have been in a chain brothel, Laethem's pawn, or both. I couldn't save myself, but I could save you."

Arasha remained silent, clicking her nails together, so Droya continued.

"Cellis will free you now that we're safe. You and I," Droya paused, recognizing the miswording, without a tingle of pain this time. "Or rather, at least with my link through Droya, can return with the ships. If you avoid Fairmar until your father's allies can free the city, it should be safe for you."

Arasha moved in closer, gazing into Droya's eyes, her own conflicted. "Drom. I need you. I don't have the strength on my own."

"You're the strongest woman I've ever known. Somewhere in this situation, you've forgotten that part of yourself. You have to remember your strength. I never had strength to bestow, much to my shame."

"No. You let me be myself without expectations." Arasha's hand reached for Droya's own in an unconscious gesture. "It's something I never experienced until I met you." Her eyes glistened with growing emotion. "God's home! Is it true I'll never be able to see you again?"

"I'm still with you, if not in physical form. Droya is yours now and will be at your side always so long as you wish it. Through her,

I'll always be there to serve your needs and help you through difficult times."

"Droya," Arasha bit her lip, "Can Drom access all of your senses or just sight and hearing?"

"Every sense I have is his as well." Guilt pressed in on Droya about playing out two identities, but none of it was untrue. "Why?"

"You sometimes share his mannerisms. Until now, I'd thought it a cruel coincidence or my imagination."

"Oh."

"Droya," The war in Arasha's expressions was clear. She might still flee. "Can you provide him all of your senses now?"

"He has them Mistress." Followed by a long silence. It was broken by a tearful rush of motion. Droya found herself in a familiar embrace from an unfamiliar perspective.

"I've missed you more than you can comprehend." Arasha's damp face pressed into Droya's neck and cheek.

It was everything Droya'd wanted since this started, but her own desires fell away. This wasn't about her, it was about Arasha. Making a soft shushing sound, Droya stroked her hair and shoulders.

"As I've missed you dove. I wish it could have been different."

"I don't care. At least I have you back. After a fashion. It's more than I could have expected for after you disappeared."

It was Droya's turn to cry.

AFTER THE INITIAL BURST of emotion, Arasha's discomfort with Droya returned. At least it wasn't raw terror now. Sleeping outside of Arasha's portion of the crew quarters, Droya's sleep was fitful. Doubt and fear plagued her. Worse was an impending sense of danger. It didn't vanish when she woke.

The trepidation kept growing stronger, even when they were summoned to the deck to aid Cellis. It refused dissipate. The feeling was so distracting Droya failed to register when Cellis spoke to her.

"Are you ready?" He repeated.

"I... Yes Ma," She paused, "What am I to call you now?"

"Cellis is acceptable."

"Yes Cellis." Saying his name was uncomfortable after using 'Master' so long. Improper. "I'm ready."

"And this will tell us how things are?" Arasha's worry was ill-restrained.

"No, but it will hint at the situation as it pertains to Lord Kirk." Cellis drew a pearl from a pouch at his belt. "The beacon is keyed to him."

"How much can we find out?" There was hope woven in the worry of her voice.

"State of health, recent movements, and sometimes emotional state. I didn't sense his emotional state when I tested two days ago. The distance might be too great."

"Did you channel through me when you used it?" Droya remembered the tingling from her time recovering.

"No, you needed rest. I spent years without a familiar. A few castings alone, strong or not, won't kill me."

"Can we start?" Arasha asked.

"Of course." Cellis closed his eyes and chanted. The tingle of magic flowed through Droya and with it the sense of danger intensified. There was also the secondary tingle outside of herself. It seemed to come from behind her.

Arasha's worry now blended with fascination. Droya's attention shifted. The sense of danger put her on edge about her surroundings. Multiple eyes were focused sidelong at them. Llwanna watched from near the steering block. The rest were from crewmen with disgusted expressions.

Numbness was starting when Cellis spoke. "He's still injured, but hasn't moved since my last check. Still no emotional reading even with Droya's aid."

"Injured and not moving? Did they catch him?" Arasha's voice was panicked.

"No way to be certain. I don't believe so though. If the circle had him, they'd heal him prior to bringing him for judgment. I doubt they'd have waited this long.

"Why didn't you tell me he was injured?"

"I had to learn more about the situation so you'd not spend two days worrying over nothing."

"You're dreading dangerously close do mudiny." Droya's acute hearing picked up on Michael's heated tones. She doubted Cellis or Arasha could have heard it. She focused in, ears swiveling so the immediate conversation was lost in favor of the distant one. Her eyes shifted to the three crewmen confronting Michael.

"Sir. We're loyal, but this is madness. Even with the extra supplies, we're at the point of no return. No one has ever gone this far to sea."

"Sday the course. We'll make landfall before the hold's empdy."

"No disrespect sir, but some of the crew's questioning your wife's loyalties." The rage forming in Michael's eyes was clear even from this distance. "We're only here on the whims of the Magus she all but hangs on. If,..."

Micheal bellowed, hand going to his rapier. All eyes moved to match Droya's own. "You dare?"

"You deserve our honest opinions Captain. Out of respect." The crewman paled, making a reflexive reach for his own blade. He managed to stand his ground though the two men with him both backpedaled.

Was this the source to the sense of danger? No. The feeling of looming threat was targeted now. The same direction of a faint tingle to the rear of the ship. Ears still focused on the captain, Droya scanned past Cellis and Arasha, squinting keen eyes on the horizon.

"You quesdion my judgmend and insuld my wife in the same breath? I should run you through. No one should dare such a slighd."

Was there something on the horizon?

"Please sir, I am ever loyal."

A speck. A wave? A whale? A trick of distorted air?

"Apologize do her!" Michael's blade was out and at the man's chest in a flash of metal.

A sail? A ship. Droya strained to focus. Keen eyes or not, a ship shouldn't be visible at this distance.

"Honey, please don't." Llwanna was now between them. "He's come ta ya because he trusts ya. Whatever it is, don't ruin that good faith."

How could a ship show up at such a distance? It would have to be huge. Droya's eyes widened. A galleon! The navy.

"Something aft, a large ship." A voice cried down from the eagle's roost. It replaced the violent tension with another form of tension. Every crewman was stirred to motion. Michael's weapon was sheathed and his rage forgotten. Even Cellis and Arasha moved towards the steering block.

In moments, the sails were let out to full and the now-familiar external tingle came from Llwanna. The ship lurched as it had done at those times while Droya had been recovering. Harder than those times. The sails bellowed, scooping energy from the summoned gale.

"What is it?" Cellis was asking Michael rather than Llwanna for once.

"We'll discover when the Salson does." Apparently the term he used for lookouts. "Assume hosdile."

"It's a galleon." Droya struggled with the growing sense of danger. It was like being stalked and catching flashes of your stalker's shadow creeping up behind you.

"Are you cerdain?" Michael's voice was cautious. Llwanna spared a glance as she chanted to sustain the wind.

"The size is right." Everyone around Droya but Cellis and Arasha looked relieved.

"The navy's following us?" Arasha asked uncertain of what it might mean.

Cellis pressed further, "What is it we're missing?"

"A galleon is powerful," Michael explained, "But it's also slow. It shouldn't be hard to outrun it."

Ten minutes brought confirmation it was a galleon, along with frowns from the crew. Twenty more minutes confirmed they flew the navy flag of Fairmar along with the flag for the Circle navy. Expressions grew dour.

"This is a fore shord of a heighd." Michael lifted a brass tube to his eye in the direction of their pursuers. "They shouldn'd be able do cadch up do us. Even with a Magus aboard, a galleon shouldn'd be capable."

"They don't just have a Magus. They have Laethem." Cellis' words brought a frown to Llwanna, though she kept chanting.

"Laethem?" Arasha eyed Droya, no doubt remembering their conversation. "How can you be sure?"

"Only a Master Magus of Aeromancy could manage a feat of such magnitude."

"Hoo do we oodpace the basdard?" Michael managed between shouting orders about armaments and preparations.

"If he's prepared, we don't." Cellis glanced at Droya. "Prepare for a heavy flow of magic. I'm going to attempt some emergency defenses and interference."

Droya nodded, urging Arasha, "Mistress, it may be best to withdraw to the cabin until it's safer." Arasha complied, though she left the door open a few inches to watch.

The flow of power hit with the shock of plunging into icy water. It was raw and less controlled than normal. Wild as a drowning beast struggling to live. She could sense the walls of force erecting around the ship, along with a surge of power that left water churning in their wake. Time became abstract, but every moment Droya caught a glimpse, the galleon was closer than before.

She was numb to physical sensation by the time there was a surge in the magic from the enemy ship. Her eyes shifted upwards to watch an arc of flaming stones deflected off of an improvised barrier. Cellis began a new casting, trying to reinforce the shield. Haphazard and last minute, it wasn't as strong as it should have been. Several more stones struck, deflecting again. This time plumes of flame managed to make it through.

Crewmen rushed to put out flames where they sprang, but the sails were the primary concern. Cellis' skills seemed ill suited to this sort of thing. At least the shield held as a third volley of flaming stone rained down. More fires sprang up, one managed to burn through a rope before it could be put out.

The rope end sprang free, the flaming tip arching to catch Llwanna's temple and bowling her over. Two things followed. The wind left the sails and Cellis paused his chanting as hers halted in a startled exclamation. The timing couldn't be worse. A volley struck, shattering the shield and stones splintered a mast.

The timber folded on itself, crashing down. Half remained tethered by a rope while the rest leaned against a secondary mast, trailing into the sea. They were dead in the water.

Chapter Seventeen
The Fear of Loss

Erica sucked at the smooth stone in her cheek. The young new body she'd used the last few years to pull strings was different, but transferring minds meant you still had your quirky habits. It didn't matter now. There was no one left who'd remember those habits anyway. To the world, she was the angular young man Erin.

She observed the plumes of smoke still rising from the city beyond the window as if it were a smoldering brush pile. For all she cared, it held the same value. A sneer crept across her lips. Everything was coming together to perfection.

By now Laethem and Maria would have caught up to Cellis. If they weren't dead already, both would be within a few hours. The spell she'd tied to Laethem would ensure chance worked against them. That would leave her only two Circle members to dispose of.

Two final obstacles between herself and all the souls she could wish for. Fuel for magic the world hadn't seen in an age. Power which would be hers alone to wield. The fools no longer remembered her, let alone recognized her.

She had much to do. She could taste success as she slid the stone to the opposite cheek and continued to plan.

"STAND DOWN." LAETHEM'S voice boomed with unnatural volume. "Surrender yourselves to justice and most of you will be free again soon."

"He has Maria with him in the eagle's roost." Cellis must have been unaware Droya could hear those words. There was a tone of resignation.

"Mas... Cellis. We are going to fight them?"

"We're hopelessly outclassed. Two Circlers sent after us. It's unfathomable they'd expend such resources to reach us, but here we are."

"I'd assumed you were a match for Laethem."

"I am. More than a match," Cellis scowled. "But that's two Master Magus over there. Both prepared for this conflict. I'm not fool enough to believe my improvised castings can hold out for long against the prepared spells of two such Magi. We have no choice. I'll negotiate a surrender and have to hope they'll be satisfied with myself alone. If so, they might let you and the others go."

Droya glanced towards Arasha as Cellis cast a small spell to enhance his own volume. She was watching through the half-closed doorway. Visibly trembling.

"I underestimated how far you were willing to take this Laethem." Cellis' on voice echoed like thunder now. "Let the others free. It's myself you want."

"Vain as ever." Laethem could be seen leaning out from his lofty perch. The woman beside him didn't move. "You're in no position to decide the terms of surrender."

The tingle of magic use came to Droya's senses and drew her attention towards it. Llwanna remained where she'd fallen. Blood flowed from the gash in her temple. Her eyes were open however and her lips moved. The chanting was inaudible even to Droya's keen ears. No one else seemed to notice she'd woken.

"Does he speak for the Circle Maria? Are you here to aide him or is this about proper Circle justice?" A faint tingle from the ship, but far less powerful than whatever Llwanna was attempting.

"You've betrayed the Order." A female voice now came from the galleon. "But everyone who's aided you in the time since is guilty of a crime as well. Surrender yourselves and I promise leniency for any of those whose involvement was not direct."

"That'll be a red day at sea." Llwanna sprang up. Her blood-streaked face contorted in anger as she flung her hands out. The galleon lurched as a gale crashed into their sails counter to their current momentum. Timbers creaked, but held. Most of the visible bodies aboard were sent sprawling. Maria and Laethem had to grab railing to prevent being thrown from the eagle's roost.

Magic surged on both ships, a massive flow of it from Cellis rushed through Droya as he cursed and erected new barriers. Pillars of water rose from the sea. Arcs of flame streamed across the sky. Glowing balls of blue floated towards their ship. Crewmen, unable to aid in the mystic battle, took to sending volleys of arrows between ships.

Some of their attacks made it through the galleon's shielding. Far more made it from the galleon through their own. Fire cut charred gashes across the deck. Arrows caught several crewmen. One of the blue orbs slipped through the defenses, bursting like a bubble in a flash of electricity. Where it had touched the deck, a charred hole surrounded by crackling pattern remained.

Droya's attention was drawn to the cabin door. Arasha was a step outside of it, fascination at the spectacle having overcome fear. She didn't react as an arrow planted into the wooden wall behind her. Two more of the luminous spheres slipped through the barrier. One floated in a slow glide towards where Arasha stood.

"Arasha!" Droya's voice was lost in the din of crackles, explosions, and voices. Dashing quicker than she'd realized she could, Droya crossed the distance between them. No time to plan. No chance to push her to safety. Droya did the first thing that came to mind. She put herself between the two, hand extended as though it could push the orb aside.

Contact. A burst of pain made it through the channeling induced numbness. The horrible sensation flowed down her arm as everything went black.

HER FIRST CONSCIOUS thought was to wish the whisper would be silent. It was raving madness at her. She could sense magic all around. She could sense it still flowing through her. All of this seemed as though she were outside of her own body.

Vision and hearing cleared like a fog burning away in the sun and dispelling the euphoria of having been able to save Arasha. Instead of returning to safety, Arasha was bent over her screaming.

"Don't die. Don't you dare." The words were faint through the ringing of her ears.

Was Droya imagining it?

"Live! Whatever god protects Ill'In save her. I can't lose Drom again."

"Get to safety." Droya's voice was harsh and raw. Her mouth was filled with a metallic taste.

"Oh thank the pantheon." Arasha's lips pressed to Droya's own in an unexpected and passionate gesture.

Droya was too stunned to respond at first. Tears filled Arasha's eyes and there was a genuine joy there. Arasha struggled to drag Droya to the safety of the cabin.

"Don't stay out here. I'll be alright." Reaching back to push up into a sitting position, Droya's body fell sideways as her left hand failed to grip. There was a tinge of horror as she inspected the damage. Her hand was charred and bloody, more like cooked meat than a working appendage. A streak of blistered black skin ran down her arm and over her body, parodying a lightning strike. She couldn't feel it though. There wasn't time to dwell on it either.

Arasha managed to pull her a bit farther as she stared at her useless hand. The jagged char of flesh traced across her body bore strange similarity to a flash of lightening frozen in time.

They were almost to the cabin when an arrow struck Arasha's shoulder. It was enough to send her sprawling from the force of impact. It drew Droya back into focus. Weak as she was, there was nothing in her to draw from.

Arasha regained herself, arm hanging limp. Not bleeding enough to be fatal at least. Bless her for it, she used her functional arm to continue pulling at Droya. Such strength of will.

Strong or not, they were going to die. Droya could sense the power flowing all around. Screams and explosions beating at her ears. Flashes of light trying to steal her vision by bouts of contrast. All of this power and she couldn't even stand up to help her wife. She watched Arasha's strained expression, unwilling to quit, and it struck deep at Droya's heart.

A raging river of magic was flowing through her. Three other powerful streams raged from the others nearby. Power enough to reshape reality four times over. Reaching out for them with in her mind, she touched all four. Power. She needed power of her own.

Cellis' magic was already within her. She managed to 'tug' at two of the others, siphoning some of them away. The last, she managed to take within herself. Tapping without interrupting, her strength was returning. Greater than she'd ever felt. In another situation, it would have led to elation. In the present, it was a means to an end.

"Arasha. Mistress." Droya rose, pushing up with her remaining hand. "You have done more than a Magus could manage, but there's one final task you must do."

"What do I have to do?" No longer dragging, she went with Droya into the cabin. Questionable safety at this point, but at least safe from the arrows. The whisper in Droya's mind fell silent, as if recognizing her thoughts.

"It's cruel to ask, but it's our best hope. I," Droya paused eying the cabin door as the sound of battle continued beyond. "Drom needs you to remove my piercer for now."

"W-what?" Arasha backed up a step.

"I can't join the fight while I wear it. Even contemplating such an action causes pain." It didn't occur to her she wasn't in pain at the suggestion. "Following through would drop me before I could make any difference."

"I can't. It was hard enough getting close enough to put it on. There's no way I can take it off."

"Drom's in control." It was another half truth, feeling like a lie, but it had to happen. "I will only act to protect you." Arasha was still hesitating. Droya closed her eyes for a moment, summoning the ghost of who she'd once been. When she opened her eyes again, she tried to hold herself in the exact manner she once had as Drom.

"Just because I was pampered does not mean I never learned how to do my fair share of the work." Droya hoped the reference wasn't lost in the heat of things. "It's too much to ask, but it's the only way. Our side is losing. If we can't do something soon, the Circle will make sure we never see one another again." 'See' wasn't the right word, but now wasn't a time to quibble. "I need your help with this. I'm so sorry there's no one else to ask."

Pain and fear roiled in Arasha's expression. It was heartbreaking. Unable to bear it, Droya turned away. Keen senses meant nothing against the turmoil outside the door. Without being able to to hear the footsteps, it was delicate fingers that first informed Droya of Arasha's choice.

The clasp came free, drawn by trembling hands. The whisper, now a voice, plead for blood. Droya held motionless, focusing inward.

-Destroy them.-

-Only the enemy.-

-All are enemies.-

-You'll have your blood, but only as much as it takes to protect Arasha.-

The voice fell silent, leaving Droya unsure of what to expect. Regardless, she was free to act.

"Arasha, thank you. Shut the door behind me and don't watch. I don't want you to endure anything that may follow."

Arasha nodded, holding the chain like a viper. One last long gaze back as Droya stepped out and into the maelstrom again.

DROYA PAUSED ON THE deck, embracing the torrents of magic flowing through her. The dead and dying remained wherever they'd fallen. All other hands were too focused on defense to attend to them. The galleon had made it close alongside them though still shy of boarding plank range.

There was nothing she could do from here. With a deep draw of air, she moved to the opposite side of the ship from the galleon. No human could hope to make the distance in a jump. In truth, she wasn't sure an Ill'In could either, but there was a thin hope in the fact the inner voice remained silent. She hoped it meant it wasn't expecting suicide. 'For Arasha' Droya thought.

She took off, tilting hard as she built speed. Her motion shifted to an animalistic one. Vision seemed to narrow as her working hand and both feet caught the railing almost as one. Curling tight and carried by the pull of her own momentum, she sprung at the galleon.

Her working fingers caught the opposite railing, threatening to slip with the jarring impact. In a desperate scramble, she was over the rail, face to face with several stunned crewmen. The numbness from channeled magic left no indications of anything different. Only the appearance of something in her line of sight informed her of an arrow. It was lodged at an angle into her left bicep. Breaking it off took only a moment, but it was enough time for the crewmen to recover their senses. As they reached for weapons, the voice returned.

-Kill.-

For Arasha's sake, Droya embraced it this time. Logic fell to the background and something feral came forward. Time lost meaning, squashing and stretching as she engaged. A crack of lightening nearby drew her back into the present.

She couldn't recall details. She decided it was for the best, given the amount of blood on her hand and tattered dress. Paradoxical to the numbness, the sensation came from the hairs on her body all standing on end. The 'voice' acted on her reflexes, moving her aside even before the thoughts could form.

Lightning crackled, striking where she'd been. Charred wood splintered with the strike, throwing shards and setting what remained aflame. Droya peered at the eagle's roost. She had their attention. No time for delay.

The tempestuous flow of magic through her wavered. One of those two flows she'd managed only to siphon without drawing in, though which magi it originated from, she couldn't say. Time was running out.

Dodging another arrow, Droya bolted towards the main mast, leaping several feet and climbing as well as she could with one hand and an injured arm. There were climbing pegs set into it at intervals. Those helped. Above, she could sense immense magical power. Those two would indeed be a match for Cellis and Llwanna.

A dozen rungs were left, but a flaming orb hurtled from above. Obvious magic. Even with the warning of sensation, there was no way to evade. Left without any other option, Droya extended her damaged left arm again. With how the lightning had gone, there wasn't much hope. What other choice was there though?

At the moment before it struck, she had the wild idea to try drawing the magic from the fire ball into herself. As the magic kissed her skin, it seemed to be working. Power flowed into her, but she'd waited too long to try. Too late.

The world exploded around her for the second time that day. This time in fire rather than electric. She was hurled outward into the ocean. A lifetime in a city without swimming experience left her thrashing. She slipped beneath the waves. It was luck alone when aimless kicks brought her into contact with the wood of the galleon.

Finger nails that should have broken against the hard surface dug in. Droya went to grab with her left hand, only to find several inches of charred tatters at the end of her wrist. The damage from the electrical shock had been dreadful, but superficial enough to hope at recovery. This was not recoverable. The shock left her numb, both on the emotional and physical levels.

That voice she'd struggled with since the beginning now brought her back to herself.

-Fight. Live.-

Fight? How could she fight? The mere act of climbing back up with only one hand seemed impossible.

-Swim. Flee and live.-

She couldn't swim. No hope there. She couldn't flee even if she were willing to leave Arasha behind.

-Fly and fight.- The voice was growing agitated.

Fly? Droya might have laughed in other circumstances. At present she wanted to cry in frustration. "I don't have wings you auditory menace." Droya wanted to strangle the voice. It responded with a silence. This, despite no collar forcing it to quiet.

-We are fae.- It finally spoke again in a whisper rather than a scream.

Nonsense. It meant nothing. Not all, or even most, fae have wings to fly with. Still, without any other hope in that moment, Droya couldn't help wishing she had wings. She could almost feel them as she let herself imagine. A thin and meaningless hope.

The image which came to her wasn't the delicate lacy wings of fairies or sprites. Instead, bat-like white wings came to mind for some reason. They were vivid enough to seem real. Two hooked 'fingers' perched atop each, with three elongated wing fingers draping below. Velvety fur coated the back of the membranes while the interior was supple and smooth.

Part of her reached out to the magical flow. Without intending to, it channeled through her will.

-Live. Fly. Fight.-

"Save Arasha."

Something tingled and itch against the otherwise numb state of her body. Both shoulders itched, burned, then erupted into flashes of pain. She struggled to maintain her grip on the galleon. Immediate numbness returned. The pale white wings that were now part of her flexed. They seemed natural, as if they'd always been there. So much so she doubted for a moment they'd not been there all along.

'Sentient beings develop based on their own wills.' Cellis' words returned to her. 'Magical beings are prone to more rapid and extreme transfigurations.' It was certain this counted as both. Studying the bloody stub that had been her hand, she drew at the flow of magic within her. The flesh bubbled as wisps of ethereal mist flowed from the hull into her arm. Corrosion ate away at the hull, showing pock-marks where the wood had been sound before. Other sections of the wood bore the same markings. It must have been drawn away when her wings formed.

Flesh knitted and reform as she watched. The scar of what had been lost was marked only by a color difference. Where her existing skin had been pale, the new growth was stark white. Tone aside, the hand was identical to what had been lost. Finally she focused on the wound in her bicep, the remaining shaft of the arrow dissolving away and flesh closing as a circular scar.

Droya flexed it and peered up. She'd siphoned energy. Presumably from Llwanna and Cellis. Doing it couldn't have helped their defenses at all. She had to reach Laethem and his companion. This had to end before Arasha was hurt further.

It was unnerving, but she spread her wings. The unnatural act came with an odd ease. The moment she pushed off, they began a swift, rhythmic beating. The first few flaps cleared the waves by only a narrow margin. Subsequent wing beats drove her skyward. Several near-misses by orbs of blue light and streaks of crackling flame. It didn't leave her time for uncertainty. Maneuvering became easier with every flap. Droya practically danced between attacks by the time she drew even with the enemy eagle's roost. Arrows flew from the deck below, but the archer's couldn't track the erratic movements well enough to connect amid all the other chaos.

For a moment, both of the Magi there had their full attention on the assault of the other ship. Maria was the first to notice Droya, reaching to grab Laethem beside her and drawing his attention. Droya made absent note of a tiny flame on the woman's shoulder. It didn't hold her attention long when the source of all her past problems was near at hand.

Her eyes locked on Laethem. Both he and Maria wore dumbfounded expressions. Laethem was first to brush off the shock and a gale sprang from his hand, buffeting her. It came with wings other than her own, raking claws and fevered biting. His pygmy drake familiar. It was all she could do to avoid the strikes. The miniature dragon didn't seem affected by its master's wind at all.

She had to drop several feet to avoid a streak of flame. Maria had recovered. Three different attacks at once now! Winds battered her into masts and made her catch on ropes despite her best effort. Teeth and claws dug thin trails in her skin, distracting her. The pungent tang of singed hair spoke of several close calls with the flames.

Unable to distinguish herself from the inner voice, the insane idea came to embrace the flames again. Madness with so many things happening at once. Even so, the next thin line of flame that burst towards her wasn't dodged. She embraced it. Not in the physical sense, but as if she were channeling magic for Cellis.

Unlike before, the flame left her unharmed. Instead it swirled around her, wispy threads of its essence trailing into her as the flame itself sputtered out. Having nowhere for the power to go, it flowed through the nearest outlet. As the drake bit again, it burst ablaze. A charred remnant fell away.

Laethem cried out, "Vlax!" Reeling from it as though himself struck. Maria let her arms fall limp, mouth working without a sound. Bellowing in rage, Laethem drew power into a tremendous crackling orb of light.

Droya could sense its power, but also the fact it was woven in a crude rush. Far simpler to embrace than the flame had been. She swooped towards Laethem, the ball roiling through the air towards her. Passing through the center, it didn't burst as those electrical orbs had. Instead it crackled and swirled, flowing into her as water circling a drain.

There wasn't the time for Laethem to attempt anything else. Their bodies met, and she channeled the power he'd donated into her momentum. She struck with such force Laethem was flung from the eagle's roost, splintering the wooden railing. He tumbled, catching several beams as he fell away, cracking into the deck hard enough to splinter the surface and remove any doubt as to his state of survival.

Droya flapped, hovering by the eagle's roost. The victory rang hollow to her. Without magic, magi were frail beings. Her attention shifted to Maria, but the Magus' arms were both forward, palms up. It was the Fairmarian show of surrender and submission.

Just like that, the battle was over. The Magus before Droya dropped her hold on the flow of magic. The puny flame on her shoulder remained, a familiar on closer inspection. It seemed to be a tiny living flame with a thin smoke tail trailing behind it.

The voice in Drom's mind cried to continue the bloodshed.

"There's been enough death for today." Though Droya was speaking to the voice, Maria seemed relieved to have it spoken aloud. The voice softened to a whisper despite the lack of a piercer chain.

Droya landed in the roost, grabbing Maria. It elicited a flinch from the woman as her new wings spread. After two flaps, it became clear flying with a second person was a terrible strain. She settled on holding her wings out and gliding to the opposite ship.

Silence fell on the deck as both ship crews realized what had happened. There was an awkward pause as they landed. Droya walked away from the captured Magus.

Arasha remained within the cabin, peering out of the remains of the door. It must have been damaged in the fighting. She wore the same expression as the crew, fear, and fascination mingling. She seemed to most fixate on Droya's wings. At least it would keep her from noticing any blood the seawater hadn't washed away.

"Mistress," Droya lowered herself to her knees and bowed her head. "Please return my chain."

The voice within her raged at this. Droya wasn't in full control. It was a struggle to push down the urge to fight or flee. Arasha stared unmoving.

"I beg you Mistress. It's what must be done." Droya didn't want to mention her former self. It made her feel dishonest. Arasha's hands moved as if some invisible force was slowing her to a crawl.

The voice wailed.

Llwanna released her hold on magic, severing half of Droya's remaining flow.

Arasha moved fractionally in what felt like an eternity. A lifetime of fears weren't helped by the new appearance or the traces of red stains on Droya's tattered clothing she seemed to only now be seeing.

"Mistress, you must," she was cut off by the sudden lurch of movement from Arasha. The snap of the clasp and the dropping of Cellis' magic overlapped. It made it impossible to determine which act had the most impact. Regardless, the result was the last crutch bolstering Droya's strength collapsed and so did she.

THE SHIP'S HOLD SAT packed to capacity now. The crew had looted supplies from the galleon's considerable stores. It was a minor dent in what had been there. Even with the magic door, there wasn't room for any more.

The smallest of the galleon's sails had been taken to replace the largest of their own. Neither of the Magi knew the right spells for repairing the broken mast, but Michael believed they would be able to make it the remainder of the distance with the existing sail. Despite the losses, the crew seemed in brilliant spirits and none questioned their tasks now. Such a major victory had that effect on people.

"We took precautions to ensure you won't follow us. At least until the bindings can all be severed and the wards dispelled." Cellis seemed less pleased with himself than another man might have been.

"I have no intention of following you." Maria shifted. Her discomfort at the rope didn't seem alleviated in the least by the motion. "Justice demands much, but far too many resources were lost to you already."

"Justice?" Droya wanted to strike the woman, but didn't. Not just because the warning sensation from the piercer chain. "Laethem and the rest of you destroyed lives and brought chaos to the kingdom."

"Everything which we did, was necessary for the greater good of everyone." Did she sound doubtful? Maybe it was Drom's wishful thinking.

"We should kill them and sink the ship." Michael could have been observing the weather by his tone.

"No," Cellis studied the horizon. "We are better than that. Besides, no matter what they do, word of today will spread from their crew. Perhaps the loss of morale will aid the true rulers in recovering control."

Arasha watched the exchange without comment and Llwanna was busy checking to be certain everything was prepared for departure. With a dismissing motion from Michael, Maria crossed the plank between ships. A dignified stride wasn't effortless while bound and balancing atop a rocking plank. She managed an admirable show anyway.

Droya drew her new wings in tight and hoped this was the last she'd be dealing with the Circle. This moment didn't seem final enough for that to be the case. A distant sense of danger had returned anew, hanging heavy in the air. Somewhere beyond the horizon. It was waiting. Maybe it was the wary glances she caught from the two Magi aboard. Were they uneasy with what she'd managed, even if the results were in their favor?

Chapter Eighteen

The Beginning of an Adventure

Maria browsed the unkempt room with a frown. She'd expected Laethem's quarters to be neater. His desk at least seemed organized, so it's where she started.

Whiskers hopped from her shoulder, a tiny ball of flame with a smoke wisp for a tail. His tiny coal eyes glinted up at her with a quizzical expression. She stroked his fluffy body, the flames being ephemeral rather than true combustion.

Reaching for the paper he'd left sitting in the center, she skimmed the contents. A letter from someone named Ries. His informant. Laethem had told the Circle about the letter. It's how he convinced them the rogue Cellis could still be brought to justice. As he'd said, it indicated where they'd gone, the fact they would cast from Godsaddle, and where they were aiming to go. No surprises there.

She set it down and walked around the desk to study the map he'd left there. Again no shocks. Ocean charts listing all the known islands, the corner of a larger newfound land mass, and the ship teleportation information.

"What do you think whiskers?" She felt drained. "You see anything that will help quell this rebellion?"

Her familiar kept its eyes on her, cocking his head.

"Me either." She dug around for over an hour. Only as she was about to leave, did she think to inspect the hearth of his office. Ashes, mostly.

Among them, she found a single scrap which had escaped burning, but in this state, it wasn't helpful. Three letters from the corner of a paper.

'Eri.'

She frowned. If it could be burned, it could be restored. She would have to do so once she could gather the needed items for the spell. Until then, she went searching for something to gather the ashes with.

HAVING LET MARIA OF the Embers retreat eased Droya's conscience some. Only by a fractional margin. The personal journals taken at the same time as the supplies confirmed she knew nothing of Laethem's plotting. Still, she was a Circler and had played a role in the Council's actions.

No pursuit had followed them, so now everyone was at ease. Weeks had passed and ease had shifted to elation when a crewman spotted the small rise of land an hour ago. She and Arasha stood in silence at the bow of the ship. Droya remained sore for a long time after the battle. Without the flow of magic to numb her, the new wings and regenerated portions of her body had suffered a terrible ache. Thinking about it prompted her to flex the chalk-white fingers of her left hand and stretch the wings.

"They're pretty." Arasha's attention had been drawn by the motion. Droya wasn't sure 'pretty' would be the word she'd have chosen. Still, Arasha was speaking of her in positive terms. Why quarrel about it?

"Thank you Mistress."

"Droya. I'm sorry if I seem," She struggled for the right word. "Timid towards you. And for avoiding you these last weeks."

"I understand Mistress. Through Drom, I already know of your past."

"That's no excuse. Not when you've proven trustworthy. You lost an arm to save us."

"Only a hand and it grew back." Droya wiggled her fingers to punctuate the statement. "Solid as a smith's anvil." The phrase came as second nature. One more phrase picked up as a child and carried long after any hope of being a smithy's apprentice had passed. Droya'd used it without giving it much thought. Arasha glanced, but didn't comment.

"Still, you couldn't have realized you'd survive the blast or even the shock. You did it anyway and you saved me."

"You are my Mistress and I share all of Drom's love for you." Droya's eyes fell to Arasha's still-bandaged shoulder. "You risked yourself for me as well."

"I," Arasha blushed and turned her head away again. "I'm ashamed to say I only did it for Drom. Sorry, but you deserve the truth."

"Mistress, you owe me nothing. I'm delighted by the opportunity to do anything which benefits you."

"I'll try to improve anyway." Arasha didn't make eye contact. Silence filled the space between them and the tiny dot of land grew and spread across the horizon. Droya made an absent note to herself that Arasha had gained back much of the weight she'd lost during the period following the auction. It was delightful to see she'd felt well enough to eat properly again. As Droya returned her eyes to the horizon, Arasha spoke again. "Magic is amazing."

"Yes Mistress." Droya considered for a moment before adding, "It has a dark side though."

"There's good and bad in everything I suppose." Arasha studied Droya again as she spoke. Her thoughtful expression wasn't cold or fearful as it had once been.

The path fate had put Droya on was an unusual one. It wasn't what she'd have chosen, but had gained her as much or more than she'd lost. Above all, she now understood Arasha in ways she couldn't have before. The Circle couldn't meddle in their lives now.

There was much more hope than there'd been in a long time. It seemed possible their gains might be worth the price they'd both paid. It was a hard sell, but not impossible.

Silence fell between them as they watched water and sky shift into the magenta and orange of sunset. The dark blob of land drawing closer split the contact point of water and air as a growing rift. Droya immersed herself in the moment and let out a contented sound.

EIGHT UNBLINKING EYES watched the mass of wood and cloth as it drew near. In the dying light, the mammals didn't seem to notice the creature. To ensure that remained the case, it stayed submerged. Only the top of its head sat above the dark water.

The mammals were favoring the landward side of their mobile island as something heaved overboard. The splash rippled loudly through the water. These things were as noisy below the waves as above. Its mandible twitched in agitation as metal scraped the stone and sand below. The reptiles never made this much racket.

The creature tread water inches below the surface, observing as the mammals shouted and pointed towards land. Without warning, one mammal with points of flesh extending to the sides of its head and mounds over its shoulders gazed directly at it. Maybe they weren't as dusk-blind as it had thought.

Ducking below the waves, the creature kicked its four, flat movement limbs and tucking the rest close to its abdomen. These new mammals could make engaging prey. Thoughts of how they might taste filled its mind as it paddled into the inky depths.

Author's Notes

It's been an interesting journey from where I started until now. The earliest concept of this book began in 2005 as a collaborative project. A few scenes were hammered out, but the other writer dropped out. The idea sat in a folder as I honed my abilities with other writing for a few years, gathering dust.

I worked on other writing projects. Ghost writing a few years for example. I also did fiction every Friday on my blog. That led to the publication of my first novella, but nothing full novel length.

Eventually, this story returned to my attention. At the time, I was incredibly slow at writing. I used a notebook. Pen and paper! Then I would find time to transcribe what I had written when I could into a file. I got halfway through the story this way before realizing I needed to completely scrap some of the early scenes and redo them.

Doing that with pen and paper was a daunting task. I ended up doing other things first. Still, I would eventually return to this book, armed with far greater skill than when I started. Revisions were made. Elements were altered. By 2024, I had a solid story written and began my editing.

At the start of 2025, I was all set to focus on the publication of the novel when a serious health matter occurred with my wife. Everything got dropped. I do mean everything. For a time, spending time in the hospital ate so far into my day job that work hours were cut to the bone.

Several surgeries and almost a year later, she'd recovered enough for my day job to be catching our finances back up and for me to focus on the last bits needed to finish this work. I found a very talented artist to do the cover and dealt with a final round of edits to ensure any typos we missed could be caught. I know there's bound to be at least one somewhere still. I'll find it the day after publication on the first page I turn to!

Anyway, the point is that this book was a labor of love and I'm glad you read to the end. I truly hope you enjoyed it. While I know not every book is right for every reader, I hope that it was a solid match. If you did like the book, I would love to see your reviews telling me exactly what it was you enjoyed.

Of course, even if you hated it, reviews help others find what is and isn't a good match for them. The exact things you hated may be something someone else loves. In other words, even if you are leaving a low star review, I still appreciate that you are taking the time to articulate what did and didn't work for you. You can't know how much it means to an author that someone is passionate enough to leave a review. That said, I hope you found it an enjoyable read.

I am currently halfway through my next intended book. If you did enjoy this one, I want to encourage you to check out my website in the link below. There, you can sign up for my newsletter. I am planning a free book of short stories that will go out to anyone on the mailing list once it's done. You'll also get alerted when new books are coming out and access to some newsletter only offers from time to time. While you're on the site, why not look around at some of my other works or the blog also?

DXLogan.com[1]

1. http://www.DXLogan.com/

Also by D. X. Logan

Nighteyes
The Platinum Chain

Watch for more at www.DXLogan.com.

About the Author

D. X. Logan has worked hard to broaden his perspective. He's sought out a wide array of life experiences in this pursuit. This includes achieving a BA in Early Childhood Education, hiking the complete Appalachian Trail and exploring professions from hospital work to corrections.

These have given him a wider base of experiences write from. Knowledge is power. He uses that power explore varied topics through novels and in crafting TTRPGs. In fiction he favors the genres of science fiction, fantasy, and horror. His nonfiction centers on hiking and homesteading.

Read more at www.DXLogan.com.

www.ingramcontent.com/pod-product-compliance
Lightning Source LLC
LaVergne TN
LVHW091118080826
845145LV00008B/1968

* 9 7 8 1 9 6 7 4 2 3 0 1 9 *